Slap shot surprise

Slap Shot Surprise

USA TODAY BESTSELLING AUTHOR

Melanie Harlow

Melanie Harlow

Entangled Publishing, LLC
644 Shrewsbury Commons Ave., STE 181
Shrewsbury, PA 17361
rights@entangledpublishing.com

Amara is an imprint of Entangled Publishing, LLC.

Visit our website at www.entangledpublishing.com.

Edited by Julia Griffis
Cover art/illustration and design by Hang Le
Stock art by Anastasia Pechnikova/iStock, bortonia/iStock,
ilyaliren/iStock, and snegok13/iStock
Edge design by Bree Archer
Map Illustration by Francesca Weber
Interior design by Britt Marczak

ISBN 978-1-64937-775-3

Manufactured in the United States of America

First Edition October 2024

10 9 8 7 6 5 4 3 2 1

an imprint of Entangled Publishing LLC

1. Cherry Blossom Inn
2. Harbor Lights Salon & Spa
3. Bayview Service Station
4. The Pier Inn
5. Lush Wine Bar
6. Main Street Coffee
7. Larry's Barber Shop
8. George Buckley's House
9. Ari DeLuca's House
10. Moe's Diner
11. The Sweet Shoppe
12. Waterfront Park
13. The Lighthouse
14. Farmer's Market
15. Chapel by the Sea
16. Buckley's Pub
17. Austin Buckley's House

For my husband, who came up with the title of this book. You make me laugh every day, but especially that day.

Chapter 1

MABEL

*I*n my defense, I thought the plane was going down.

Otherwise, I *never* would have said those things about my sex life to a perfect stranger.

And not just any stranger.

Already on edge, I'd boarded the plane only to discover that my last-minute upgrade had resulted in my getting a window seat instead of the aisle. I always preferred an aisle seat, since it would allow me to reach the nearest exit row more quickly in case of an emergency. Were the perks of first class going to make up for the anxiety I already had about this flight? Gravity wasn't going to give a shit about my gold member status. People in the posh rows fell out of the sky at the same rate as the people in the back.

My plan had been to ask whoever had seat 3B if they wouldn't mind switching with me in 3A. Then I'd immediately locate the nearest exit row and plan my evacuation route. However, I'd been struck dumb by the sight of the gorgeous, broad-shouldered guy who'd boarded a few minutes later, walked down the aisle, and stopped at my row. After tucking his roller bag into the overhead bin, he offered me a smile before dropping into 3B.

My heart fluttered. I felt strangely honored, like he'd *chosen* that seat. Like the cutest, most popular boy in school had gotten on the bus and slid in next to me despite all the other open seats.

He pulled out his phone and tapped at the screen while I stared unabashedly at the chiseled jaw with a hint of stubble, the tousled brown hair, the small scar near his temple.

He wore jeans and a white button-down shirt with the sleeves cuffed, revealing tanned, muscular forearms and a fancy black wristwatch. His legs were long, and I liked the way the denim hugged his thighs. He looked effortlessly sexy and cool.

Glancing down at my own clothes, I took a moment to inwardly bemoan this morning's choices—I'd come straight from a conference session, so what I had on could loosely be described as business casual, but there was nothing cool or sexy about my camel trousers and pink blouse. Worse, I'd already traded my heels for sneakers and thrown my hair up in a ponytail. I'd worn my glasses instead of my contacts.

The guy stood up again to grab something out of his bag overhead, and I realized there was something familiar about his face. Did I know him from somewhere? I racked my brain, but I couldn't place him. He was handsome enough to be a movie star, but I didn't think that was it. Certainly it wasn't anyone attending the conference I'd been at this week. The Small Museum Association had many smart, passably attractive professionals, but *nobody* in this guy's league.

He glanced down and caught me looking at him. It was the perfect opportunity to ask about a seat switch, but when I opened my mouth, nothing came out. Embarrassed, I adjusted my glasses and focused my attention out the window, where heavy sheets of rain were slanting down angrily from dark skies. Lightning flashed, and I sat back abruptly and yanked the strap on my seat belt to tighten it.

Why hadn't I waited this and flown home tomorrow morning? I still would have had plenty of time to make the wedding. Or I could have hopped on a train. Rented a car. Hitchhiked. Anything would have been safer than this airplane!

The hot stranger took his seat again, calmly buckling up. "Looks bad out there, doesn't it?" He had a nice voice.

I nodded and braved another look at his face. His eyes were midnight blue, his brows thick and dark. I wondered how he got that scar on his temple. He had a second scar, a tiny vertical white line, just above his upper lip. Maybe he'd been in a car accident or something. Or maybe he was a boxer.

I realized I'd been staring at him for too long without speaking. "Yes, it does," I said, "and unfortunately, I'm—" *Hiccup!* I slapped a hand over my mouth. "Sorry. I get the hiccups when I'm nervous."

He laughed, but in a nice way, and handed me one of the little mini bottles of water resting on the armrest between us. "Here. Drink this."

"Got anything stronger?" I asked. But I unscrewed the cap and chugged half of it down.

"Such as?"

"I wouldn't say no to some vodka." *Hiccup!*

"Just vodka?"

"Maybe with soda." I looked toward the galley. "But it might be too late. They already came around and asked us if we wanted anything before takeoff."

"I can probably make it happen." He put his hand up and made eye contact with one of the female flight attendants, who wasted no time in approaching him with an eager-to-please smile. She was pretty and young, with cascading waves of beachy blond hair, long black eyelashes, and a golden tan. Flight attendant Barbie. "Can I get you anything, Mr. Lupo?"

"Yes." He looked at me. "My friend here would like a vodka soda, and I'll take a whiskey neat."

"Of course."

"You don't by any chance have a lemon, do you?" He looked at me and explained, "My mom always made us suck on a lemon if we got hiccups."

"We don't," said the flight attendant, clearly sad to disappoint him. "I'm sorry."

He shrugged. "Just the drinks, then. Thanks."

"You got it." She managed to tear her eyes off him and give me a tiny nod before hurrying away.

"See?" He looked at me and shrugged. "Easy."

I had a feeling that kind of thing was always easy for him.

The flight attendant had called him Mr. Lupo. The name was slightly familiar to me, but I wasn't sure how. Outside the window, lightning flashed again, and I jumped. A small squeaky sound escaped my throat.

"Don't worry," he said. "I fly through thunderstorms all the time."

And before I could stop myself, I was blurting out facts, which I tend to do when I'm nervous. "But thunderstorms can contain fierce updrafts and—*hic!*—downdrafts that can cause violent turbulence and potential structural damage. And the high concentrations of—*hic!*—supercooled water droplets can instantly freeze upon contact with the aircraft, causing a—*hic!*—rapid buildup of ice on wings, engines, and other surfaces, affecting the aircraft's aerodynamics and performance."

He laughed again. "Are you a meteorologist or something?"

"No. I'm a museum curator." Inhaling and exhaling slowly, I gripped my knees. "I'm just really, really afraid of flying."

"I can tell."

"When I was in middle school, this kid who said he could read palms told me I would die in a plane crash."

He shrank back a little, his expression skeptical. "I hope you didn't pay him."

"I had to. Everyone else was doing it, and I didn't want to be left out. But it scared the bejesus out of me. I thought he was just going to tell me, like, who I'd marry or how many kids I'd have."

He shook his head. "I'm pretty sure he did not have any of that intel."

"You're right. I'm sure you're right," I said, knowing I was babbling to a complete stranger, but unable to stop myself. "But ever since then, I've been afraid of flying. And while I was sitting at the bar waiting out the delay on this flight, I Googled 'flying through thunderstorms.'"

"That was probably a bad idea," he said, as the flight attendant appeared with our drinks.

"I haven't even told you about the hailstones, lightning strikes, and wind shear."

He handed me the vodka soda. "Here. This will help."

I took a sip, the soda bubbles fizzing on my tongue. "Thanks."

"A museum curator, huh?" He took a swallow of whiskey. "I think you might be the first one of those I've ever met."

"What do you do?"

"I play hockey."

I pushed my glasses up my nose. "Like, professionally?"

Another grin. "Yeah. Like professionally."

"That's cool." It had to be the reason his name seemed familiar. I wasn't really a hockey fan, but maybe I'd seen him on the news or something. It might explain the scars too. Hockey was sort of brutal, wasn't it?

"Do you follow hockey?" he asked.

"No," I admitted as the plane pushed back from the gate. "Sports are not really my thing."

"That's okay," he said. "Museums aren't really my thing."

"Do you play for Chicago?" I asked.

"Yes. But I grew up in northern Michigan."

"Me too." I was about to ask him where in northern Michigan he was from when the flight attendant appeared again. "I'm sorry, I'm going to need to collect your glasses before we take off. Due to the storms, there may be some rough air, and the pilot would like the crew to remain seated."

"No problem." He tossed back the rest of his whiskey and handed her the glass.

Trying not to freak out, I finished my vodka soda in two long gulps, feeling the alcohol go straight to my head. After handing her my glass, I decided to put in my earbuds and listen to my meditation playlist. I couldn't keep bothering this guy, and it was too late to ask him for his seat. He'd already turned his attention back to his phone, so I popped my earbuds in, needlessly tightened my seat belt again, and closed my eyes.

Above the soothing swell of the music, I heard the captain make announcements about the flight time (one hour and eleven minutes), the weather in Traverse City (clear and sixty-seven degrees), and the expectation for a bumpy ride getting out of Chicago (he was sorry).

As the plane gathered speed, I said a quick prayer, turned up the volume, and tried to remember to breathe.

• • •

The turbulence started within minutes.

Takeoff had been bad enough, the entire plane shuddering like it was made of plastic and might split apart, but things only got worse once we were up in the air. The plane lurched and groaned and shook so badly my teeth rattled. The cabin was roaring with scary noises. I gave up on my relaxing music and shoved my earbuds and phone back into my bag. Pressing my back into my seat, I gripped the armrests. My heart was beating way too fast, and I felt like someone was sitting on my chest. I couldn't get enough air. Was I underwater?

Other people started to freak out too. Overhead bins fell open, and bags tumbled down. A woman screamed, and a baby began to cry. The aircraft dropped, and I yelped, certain we'd fallen a thousand feet and were heading for the ground.

I felt a cool, heavy hand on my white knuckles. "Hey. It's okay."

My eyes flew open and I looked at my hot seatmate. "I don't want to die," I whimpered.

"You're not going to die." He kept his voice calm and his palm over my fingers.

"I am, I am." I shook my head wildly. "I didn't pay attention to the safety lecture and I don't know where my exit row is and my seat cushion doesn't seem like enough of a flotation device to save me." I looked up. "Where are the oxygen masks? They should have dropped by now! Everything is malfunctioning!"

"Everything is going to be okay."

"It's not. Human beings are not meant to be in the air. We are ground-dwelling creatures. And now the gods are punishing us for our hubris."

He stroked my hand. "What's your name?"

"Mabel Jane Buckley."

He tried not to smile, which resulted in a crooked half grin. "Mabel Jane Buckley, my name is Joe Lupo. It's nice to meet you."

"Nice to meet you too," I squeaked, my throat tight with panic.

"I wish we didn't have to die so soon after getting acquainted."

"We're not going to die." But at that moment, the plane dropped sharply again, causing more people to scream.

"We are, we are," I moaned, unable to stop my brain from careening toward catastrophe. "And it's not fair. You're too hot to die like this, and I just bought a house. I have a cat. Who's going to feed Cleopatra when I'm gone?"

"You're not going anywhere. You'll feed her yourself."

"Oh God, I lived such a sheltered life. I'm way too practical. I never splurged on designer shoes or a nice purse or a new car. I don't even know what a new car smells like!"

"Shhh." He kept moving his hand over mine. "You'll have all those things someday."

"And there's so much I didn't get to *do*," I wailed. "I never got married. I never had kids. I never had a crazy one-night stand with a hot stranger!"

"I'm definitely not your guy for A or B, but C isn't necessarily off the table," he said, cracking a smile. ...

"You don't understand, I haven't even had good sex!"

"Now if ever there was a reason to live..."

"I'm serious." Wild-eyed and hyperventilating, I stared him in the face. "I've never even had an orgasm with a guy. I've been faking it for years."

That one stumped him.

"I haven't even had that many boyfriends. And the ones I had just...couldn't figure it out."

"That's—that's, um—" Joe struggled for words and shook his head, like the concept was entirely foreign.

"I didn't want to hurt anyone's feelings, you know?" Now I was rocking back and forth, words gushing out of me like water over Niagara Falls. "I tend to date guys who just aren't that exciting or talented in bed—like they have the right equipment and all, but they're not sure how to use it."

He smiled. "Like the shot's all lined up, but they can't put the puck in the net?"

"Exactly! And I thought I'd have more time to remedy that. I'm only thirty! I thought there would be more pucks! Better pucks!"

"You've got plenty of time," he assured me.

"I don't, I don't," I howled, squeezing my eyes shut. "This is it. My life is flashing in front of my eyes. I'm going to die right here in this seat without ever experiencing a *good puck*!"

And just like that, I realized the plane wasn't shuddering anymore. The ride had smoothed out and the cabin was quiet. All around us, people were talking and laughing in relief.

Or maybe they were laughing at me.

My eyes flew open. I gasped. "Oh God."

The hot stranger holding my hand laughed.

"Oh. *God*." I lowered my lids again. "I'm not going to die, am I?"

"Nope."

"But now I want to." I peeked sideways at him. "I'm *so* sorry."

Another chuckle, warm and genuine. He took his hand off mine. "It's okay. You kept me entertained."

"Oh God." I wrapped my arms around myself, wishing I could curl into a little ball and roll under the seat. "What was your name again?"

"Joe Lupo."

I looked at him in complete despair. "Joe Lupo, you have to promise me you will forget all about this."

"I mean, I could try. In all honesty, I've never had a great memory, and I've taken a few bumps to the head that make it even worse." One side of his mouth hooked up, and his blue eyes twinkled. "But something tells me I'm gonna recall this."

I slumped in my seat.

"Ladies and gentlemen, we do apologize for the rough air." The flight attendant spoke calmly. "The captain has informed us that we've cleared the storms and it's now safe to move about the cabin, so he's turned off the fasten seat belt sign. We will offer a quick beverage service, so please keep the aisles clear."

"Would you like another drink?" Joe asked.

"No, thank you," I said, plucking my blouse away from my chest. Beneath the silk, my skin was sticky. I probably had armpit sweat rings.

Flight attendant Barbie was back with her flirty smile and perky banter, and Joe seemed to eat it up. I took my glasses off and cleaned the lenses, just for something to do. Then I dug my earbuds and laptop from my bag and listened to music while I went over some of the notes I'd taken at the conference.

But I was distracted.

Next to me, Joe Lupo sipped a cup of coffee and chatted with the pretty flight attendant, who seemed to have an awful lot of free time. Wasn't there something else she should be doing? Out of the corner of my eye, I saw his big hand wrapped around the cup and recalled the way he'd touched me.

Envy rippled low in my belly. He'd probably ask for her number. Maybe they'd hook up later tonight. They'd have a hot one-night stand during which she wouldn't be shy about what she liked or wanted, and she'd probably have a mind-blowing orgasm.

Probably? I snuck a peek at those muscular thighs again.

Make that definitely.

Joe Lupo struck me as a man who knew how to score.

Chapter 2

JOE

I'd missed the rehearsal dinner completely, but I met up with the wedding party at a bar called Buckley's Pub.

Which was kind of a weird coincidence.

I'd been thinking about that girl on the plane almost the entire drive up to Cherry Tree Harbor. The one with the dark hair and dimple in her cheek. The one who'd blurted out all those things about her sex life when she'd thought the plane was going down.

Mabel Jane Buckley.

Not my usual type, I'll admit, but there was something about her. She was cute in that girl-next-door kind of way, like the nice nurse at the pediatrician's office when you were a kid, the one who gave out the suckers. Or your favorite elementary school teacher, the one who said good things about you at parent-teacher conferences, even though you had trouble following all the rules.

She was thirty years old. Never had an orgasm during sex. Faking it for years with unexciting guys. Never had a one-night stand with a hot stranger. My interest had definitely been piqued.

But once the flight had smoothed out, she'd kept her earbuds in and her laptop open. Then after we landed, she'd avoided eye contact as she hurried through the jet bridge and into the terminal.

Too bad, I thought, pushing open the door to the pub. I wouldn't have minded playing the role of hot stranger for her. I had zero interest in being anyone's boyfriend, but putting the puck in the net was my specialty.

Inside Buckley's, an upscale place with lots of leather, dark wood, and brick walls, I spotted my twin brother Paul standing by the bar. We looked alike but weren't identical. Both of us had brown hair, our dad's muscular build, and the Lupo nose and mouth, but I had our mom's blue eyes where his were dark. We also had an older brother, Gianni, and a younger sister, Francesca.

Paul smiled when he saw me, grabbing me in a bear hug. "You're late, asshole."

"Sorry," I said. "Flight was delayed out of Chicago. We didn't even land in Traverse City until after eight, then it was a ninety-minute drive up here. How did everything go?"

"Fine." He shrugged and tipped up his beer. "Footsie seems pretty chill about everything, and our part is easy—we just stand behind him during the thing and then follow him back down the aisle when it's done."

Footsie—his actual name was Daniel Foote—was the groom, and his wedding was tomorrow afternoon. Paul, Footsie, and I had been friends since elementary school. We'd all played hockey together before I went on to Juniors and they played for our high school team. But we'd stayed close.

"Cool," I said. "I'll just do what you do. I'm gonna go find Footsie and say hi."

It was easy to spot him—he was always the tallest guy in any room. At six foot three, I wasn't short, but Footsie had a few inches on me, and he was built like a fucking tank. With his wide shoulders, blond hair, and thick beard, he looked like a Viking.

"Lupo!" Footsie's long arms engulfed me. "Good to see you, man!"

"You too. Sorry I missed the rehearsal."

He waved a hand in the air. "Don't worry about it."

"Joe Lupo! You're late!" Footsie's fiancée Lisa approached and wagged a finger at me. I hadn't been around her all that much, just enough to feel kind of sorry for my old buddy. She was always on his ass about something. Perfect example of why I didn't want a girlfriend.

"Sorry, Lisa." I gave her a quick kiss on the cheek. "Flight was delayed."

"Just be on time tomorrow, okay? And at some point tonight I want to introduce you to Jackie—she's your assigned bridesmaid for tomorrow night." She giggled. "She's *very* excited."

"Okay." I did not want to be assigned a bridesmaid, but I tried not to let it show on my face.

Lisa tugged Footsie's elbow and looked up at him. "Babe, I need you for a minute."

Exhaling, he looked at me. "Sorry."

"No worries." I held up my palms. "I'm going to grab a beer."

Back at the bar, I caught the bartender's eye and ordered a beer. When he brought it, I could tell he recognized me.

"Dude," he said. "Are you Joe Lupo?"

I nodded. "Hey."

"*Dude*," he said again. "That goal you scored in the last game against Toronto in the Western Conference finals was insane.

Fucking bar down."

"Thanks."

"Sucks you didn't win the cup. I was rooting for Chicago over Florida."

"We'll get it next time."

The bartender shook his head. "Fucking Florida, man. Do they even have ice?"

I laughed. "They do."

He shrugged. "Anyway, good to meet you. Beer is on the house."

"Thanks, I appreciate it." Bottle in hand, I walked back to my brother and puffed up my chest. "Sorry that took a while, I had to sign a few autographs at the bar."

"Fuck off," he said good-naturedly. "Did you really?"

"Nah." Laughing, I tipped up my beer. "The bartender recognized me though. I got a free beer."

"Like you can't afford to buy a beer." Paul shook his head. "Man, your life is something else."

"Hey, I worked my ass off to get where I am. And I have to work even harder to *stay* where I am." It was the truth. Competition for roster spots in the NHL was tough, and at thirty-two, I wasn't a young phenom anymore. Every year, a new crop of rookies came up, every single one of them hungry for their shot. They were fast, aggressive, and talented as fuck.

It only made me fight harder to stay in the game.

The Stanley Cup was the greatest prize in any sport, and I wanted that ring before I hung up my skates. I'd worked my entire life for it. Sacrificed blood, sweat, and tears. Spent thousands of hours on the ice—not to mention thousands of my parents' dollars on training, travel, and equipment. I didn't just want it for me—I wanted it for everyone who'd ever believed in me, from my family to my coaches to my friends and teammates.

I also wanted it for every naysaying asshole who'd scoffed at my dreams and told me I didn't have what it took. If I didn't have something, I worked on it until I got it, for the sheer love of the sport. For the rush I got from the win. For the unbeatable thrill of being one of the best in the game.

For as long as I could hang on to it.

"How's that shoulder?" Paul asked.

"Fine. It was only a partial tear. All I needed was some PT this summer."

"How many more years do you think you have in you, old man?"

I tipped up my beer. "As many as it takes."

"And then what?"

"Fuck if I know. I don't think about it."

"Well, you can always come back home and play on our rec team."

"The Dad Bod Squad?" I laughed. "No thanks."

"Come on, we have a good time!"

I gave him a smirk. "We have a better time in the NHL."

He shook his head. "Sometimes I still can't believe you got there. You're so damn lucky. I mean, I had the exact same genes. Why did I get the skinny legs and the crap eyesight?"

"We can't all be winners, Paul. Somebody has to sit in the stands and cheer when I score."

If we were twelve, he'd have tackled me. Now he just laughed.

"Is Alison here?" I asked.

"Yeah." His eyes scanned the crowd for his wife. "Over there on the couches talking to some of the bridesmaids. I just can't take any more wedding talk. I swear all women lose their minds about this shit. And none of it matters! Like, who cares about the fucking tablecloths or centerpieces? Footsie told me last week Lisa cried about the weather forecast and didn't speak to him for two days over some bullshit about who's sitting where at the reception. Also, she told him she doesn't want to have sex until they're married. Even though they've already been having sex for years."

"What?" I shook my head in disbelief. "Why?"

"Apparently it's a thing. You deny yourselves for months leading up to your wedding to 'up the ante' and make yourself want it more."

I snorted. "That's fucking stupid. Why would you have to make yourself want it more?"

"I have no idea. But Lisa claims it's going to make their wedding night sex better."

"It's going to make it faster, that's for sure." We laughed, and I felt the stress of the long trip here dissolve. It was good to be with my brother again. Growing up, we'd spent every day beating the shit out of each other—Gianni too—because we were all so competitive, but we were tight.

"So you didn't bring Courtney with you, huh?" he asked.

"Nope." At the mention of my ex, I took a long pull on my beer.

"I take it that means you're off again?"

"Permanently."

"I've heard that before."

"I'm serious. I haven't even spoken to her in months."

"What happened?"

I shrugged. "The relationship was just too much work, and I need to focus on hockey. She'd say she understood, and then five minutes later, she'd complain I wasn't giving her enough attention. She was moody as hell."

"All women are moody." He stopped with his beer halfway to his mouth. "But don't tell my wife I said that."

"It wasn't *just* the moods," I told him. "She was constantly jealous and accusing me of cheating on her when I traveled, even though I never did. I got tired of it."

"Come on. Not once?" My brother looked at me sideways. "All those puck bunnies hanging around and you never got tempted?"

"I didn't say I never got tempted—I said I never *cheated*, and that's the truth. I'm loyal. And I was sick of trying to prove it to her." I rolled my neck, which was stiff from travel. Definitely not from age.

"That's fair."

"She also wanted to move in, and that was a *hard no* for me. I need my own space." I smiled as my sister-in-law walked up behind my brother. "Hey, Al."

"Joey!" She threw her arms around me and gave me a squeeze. "Good to see you."

"You too." I loved Alison—she'd been around almost as long as Footsie, and she'd spent years saying no to my brother before finally agreeing to go out with him. Later on, she admitted she'd liked him the whole time, but she wanted to be the last person he dated, not the first. You had to admire the long-game strategy there. "Thanks for sending the videos of Hudson. I can't believe he's walking already."

Alison smiled. "I know, me neither."

"Time to get him on skates."

She laughed. "Paul said the same thing. Let's maybe give the kid a chance to get used to shoes first. There's more to life than hockey."

My brother and I exchanged a confused look, like we didn't understand that concept.

"So I hear you're sticking around a few days after the wedding," Alison went on.

I nodded. "I don't have to be back in Chicago until

Wednesday. My mom said everybody is coming to dinner at their house Sunday night?"

"Yes." Alison smiled. "You'll get to see all your nieces and nephews."

"Can't wait." Being an uncle was the best—you could just hang out with kids for a little while, let them climb all over you, take them for ice cream, and then give them back at the end of the day, sticky and tired, but someone else's problem. Gianni and his wife Ellie had three kids, Paul and Alison had one, and my little sister and her husband had a newborn daughter I hadn't even seen yet. Which reminded me, I should pick up a little gift for her. "Hey, what time do we have to be at the venue tomorrow?"

"Ceremony is at four," Paul said, "but we're meeting for photos at two thirty. You're staying at The Pier Inn, right?"

"Right."

He nodded. "Us too. I'll ride over at two thirty with you and leave our car for Alison, so she doesn't have to get there so early."

"Works for me," I said, stifling a yawn. "God, I'm tired. It's been a long day."

"You're lucky you got out of Chicago," Alison said. "I heard the storms were bad."

"They were. The flight was rough. This woman next to me was terrified. She started listing all these things she'd never done because she was scared she'd never get a chance to do them."

"Like what?" Paul asked.

"Buy a new car, get married, stop faking it in bed."

Alison's eyebrows shot up. "She told you she fakes it in bed?"

"Yes. She said she always dates nice guys who don't know what they're doing, and she doesn't want to hurt their feelings, so she doesn't say anything."

"Damn, she really spilled her guts," Paul said.

"She did." I couldn't help chuckling at the memory. "I had to hold her hand and try to calm her down."

Alison laughed too. "You held her hand? Did she know who you were?"

I shook my head. "Not a hockey fan. Although she *did* tell me I was too hot to die."

Paul rolled his eyes. "Of course she did."

Finishing my beer, I took out my wallet and grabbed a ten for the bartender. "I think I'm gonna take off. I'm exhausted, and I need my beauty sleep."

"Wait until you have kids," my brother said. "You don't know the meaning of exhaustion until you're a parent."

"That is a life choice I don't plan on making."

"Ever?" Alison sounded surprised. "You don't want kids?"

I shrugged. "Maybe someday in the distant future, when I'm too old and decrepit to play hockey anymore, and I'm bored of things like sex, sleep, loud music, and doing dumb shit whenever I want."

My sister-in-law clucked her tongue. "Forget I asked."

"See you tomorrow," I said with a grin. After leaving the ten on the bar beneath my empty beer, I headed outside.

On the walk back to my car, I wondered again about Mabel Jane Buckley and hoped she'd gotten home okay. Was she already tucked in bed, her cat curled up beside her? Was she watching TV? Scrolling social media on her phone? Would she search my name? Did she even remember it?

She was still on my mind when I got into bed in my hotel room. After undressing completely and sliding between the sheets, I grabbed my phone and typed "Mabel Buckley museum curator" into the Google search bar.

The top result was the staff page on a website for something called the Cherry Tree Harbor Historical Society. I clicked on it, and there she was, looking just as cute but much more relaxed than she had on the plane. It was a headshot that sort of looked like a yearbook photo. The top half of her hair was tied back from her face, and her smile showed off that dimple in her cheek. She wore her glasses with the thick black frames and a pearl necklace that immediately put a dirty thought in my head.

You're a dick, I told myself. *Put the phone down and go to sleep.*

I set my phone on the charger, turned off the lamp, and stretched out on my back. It felt great. I liked taking up the entire bed, and I didn't like anybody clinging to me during the night. Courtney used to practically strangle me.

I didn't even miss the sex, which hadn't been that good in the end anyway. She'd started playing all kinds of games, pretending like she wasn't interested, using sex as a weapon, becoming infuriated when I refused to beg for it, accusing me of "getting it somewhere else." There would be a lot of door slamming and tears and reminders about how hard it was to have a boyfriend who was gone all the time and emotionally unavailable even when he was home. I'd always end up apologizing, even though I wasn't sorry. But the accusations got worse and the arguing more frequent, and finally, I'd had enough. Before the season was over, I told her I wanted out. The stress was starting to affect my game.

She called me a self-centered, egotistical bastard and threw a plate at my head—which I blocked with an elbow, but it still fucking hurt. "You never loved me!" she sobbed. "You only ever loved the game!"

I didn't argue.

She screamed a few more insults, told me I'd end up miserable and alone, and stomped out. I hadn't heard from her since.

Which was fine by me.

My apartment was *mine* again. Quiet when I wanted quiet. Loud when I wanted loud. I could play video games without her sulking because I was ignoring her. I could grow a playoff beard and not hear complaints that I looked grungy. I could cook my dad's pasta with meat sauce for dinner without listening to her whine that she couldn't eat carbs. I could come and go as I pleased without any hassle. And I slept better at night with the bed to myself.

Don't get me wrong, I wasn't planning to be celibate, just single. If I met someone who was up for a no-drama, no-strings-attached good time, I'd indulge. Otherwise, being alone suited me just fine for now. I got my fill of love from the game, from the fans, from the crowd. I respected what my parents and siblings had, but that didn't mean I had to follow in their footsteps. I liked the idea of being my own man. Forging my own path.

Placing my hands behind my head, I spread my legs a little wider and closed my eyes.

Life was fucking great.

I wouldn't change a thing.

Chapter 3

Mabel

"*Y*ou said *what* to a total stranger?" My best friend and sister-in-law, Ari, glanced over at me from behind the wheel of her car. We were on our way to her cousin's wedding—I was her date, since my brother Dashiel was out of town.

"I told him I'd never had good sex," I repeated, cringing in the passenger seat.

She burst out laughing. "You didn't!"

"Oh, it gets worse. I also told him I'd never had an orgasm with a guy, and I'd been faking it for years."

"What?" Ari shrieked.

"Seriously, I've never been so embarrassed in my life. Then I told him—"

"Wait a minute, back up. Is that really true? *Have* you been faking it for years?"

I squirmed a little. "Yes."

"Why didn't you ever tell me that?"

"Because it's embarrassing, okay? And I don't like talking to you that much about sex because you're married to my brother. I love that my best friend is now my sister, but there are just some details I don't need."

"But we can still talk about sex in a general way," she countered. "I was your best friend *way* before I married Dash. You've really never had good sex?" She sounded both surprised and sad for me.

"It's not like it's been terrible," I said, a little defensively. "I don't have any trauma about it or anything. I just haven't been with anyone who knew how to..." *Put the puck in the net*, I heard Joe Lupo say in my head. "To get the job done on my end."

"It's not a job, Mabel."

"You know what I mean. And maybe it's partly my fault." I pulled down the visor in the passenger seat and used the mirror to apply my lip gloss. "I'm not good at saying what I want. I'm a talker in every other situation in life except that one. I get shy."

"Well, in the future, I encourage you to speak up." She laughed. "Just maybe not to strangers on a plane."

"I thought I was gonna die, okay?" I flipped the visor back up and stuck my gloss back in my clutch. "All these things were running through my head that I wasn't going to live to do. I was too distraught to think straight. I practically propositioned him!"

"Like you asked him to join the mile high club?"

"I'm guessing he's already a member, but no. I just told him I'd never had a one-night stand with a hot stranger, and he made a joke about how it wasn't off the table."

"Are you sure it was a joke?"

"Definitely. Trust me, this guy was way out of my league. He just felt sorry for me."

"Well, I'm sorry too. I know how much you hate to fly." Ari turned into the parking lot next to the Chapel by the Sea. "What did he look like anyway?"

"Brown hair. Blue eyes. Great smile." I'd been thinking about his face nonstop. "His nose was kind of crooked, and he had a scar on his lip, but he was gorgeous. The most gorgeous guy I've ever met."

Pulling into an empty spot, she put the car in park. "Did you get his name?"

"Joe Lupo."

"Hold on. *Joe Lupo?*" She grabbed my arm. "The hockey player?"

Surprised, I looked over at her. "He did mention being a hockey player. Do you know him?"

"Well, I've never *met* him, but I know who he is. He plays for Chicago, right? He's a forward?"

I shrugged. "Maybe."

"It's gotta be him. He's from around here, and Dash knows his older brother Gianni. They were housemates at some point in L.A." She started to laugh again. "You blurted those things out to Joe Lupo?"

"Don't make it worse, Ari." We got out of the car into the humid July heat and started walking toward the chapel steps, avoiding the puddles. It had rained off and on here today, and there was supposed to be another storm coming. "It was the most mortified I've ever been. I could not even look him in the eye afterward."

"I'm sorry. But can I please tell Dash about this?"

"No! You can't tell anybody! I just want to forget it ever happened. And I hope I never run into Joe Lupo again." I lowered my voice as we entered the sanctuary, which was blissfully cool. "Now remind me whose wedding we're at."

"My cousin Lisa. She's kind of annoying," Ari whispered, "but she's family, and my parents said I had to come and represent the DeLucas, since they're on vacation. Thanks again for coming with me."

"I don't mind. Dressing up, cake, champagne…what's not to love?" I picked up a program from a basket resting on a table just as an usher wearing a dark suit approached us.

"Bride or groom?" he asked.

"Bride," said Ari. "I'm her cousin."

"Right this way. Family is up front." We were led up the aisle and shown to a pew three rows back. Ari went in first, and I followed her, which put me on the end.

"Where's Dash again?" I asked as we sat down.

"Film shoot in L.A. until next Thursday. It ran over." Her expression was pained as she lowered herself onto the bench. Her stomach was big and round as a beach ball. "I hate when he's gone so long. What if I go into labor early and he's not here?"

"I'm here." I patted her shoulder. "How many more weeks to go?"

"Four," she said with a sigh. "And I hope they go quickly. I'm so uncomfortable. How ridiculous is it that I'm wearing flip-flops with this dress?"

"Not ridiculous at all, you look beautiful." I smiled at her. "That color blue is stunning on you."

"Thanks. You look good too." Her eyes traveled over my strapless black skater dress and lingered on my high-heeled sandals. "Tell me I'll have a waist again someday. And feet that aren't swollen. And a face that isn't puffy."

I laughed, tucking my clutch between us. "You will. Now you tell me that someday I'll meet *the one*—that guy who will fall as crazy in love with me as Dash did with you. And that we'll get married and have kids as adorable as yours." Dash and Ari already had a two-year-old daughter Wren, a darling, precocious little thing with her mom's brown curls and the Buckley dimple in her cheek.

"You will meet the one," she said confidently. Then she leaned over to whisper in my ear. "But first, you're going to have good sex."

"Shhhhh!" I glanced around to make sure no one had heard. "Ari, we're in a chapel, for God's sake."

"Which is a perfect place to pray for something you want."

I glanced at the cross behind the altar but didn't feel quite right about asking God for a headboard-shaking orgasm. Instead, I said a quick prayer that *the one* existed somewhere out there and that I'd get to plan my own wedding someday. Then I glanced at the ivory card stock program in my hands.

Welcome to the wedding of Lisa and Daniel, it said at the top. I was scanning the order of events listed on the front when the organ music began. Like everyone else, I looked toward the back of the chapel, where ushers were waiting to seat the grandparents, then the groom's parents, then the bride's mother. Next came three bridesmaids and the maid of honor, all wearing a different dress in the same shade of dusty rose. They were followed by an adorable ring bearer and flower girl, who dropped pale pink rose petals from a little white basket. When the bride appeared at the back of the chapel on her dad's arm, all the guests rose to watch their procession.

I love this moment at a wedding, where the groom gets to see the woman who will become his wife walking toward him. Maybe I'm just a sappy romantic, but it always gets to me, especially when the groom tears up. All four of my brothers had gotten weepy at their weddings, and I hoped someday my groom would, too. I wanted a husband who loved me that much.

As I rose to my feet, I glanced toward the altar, where

the groom stood solemnly in a black suit, the four guys in his wedding party lined up behind him like dominoes. They were all tall, wide-shouldered, and somber-faced. My eyes traveled over them, cataloging their features. The groom was blond with a beard. The best man had longish, layered brown hair and scruff. Groomsmen two and three were clean-shaven and—

Wait a minute.

I blinked. It couldn't be.

I leaned forward, my vision going a little fuzzy at the edges.

It had to be some trick of the light. Some figment of my imagination. Some crossed wires in my brain that conflated a memory from yesterday with what I was seeing now.

Joe Lupo was groomsman number four.

Was this God's idea of a joke?

As if I'd summoned his attention, he suddenly looked straight at me. Our eyes locked. And there was no doubt about it—it was him.

His brow furrowed slightly, as if trying to place me. Then the corners of his mouth twitched.

"Oh no," I whimpered. Pretending I had an issue with one of my contact lenses, I looked at my lap and fussed with my eye. Then I whispered frantically to Ari, "Change places with me. Hurry." Taking her by the shoulders, I started squeezing behind her so she would be on the aisle and I could hide behind her girth.

"Mabel, what on earth?" Ari struggled to get around me.

"Don't ask." I ducked down behind her, although she was in flip-flops and I was in heels, making it awkward. "I'll explain later."

The bride arrived at the altar, but I didn't dare peek at her dress or her veil or her bouquet, details I normally loved to obsess over. Instead, I fished my oversized sunglasses out of my clutch and put them on.

Ari stared at me. "Why are you wearing those?"

"It's very bright in here," I whispered. "Do you happen to have a big hat?"

She looked at me like I was nuts. "No! Are you okay?"

"I'm fine." But I wasn't. A quick look at the back of the program confirmed that Joe Lupo was indeed a member of the wedding party.

How could I be so unlucky?

My face was on fire. Sweat trickled down my chest. For the rest of the ceremony, all I did was concentrate on leaning and slouching in whatever way would keep me blocked from Joe's view. After the bride and groom were pronounced Mr. and Mrs. Daniel Foote, the guests all cheered and the newlyweds made their way back down the aisle.

I clapped along with the rest of the crowd, but I kept my eyes on the floor and my chin tucked. When our row was dismissed, I followed closely behind Ari, my head down, until we made it outside. Then I made a beeline for the car.

"Mabel, where are you going? I can't move that fast!"

"Sorry." My leg bounced nervously while I waited for her to catch up. The wedding party was standing on the pavement in front of the chapel, and out of the corner of my eye, I saw Joe scanning the guests spilling down the steps, like he was looking for someone. Quickly, I turned around so he'd see only my back.

When Ari reached me, she was out of breath. "What is going on with you?"

"He's here," I said through my teeth.

"What?"

"He's. *Here*," I said a little louder.

"Who's here?"

"Joe Lupo," I stage-whispered. "The hockey player guy. The

hot stranger from the plane. He's a *groomsman*."

"Stop it." She immediately looked over my shoulder toward the chapel lawn and gasped. "Oh my God! I think I see him!"

"Ari! Don't be so obvious!"

"Dang, you were right. He *is* hot."

"I have to get out of here. I think he spotted me during the ceremony."

"Is that why you put on the sunglasses?" She started to laugh. "I think you made yourself *more* conspicuous, not less. It's not even sunny outside today, let alone in the chapel." Then she gasped again. "He's looking over here."

My heart rapped hard against my ribs. "I can't face him, Ari. I'll die."

Still looking over my shoulder, her eyes lit up. "Well, brace yourself, because he's walking this way."

Eyeballing the parking lot, I considered making a run for it, but given the platform heels I was wearing, that plan didn't seem wise. Face-planting on the asphalt would only make things worse. Taking a breath, I turned around.

My knees almost buckled as he closed the distance between us. If my life was a movie, I'd have grabbed the remote and pressed pause just to swoon over the way he looked as he came toward me, or maybe even played his approach in slow motion. He'd been hot in jeans and a button-down, but he was downright scorching in a suit and tie. He was also a lot taller than I'd realized. Even in my thick-soled heels, the top of my head didn't clear his shoulder.

"Mabel Jane Buckley," he said, his mouth curving into a boyishly sexy grin. "We meet again."

"So we do." I laughed nervously and lifted my shoulders. "What are the chances?"

"Hi." Ari held out her hand. "I'm Ari. Lisa is my cousin."

He shook her hand. "I'm Joe Lupo. Old friend of Footsie—I mean Dan."

"Nice to meet you," Ari said. "I've actually met your brother Gianni before. He and my husband Dash are friends."

"Dashiel Buckley, the actor?"

Ari smiled. "Yes."

Joe looked at me, putting it together. "And is that your... brother?"

"Yes," I said. "He was supposed to be here, but his film shoot ran longer than expected, so Ari asked me to be her date tonight."

He smiled. "I'm glad."

"You are?"

He laughed at the surprise in my expression. "Yes. It's nice to see you again, now that we're safely on the ground."

"Um, if you'll excuse me a moment, I'm just going to run over and say a quick hello to my aunt and uncle," Ari said, giving my upper arm a hard pinch. "Back in a few."

After she walked away—giving me two very enthusiastic thumbs-up from behind his back—Joe took a step closer to me. "So...this is a coincidence."

"Yes." I stared at the tiny scar on his lip and imagined running my tongue over it in a highly inappropriate manner.

"You look beautiful."

"Thanks. So do you." Oh, shit. "I mean, not beautiful." Dammit, I made it worse! "Good," I managed to get out, although it was an understatement. "You look good."

"Thank you." He smiled, tucking his hands in his pockets. "You know, I was thinking about you last night."

"You were?"

"Yes. The wedding party went to a place called Buckley's Pub."

"Oh!" Now it made sense. "That's my brother Xander's bar."

"Cool place."

"I thought maybe you were wondering if the weirdo in seat 3A got back to her home planet okay," I joked.

"I didn't think you were weird. Just scared."

"Again, I'm *really* sorry about unloading all that personal stuff on you. I honestly thought I wasn't going to make it."

"Well, it's a good thing you did. Now you can start working on that list."

"What list?"

"Of all the things you haven't done."

Our eyes met, and my belly flipped.

"Hey Joe!" someone yelled from behind him. "We need you for pictures before it starts raining!"

"Be there in a minute!" he called over his shoulder. Facing me again, he asked, "So will I see you at the reception?"

Somehow I found my voice. "Yes."

"Good. Maybe we can have a drink while your life isn't flashing in front of your eyes."

I smiled, trying to sound breezy, like hot NHL players asked me to drinks all the time. "Okay, but you have to promise you won't bring up anything I said last night."

"Well, now you're just taking all the fun out of it." Grinning, he started walking backward, his eyes turning my insides molten. "See you there."

• • •

"He was *definitely* flirting with you," Ari said as we made the short drive over to The Pier Inn. I'd repeated my conversation with Joe for her, word for word.

"I don't know." I remembered how he'd flirted with the pretty blond flight attendant. "I think that's just his personality."

"Listen, I was standing right there. I saw the way he looked at you. I heard him say he was glad to see you. And he said you looked beautiful, right?"

"I think so. I might have dreamed it."

"And he said he'd been thinking about you."

"Only because he was at Buckley's Pub last night and remembered my name."

She thumped a hand on the steering wheel. "Mabel Buckley! Is it so impossible to believe that he'd be attracted to you?"

"Kind of." I shrugged. "I'm not saying that to be down on myself—it's just facts. This guy is some kind of NHL superstar, and hot jocks usually go for a different type of girl."

"Stop it. You're gorgeous and funny and smart."

I smiled at her. "You're my best friend. You are not a good judge of me."

"I'd argue I'm the *best* judge. And I don't think you should ignore this kind of sign from the universe."

"What are you talking about?"

"Think about it. Less than twenty-four hours ago, you thought you were going to die without ever having a one-night stand with a hot stranger, and lo and behold, a hot stranger hath appeared before you—twice! This is fate taking the reins of your life, Mabel Buckley."

"That's ridiculous," I said, laughing at her dramatic assessment. "It's not fate, it's geography. We both grew up in this area. His friend married your cousin. We happened to be on the same flight from Chicago."

"You say tomato, I say to-*mah*to." Ari turned into the parking lot of The Pier Inn and pulled up at the valet.

"Because I know a tomato when I see one. I'm not saying I won't enjoy his company over a glass of bubbly, but don't get your hopes up. Nothing is going to happen."

However, inside the ladies' room of The Pier Inn, I fussed with my hair, reapplied my lip gloss, and swiped my roll-on perfume oil behind my ears, across my throat, and inside my wrists. Then, after a furtive glance around to make sure I was alone, I stuck it down the front of my dress and rolled the scent between my breasts.

I was pretty sure this situation was a tomato.

But if it *was* a to-mahto, I wanted to be prepared.

Chapter 4

*P*hotos took for-fucking-ever.

The poses were stupid. My cheeks hurt from smiling. I was sweating beneath my suit. Lisa complained constantly about the humidity, the coming storm, the lack of good light. I kept my opinions to myself and my attitude positive for Footsie's sake, but all I could think of was getting to the reception, ditching this jacket, and grabbing a cold beer.

But when we arrived at The Pier Inn, the wedding party was instructed to wait at the top of the stairs of the second-floor ballroom until we heard the DJ announce our names. Then we had to head straight for the dance floor with our assigned partner for an entire song. It was the last thing I wanted to do, but I smiled and swayed to the music with Jackie, the bridesmaid I'd been matched with. She giggled uncontrollably the entire time.

Over the top of her head, I spotted Mabel seated next to her pregnant sister-in-law at a table near the edge of the dance floor. Our eyes met, and she smiled at me. She was so fucking cute.

"Ow!" Jackie stopped dancing and looked down. "You stepped on my foot."

"Sorry—I got distracted for a second. Are your toes okay? I have big feet."

The giggle returned. "I'm fine."

For the rest of the song, I concentrated on where I stepped. When the music ended, I escorted Jackie off the dance floor, and—as instructed—we stood near the bandstand to watch the newlyweds' first dance as husband and wife. Tons of phones were aimed at them, and the official photographer and videographer were also right in their faces. After that, we had to go over to the cake table and applaud as Lisa and Footsie cut the cake, fed each other small bites, and posed for more pictures.

When all the stupid pageantry was done, I dropped my suit jacket onto the back of my chair at the head table and cuffed my sleeves. Looking around the room, I spotted Mabel standing by herself at one of the huge windows overlooking the harbor, a glass of champagne in her hand. Straightening my tie, I decided I'd grab a beer and go talk to her. However, I was mobbed at the bar by a dozen different people who wanted to talk hockey, family, or old times—sometimes all three.

"Lupo, I wondered if you'd be here! Long time, no see!"

"Great goal against Mayer in the finals!"

"How's your mom and dad?"

"We were at that game in Detroit when you scored in overtime!"

"You'll get 'em next season, huh?"

"Hey, remember that night we snuck out and took your old man's new truck?"

"I hear your sister just had a baby!"

"Man, I remember watching you skate when you guys were just Mites. I said back then, I said that Lupo kid's going all the way, and I was right, wasn't I?"

I nodded yes and answered questions and fielded compliments, all while keeping one eye on Mabel at the window. At one point, she looked over her shoulder at me. A little buzz shot through my bloodstream—the same one I'd felt in the chapel when I realized who the pretty brunette was, staring at me from the third row. I excused myself from the conversation I was in and headed her way.

She looked different tonight. Her dress was strapless, tight on top and loose on the bottom, the kind of skirt that would twirl out if she spun around. It wasn't too short but showed a nice amount of leg—hers were gorgeous, with calf muscles that made me wonder if she was a runner. She wore her hair down, and it hung in a straight, shiny curtain that skimmed her shoulder blades. But my favorite thing was her shoes. They were fucking hot—black high heels with a platform sole and a ribbon tied in a bow around her ankle. For a moment I imagined those ankles on my shoulders.

But when I reached her side, I behaved like a perfect gentleman. "Hello."

"Hello." She turned and smiled, causing that dimple to appear. "How were pictures?"

"Endless." I shook my head. "Lisa is very...particular."

She laughed. "Most brides are."

"It's just so much. All the posing and announcements and things you *have* to do."

"Weddings do have a lot of traditions associated with them."

"I'm never doing any of it, even if I do get married someday," I said grouchily. "It will be elope or no deal."

She smiled and sipped her champagne.

"Lisa is taking the threat of rain personally, like Mother Nature made it her mission to ruin this wedding."

"Maybe it will turn out to be good luck," Mabel said brightly. "That's actually a common superstition in a lot of cultures—that rain on your wedding day is a good thing."

"It is?"

"Yes." She lifted her shoulders. "Rain is often associated with growth and abundance, so maybe it means their family tree will bear a lot of fruit. Rain can also be seen as a symbol of renewal, so it could also mean a fresh start—the past is washed away and the future can begin. I've also heard it said that a wet knot is harder to untie, so maybe it's as simple as that. The knot they tied today will never be unraveled."

Now it was my turn to smile, because she sounded just like a teacher. "I bet you had perfect grades in school."

The comment seemed to fluster her, and she faced the window again, laughing nervously. "Sorry. I nerd out about certain kinds of stuff, and I forget that other people don't find cultural beliefs as fascinating as I do."

"Don't be sorry. I learned something new." Tipping up my beer, I looked out the window again. Today was definitely not the best day Lake Michigan had to offer, but the view was still impressive. The water was choppy and gunmetal gray, white caps cresting along its surface. To the right a peninsula jutted out into the water, a lighthouse at its tip, waves crashing dramatically against its base.

"Did you grow up around here?" I asked.

She nodded. "About half a mile up the road. I used to work at the restaurant here as a hostess during the summer. I'd ride my bike."

"I worked in restaurants too when I was young."

"Really?"

"My dad's a chef and owns an Italian restaurant, so my siblings and I all worked there at one time or another. Ever been to Trattoria Lupo?"

"In Traverse City? Yes! I love that place—the food is so good. That's your dad's restaurant?"

"Yep."

"And you worked there?"

"Welllll…" I tilted my head from side to side. "We were *supposed* to be working. But my brothers and I did a lot of fucking around in the kitchen. Then when the place would empty out, we'd play hockey on the dining room floor. My dad used to get so mad."

She laughed. "I bet. How many brothers do you have?"

"Two. A fraternal twin—Paul, he's around here somewhere—and an older brother, Gianni. I also have a little sister."

"Is your twin one of the other groomsmen?" she asked.

"Yes."

She nodded slowly. "I think I know which one. I saw him when I—recognized you."

I grinned when I saw the way her cheeks reddened. "That must have been a shock, huh?"

"Uh. Yes." She laughed sheepishly and tucked her hair behind her ear. "I sort of wanted to disappear."

"I noticed the sunglasses."

"Can you blame me? I'm *still* embarrassed."

I took a sip of my beer. "Want me to tell you something embarrassing about me? Even the score?"

She faced me. "Yes, please."

I exhaled, glancing out at the churning lake again.

"Come on, you can tell me," she coaxed. "I'll take it to the grave."

"I trust you. I'm just trying to come up with something."

"Is it that hard to come up with something stupid you've said or done?"

"Oh, I've done a ton of stupid stuff. I'm just not easily embarrassed."

She sighed, her posture deflating. "Never mind."

"No, wait—I've got something." I took a deep breath, like this was a dramatic announcement. "My real name is Giuseppe."

Her jaw fell open. She had an adorably round mouth with shiny, strawberry-red lips. "That's it? That's the most embarrassing thing about you?"

I shrugged.

"I think I feel worse knowing that." She tossed back the rest of her champagne. "I have to go throw myself in the lake now."

When she tried to walk past me, I laughed and grabbed her arm. "Hang on, hang on. I thought of something else."

"I'm listening."

I kept my hand around her forearm. Her skin was warm. "When I was a senior, I made this big sign to ask my girlfriend to prom, and I spelled her name wrong."

That strawberry mouth twitched. "Did she still say yes?"

"Yeah, but she put that sign all over social media and I felt like a dumbass."

"How long had you been dating her?"

"Long enough to know how to spell her name if I'd been paying attention."

"What was her name?"

"Lindsey. With a fucking *E*."

She laughed, her head falling to one side, and I had the urge to press my face into the curve of her neck and brush my lips across her throat. I wondered what she smelled like. How she kissed. What sounds she'd make in the dark.

Whether that one-night stand with a stranger was still on the table.

Dammit, I *knew* I could give her that orgasm if she'd give me a chance. It might take some time, but I was patient. I was skilled. And I was competitive as fuck, so the opportunity to succeed where others had failed was eating at me.

But despite what she'd said on the plane, Mabel Buckley did not seem like the type of girl to jump into bed with a guy she'd only just met, so I took my hand off her before my mouth said something my brain would regret.

"I could use another drink," she said, glancing at the bar across the room. "What about you?"

"I could, but I'm afraid if I go over there, I'll be swarmed by people who want to talk to me." I met her eyes. "And I'd rather just talk to you."

Her cheeks turned pink. "I could go grab us a couple drinks, and we could take them out on the balcony," she suggested. "It's not raining yet, but I bet not a lot of people are out there because of the heat."

"Works for me." I grabbed a five from my wallet and handed it to her. "Here. Tip the bartender."

She nodded. "I'll meet you outside."

. . .

As Mabel had predicted, we had the balcony all to ourselves.

Leaning my elbows on the railing, I looked over at her. "You know, I almost missed that flight yesterday."

"Really?"

"Yes. I was coming from a charity event that ran over. I'm glad it was delayed."

"Me too," she said, tucking her hair behind one ear.

"So you don't follow hockey, huh?"

She shook her head. "No. I mean, I could follow a game. I know the basics, I just don't know any player names or team standings or anything."

"So like, if I quiz you on the basics of ice hockey, you'd get an A?"

She considered this as she sipped her champagne. "Try me."

Straightening up, I turned around and parked my hips against the railing. "How many periods are there?"

"Three."

"How long is each one?"

She chewed her lip. "Twenty minutes?"

"Not including the goalie, how many guys does each team start with on the ice?"

She thought for a second. "Five."

"Okay, perfect score so far. I better give you a hard one." I tipped up my beer and pondered my options. "What's it called when one team has more players on the ice than the other because someone is serving a penalty?"

Her nose wrinkled. "I don't know that one."

"A power play."

"Ah." She snapped her fingers. "That's right."

"So you've at least heard of it."

That earned me a flick on the shoulder. "Hey, I might not know everything about hockey, but I did grow up in Michigan."

I laughed. "Okay, last one. What's the trophy called that the playoff champion gets?"

"The Stanley Cup," she answered triumphantly.

"Excellent. Four out of five right. Is that an A?"

"It's a B-," she said with a grin. "But I'll take it."

"Believe me, it's way better than I'd do on any kind of history quiz or whatever you studied."

"I studied a lot of history. Majored in anthropology."

"That's what your degree is in?"

"One of them."

"How many do you have?"

"Beyond the B.A., I have an M.A. with a specialization in Historical Anthropology and a Ph.D. with specializations in Historical Archaeology and Museum Studies." She said it like it was no big deal, but I could only imagine how much work it had been.

"Damn. That's impressive. Does that mean you're, like, a *doctor*?"

"I mean, technically. Academically." She seemed slightly embarrassed. "But I don't use the title day to day. Only when I'm teaching at the college level."

"So you're a professor too?"

"Just part-time." Thunder rumbled in the distance, and she glanced out over the surging lake. The wind had picked up, and the metallic clank on the harbor flagpole was louder and more frequent. "Sounds like the storm is getting closer. Should we go in?"

"In a minute." I didn't feel like talking to anyone else…or sharing her. "Did you play a sport in high school?"

"I ran cross country."

I nodded, recalling her muscular calves. "I bet you were fast."

"Not really." She laughed. "I always thought I'd have done better if I was a little taller. But my brothers got all the height."

"Ah."

"I was also in the school musicals. And I was president of the French club."

"Can't say I've ever been in a musical, but I do know some French words—not that I'd say them in front of you."

She smiled. "Where'd you learn them?"

"I know a bunch of French-Canadian hockey players. Those

motherfuckers have filthy mouths." I sipped my beer, enjoying her girlish laugh. "So is your family still around here?"

"Yes. My dad lives in the house where I grew up. One of my brothers lives in town, and the other three live within an hour of here."

"You have *four* older brothers?" Lightning flashed silently over the water, the roll of thunder following a few seconds later. The smell of ozone permeated the air.

She nodded. "Yep. And we were raised by a single dad. A *lot* of testosterone in that house. Dating was, to say the least, difficult."

"I can imagine," I said, recalling how Gianni, Paul, and I used to stare down the chumps who came sniffing around Francesca in high school. I wondered what happened to her mom but didn't feel like I should ask.

"They were always threatening to beat up anyone I brought home. They thought everybody had an attitude." She sighed, looking out at the lake. "Sometimes I think that's why I date a certain type of guy."

"What type is that?"

"Quiet. Reserved. Nice. No alpha male energy."

"Nothing wrong with nice guys," I said, although clearly there was plenty wrong with the dumbasses she'd been in bed with.

"No, and I would never date an asshole, but…" She seemed to struggle with what she wanted to say next.

"But what?"

"This is going to sound bad."

"Try me."

She tucked in her lips for a moment, her eyes on the approaching storm. The air was thicker now. Charged with electricity. "Sometimes—in certain situations—I wish they'd stop being so reserved and go a little alpha male on me."

"What kind of situations?"

Her shoulders rose. She looked at me sideways. "You know. When they're lining up the shot."

"Ah." Wind came out of the south, blowing her hair in front of her shoulders and carrying the scent of her perfume. I breathed it in—something sensual and sweet that made my mouth water. Vanilla maybe?

She looked down at her feet. Her toes were painted bright pink. "Of course, maybe I'm talking out both sides of my mouth, since I also want someone unselfish who cares about how I feel too. Maybe that's too much to ask for."

"I don't think so." I hesitated. "Can I ask you something personal? If you don't want to answer, you can tell me to fuck off."

She finished her champagne. "Go ahead. I'm the one who put all my personal business out there last night."

Lightning flashed again, the reverberation of thunder close behind. I felt it rumble beneath our feet. "Has anyone ever come *close* to the goal?"

"Yes," she said tentatively. "The goal has seemed attainable a few times. Like, things were in place, and it felt like the timing was going to be right. But somehow..."

"They still managed to miss the shot."

"Exactly. But—never mind." She faced the water.

"Oh, come on. You can't do that to me." I nudged her with my elbow. "We almost died together. We're bonded for life."

She laughed. "It's nothing. I was just going to say that I know it's possible, because I can get there on my own just fine."

The scene immediately came to life in my head—Mabel Jane Buckley sprawled out on her bed with her hand between her legs—and my cock sprang to life in my pants.

Fuck, fuck, *fuck,* I wanted to get this girl going. And I wouldn't stop until she was good and gone.

"God, sorry—that's TMI," she said, mistaking my turned-on silence for discomfort. "I don't know why I just said that. I made things even more weird, which I wouldn't have thought was possible."

The door to the balcony opened, and Paul poked his head out. "There you are," he said. "Lisa wants us to sit down now."

"Of course she does," I muttered. To my brother, I called, "I'll be there in a minute."

Paul disappeared again and I looked at Mabel with an apologetic expression. "I guess I should go in."

"It's fine."

I reached out and touched her arm. "Can we continue this conversation later?"

She looked surprised I'd asked, blinking once. "Sure."

Fat drops of rain began to splatter the deck, and we moved quickly for the door. I reached it first and held it open. As she passed by me, I caught the scent of her perfume again.

And I realized what she smelled like.

Yellow cupcakes, fresh out of the oven and still warm, the kind my mom used to make for us to bring to school bake sales.

Behind me, thunder growled like a hungry wolf, the sound resonating in my bones.

Chapter 5

"Tell me everything!" Ari demanded when I took my seat next to her. "You were gone forever."

"I wasn't *gone forever*; it was like twenty minutes."

"A lot can happen in twenty minutes. For example, I can Google someone's name and find out internet gossip about them."

I rolled my eyes and spread my napkin on my lap. "Ari, come on. We're grown women. We can be more mature than that."

"But we're not."

"True, so tell me what you found."

She picked up her phone from the table and tapped the screen. "Okay, aside from a lot of boring hockey stuff, I did find an Instagram account, but he's not super active on the app. Mostly more hockey stuff, but also it looks like he's a good uncle."

"Let me see."

She flashed the screen toward me, and I saw a photo of Joe sitting on the couch surrounded by four kids—a girl and boy who looked elementary school age seated on either side of him, a younger girl on one knee with her arms looped around his neck, and a baby in the crook of one arm. The kids were all wearing Christmas pajamas, and the caption read "merry xmas from the zoo" with a few holiday-themed emojis. He was laughing in the photo, his mouth open and his eyes crinkled at the corners.

"Cute," I said. Something about seeing Joe with kids all over him made him even more attractive, if that was possible. I glanced over toward the head table. From where I sat, I could see him only from the side, but he had a fantastic profile thanks to his angular jaw and strong nose. My insides twisted.

"I think those older ones belong to his brother Gianni." Ari took the phone back from me. "Dash mentioned they have three kids. Not sure about the baby."

"Might belong to his twin brother. What else did you find?"

Ari made a face and exhaled. "There's a girl."

My heart plummeted. "A what?"

"There are some photos with a girl—not a ton, though, and none in the last couple months."

"Show me."

Ari frowned and scrolled, then handed me the phone again. "Here."

When I looked at the screen, it made perfect sense. The woman was tall, blond, and beautiful. Big eyes with perfectly sculpted brows, gorgeous sun-kissed skin, plush, pillowy lips, and long, golden, Rapunzel hair. She looked like a Miss America contestant. In a couple of the pics, Joe had his arm around her shoulder. "She's very pretty," I said, handing the phone back.

"I can't tell if she's his girlfriend or not."

"It's pretty obvious she is," I said, lowering my hopes for this evening from to-mahto back to tomato. "But it doesn't matter."

"Maybe you could ask him."

"Ari!" I laughed as the servers began setting salads down in front of each person at our table. "I'm not going to ask him who the girl is on his Instagram I saw while I was internet stalking him."

"No, I guess you can't." She sighed and picked up her fork. "I wonder why he was flirting with you if he's got a girlfriend. Unless he's a jerk."

"Like I said, he might not have been flirting. It's fine." I speared a cherry tomato and stuck it in my mouth. I really didn't want him to be a jerk.

"Well, there are some other cute single guys here. My cousin Eric is single! I could introduce you. He's a financial advisor in Traverse City."

"Sure," I said, poking at the second tomato on my plate. "Why not?"

. . .

During dinner, I forced myself not to look in Joe's direction. Once, during dessert, I peeked at him and discovered he was looking at me. He smiled, but I had a mouth full of cake, so I just tipped up my lips and turned my attention back to one of Ari's aunts, who was talking about her gall bladder removal.

After the dessert plates had been cleared away, the DJ switched from dinner music to dance music, and the floor filled with young people who jumped around with drinks in their hands and sang along to songs that made me feel old at thirty. I scanned the dance floor and noticed Joe wasn't among the dancers, but I didn't search the crowd for him. What was the point? If he had a girlfriend, I didn't feel right flirting with him.

Instead, I went to the bar for another glass of champagne. When I returned to the table, Ari had dragged her cousin Eric over to meet me. She introduced us and said she'd be right back, she needed to use the restroom.

"Again?" I asked her.

She patted her belly. "It's constant. I'll leave you two to get acquainted."

I saw right through her scheme, but Eric was friendly enough, and even if he wasn't Joe-Lupo-level hot, he had a nice face. I took a seat and invited him to sit down next to me.

We chatted for about fifteen minutes—sometimes shouting to be heard over the music—about where we lived and what we did, about how hot the summer had been, about a thriller we'd both read recently. He was perfectly pleasant, but there were absolutely no sparks.

Which made sense because the next thing he said was, "The woman I just started dating wants to take a weekend getaway up here this fall. She's into the foliage and stuff. What's your best recommendation for a romantic inn in Cherry Tree Harbor?"

I gave him some recommendations for places to stay, restaurants I liked, and fun things to do. At some point in the conversation, I began to feel like someone was staring at me. I assumed it was Ari's gaze I detected, but when I glanced over Eric's shoulder, I saw Joe Lupo looking at me from across the room. Our eyes locked. His close-lipped smile made my inner thigh muscles clench. He jerked his head slightly toward the hallway. *Meet me outside.*

Something about the gesture was so confident, so hot, I couldn't resist.

Offering Eric my hand, I wished him well and told him I hoped he and his friend would have a lovely trip this fall. "I should probably check in with Ari now. She gets tired easily."

"Of course," he said. "Nice to meet you."

My pulse quickened as I skirted the dance floor and weaved through tables. Out in the hallway, Joe was waiting for me. "Hey, you. Having fun?"

"Yes," I lied. "What about you?"

He shrugged. "It's a lot of people."

"It is."

He took a step closer, sliding his hands in his pockets. "Want to go out on the balcony again? I think it stopped raining."

I hesitated, and he noticed.

"Or not," he said, backing off. "If you'd rather dance or something, we can go back into the ballroom. I just—"

"It's not that," I blurted. "It's your girlfriend."

"My girlfriend?" He looked confused.

"Yes. I—" Squeezing my eyes shut, I realized I had to confess now. "This is a bit embarrassing, but I suppose that's on-brand for me at this point." *Hiccup!*

"Go on."

"Ari looked at your social media and saw a bunch of photos of the same woman. It looks like you have a girlfriend, and maybe I shouldn't read into things, but I just feel weird about—*hic*!"

"Hey." He touched my shoulder. "You hold your breath, and I'll explain."

I inhaled, trapping the breath in my lungs.

"I was dating someone for about eighteen months. That's whose picture you saw. We split up in April, and we are staying that way." His big shoulders lifted. "To be honest, I probably should have broken it off a lot sooner, but I didn't want a messy breakup in the middle of playoffs."

I nodded, letting him know I understood, but continued to hold my breath.

"I'm too focused on my career to be in a relationship," he

explained. "If you asked my ex, she'd give you a long list of my flaws as a boyfriend. And I probably should have scrubbed her from my posts, but honestly, I just don't care that much. Seems like a waste of time."

At my limit, I exhaled slowly and nodded. "I get it. It's not like it erases the past."

"Exactly. Anyway, I do not have a girlfriend, but if you'd rather not hang out alone with me, it's totally fine. I just like talking to you."

My decision was made in a fraction of a second. "Let's go out on the balcony," I said. "Should I grab drinks again so you're not attacked at the bar?"

"I'll get them this time. If anyone tries to stop me, I'll fight them."

I laughed. "Okay. I'm going to use the bathroom real quick. Meet you out there in a few minutes?"

"Sounds good."

Inside the ladies' room, I fluffed my hair, checked my teeth, and swiped my perfume rollerball across my collarbones. I thought about reapplying my lip gloss, but just in case this night turned crazy and Joe Lupo wanted to kiss me, I left my lips bare.

Suddenly, Ari swept in. "What is happening? I saw you and Joe Lupo both come out here, and only he came back in!"

"He doesn't have a girlfriend—those posts were old—and we're going to have a drink on the balcony." I tucked my perfume back into my clutch. "By the way, your cousin Eric is dating someone."

"Oops—sorry." She looked sheepish. "Didn't realize."

"It's fine. We didn't really have chemistry anyway." I turned to face her. "How do I look?"

She fussed with a strand of hair near my face. "Perfect."

"Thank you. Okay, I might be gone for a little bit, but text me if you get tired and want to leave. I'll come find you."

"Okay." She grinned. "Have fun."

We walked back into the ballroom together, and I made my way toward the doors that led to the balcony and pushed one open. Outside, it was dark and humid, the air heavy with mist. No moon or stars shone through the clouds, but two strands of party lights crisscrossed the air above our heads, their little round bulbs hazy in the fog.

Joe was already standing by the railing, holding a glass of whiskey on the rocks in one hand and a champagne flute in the other. After handing it to me, he pulled a napkin-wrapped slice of lemon from his pocket. "I brought you a present. Just in case you get the hiccups again."

I laughed. "Thank you. So do you have all summer off from hockey?"

"Yes and no. We do take some recovery time—and I had to get some PT for a shoulder injury—but we have to keep training to stay in good physical condition."

"Is it harder as you get older?" Realizing what I'd just asked, I shook my head. "Not that you're old," I said quickly. "You're not. I mean, I don't know how old you are, but you're not old."

He laughed. "It's okay. I'm thirty-two, which *is* kind of old for professional hockey."

"Really?"

"Yeah. Most careers only last about five seasons. Some are done in one."

"Wow." I sipped my champagne. "So you must be really good."

"I'm pretty good," he said, his grin sheepish and cocky at the same time.

"So how much longer will you play?"

"Hard to say. As long as my body holds up, I guess."

"And then what?"

"I'm not sure. I've never really thought about it." He shrugged. "Hockey is really all I know. It's the only thing I've ever wanted to do."

"Do you want to stay in Chicago?"

"I'll go wherever the game takes me." He sipped his drink. "So tell me more about what you do. I don't know anything about museums except that my parents dragged us around to a bunch of them when we took a vacation to Italy."

"You didn't enjoy them?"

"Not really. I confess, I was more interested in Italian girls than Italian art." He swirled the whiskey in his glass. "In my defense, I was only sixteen at the time."

"So now that you're older, you're into Italian art?" I teased.

"Definitely. Leonardo, Michelangelo, Donatello, Raphael— all the Ninja Turtles." He grinned. "But those are the only ones I know."

I laughed. "It's okay. I definitely couldn't name more than four hockey players. Actually I might be able to name only one."

"Which one?"

"Gordie Howe."

"Wow. You went for an oldie. But a goodie," he added. "Especially if you're a Detroit fan."

"My dad has an autographed card. My brothers are always arguing about who should inherit it."

He laughed. "Maybe it should go to you. Aren't you the one who loves memorabilia?"

It made me smile to hear the artifacts I worked with described as memorabilia. "Yes."

"Were you always like that, even as a kid?"

"I'm not sure I loved *art* museums that much when I was a kid. I liked looking at things people used in everyday life better.

And digging in the dirt to find them seemed like treasure hunting to me. I used to pretend I was Indiana Jones in the backyard," I confessed. "I made such a mess, I think my dad was sorry he ever showed me those movies. But that's how I knew what I wanted to do with my life. I even came up with my own name."

He grinned. "Oh yeah? What was it?"

"Montana Swift," I said, cringing a little. "And I had all kinds of adventures for her. There was *Montana Swift and the Raiders of the Rosebushes*, *Montana Swift: Treehouse of Doom*, and then there were a whole slew of Harry Potter crossovers, like *Montana Swift and the Mystical Mudpie Shop*. Ari liked to make mud pies," I explained with a shrug, "so I had to work that in."

His eyebrows rose. "Damn. All that my brothers and I did in the backyard was climb trees and beat the shit out of one another."

"My brothers did a lot of that," I said as a cool breeze caressed my shoulders. "I just always liked hunting for things and making up stories about them. So I decided to do it for a living, and it took me all over the world—and then right back here where I started."

He tipped up his glass. "How'd that happen?"

"About a year ago, I just got the yearning to move back home. My brothers were all getting married and having kids, and I felt like I was missing out on a lot. I'm close to my family." Thunder rumbled over the lake, and both of us glanced out toward the water. "Then my dad heard about this potential new position being created at our local museum and told me I should apply."

"That's the Cherry Tree Harbor Historical Society?"

I looked at him in surprise. "How did you know?"

"Oops." He grinned sheepishly. "Guess I gave myself away. I was curious about you after I got back to my hotel room last night. I sort of Googled you."

I laughed. "Well, I've got no room to be offended, since Ari and I did the same thing earlier." Actually, not only was I not offended, I was *flattered*. "Anyway, yes, the Cherry Tree Harbor Historical Society. Previously, it was run solely by volunteers, but the board wanted to expand the society's reach with bigger, better exhibits and events. So I applied for the job, and they offered it to me. So I moved back home, bought a house—"

"And a cat," he added. "I remember there was a cat."

"I already had Cleopatra—Cleo for short—but yes, she made the move too."

He sipped his whiskey. "Do you like the new job?"

"Yes. It doesn't pay a lot, but we're always trying to raise more funds."

"How do you do that?"

"We appeal to the community, try to target donors. I'm planning a 1920s-themed fundraiser right now called The Bootleggers Ball."

"Oh yeah? Like gangsters?" Thunder boomed again, louder this time.

"Many of them were," I said, finishing off my bubbly, "but some were just average guys who made good money funneling in whiskey from across the water. Did you know that Michigan actually played a big role during Prohibition? Lots of action because of our proximity to Canada."

"My parents have always said there was someone in our family tree who did that." He cocked his head. "On my dad's side, I think."

"Really? That's so cool!"

"I never paid much attention to the story, but it was something like that. I remember it involved bootleg whiskey." He lifted his glass, as if to toast me. "I like the idea."

"Of bootleg whiskey or my fundraiser?"

"Both," he said, moving closer to me.

And of course, because I was nervous and tipsy, I hiccuped.

He chuckled and looked around. "Where's that slice of lemon?"

"It's here." I set my empty glass aside, tucked the napkin in it, and sucked on the lemon. My mouth immediately puckered. "Ew."

"Count to ten," he said, as thunder growled directly above us. "That's the only way it works."

I counted fast and then stuck the lemon into my glass. "Yeesh. That was awful."

"But it worked, right?"

I gave it a few seconds. "I think it did. Your mom's a genius."

He tossed back the rest of his whiskey and set the glass aside. "I'll tell her you said so."

A few drops of rain splattered the railing and the top of my head. I looked up and felt them fall onto my face. "Shoot," I said, "it's starting to rain."

He moved even closer, tucking my hair behind my ear. "Do you want to go inside?"

"No. Do you?"

"No." His hand slipped behind my neck. "I want to kiss you."

My heart stopped. "Oh."

"Is that okay?"

"Yes, I was just—"

But that's all I got out, because suddenly Joe's lips were on mine. A surprised sigh escaped my throat, and my eyes fluttered closed. It was exactly the kind of alpha move I always wanted a guy to make, not at all diminished by the asking first. His fingers kneaded the back of my neck, and I put my hands on his chest. Warmth from his skin seeped through his dress shirt, and I imagined the bare skin beneath the fabric. It sent little bolts of lightning shooting through me.

As his mouth opened wider, my heart thundered like the storm building above us. He slid his other arm around my waist and pulled me closer. Raindrops fell faster and harder, running in rivulets down our faces, mingling between our mouths. But he kissed me slowly and deeply, like nothing else mattered—not time, not the weather, not anyone who might see us. He slanted his head a little more, stroking my lips with his tongue. I tasted lemon and whiskey and rain and champagne, and it seemed like the most delicious combination of flavors in existence.

His hand slid into my hair and tilted my head, exposing my neck. He moved his lips and tongue across my jaw and down my throat with that same insistent but unhurried pace, like he was going to have what he wanted, everything else be damned. *If he was a vampire*, I thought, *I'd let him sink his teeth into me right here and now. I'd welcome death.* That's how good this kiss was.

My entire body shivered, although I wasn't cold.

He brought his lips back to mine, his tongue teasing its way inside my mouth in a suggestive manner that set off a flutter between my legs. I wound my arms around his neck and pressed my body against his, melting into him. I put my hands in his thick dark hair. Desire filled me from the soles of my feet to the tips of my fingers, simmering beneath my skin.

Lightning split the sky with a terrifying crack, startling us both. Our lips parted, but he kept his arm locked tight around my back, his other hand still in my hair. Thunder boomed, shaking the boards under our feet.

He rested his forehead on mine. "What do you want to do?"

"I don't know," I said breathlessly. "What do you want to do?"

"Do you want the honest answer?"

"Yes."

He tightened the hand in my hair into a fist, moving his lips to my ear. "I want to take you up to my room, line up the shot, and put the puck in the net—deep."

I shivered again. "What if I said yes?"

"Then I'd say let's go." He loosened his grip in my hair and leaned back slightly, looking down at me so he could meet my eyes. "But just so we understand each other, it would be all in fun, right?"

I knew what he meant, and it was fine with me. "Right. Like one of those games that isn't official."

He laughed. "A scrimmage?"

"Yes. A scrimmage."

"So is that a yes?" he drawled in my ear. "I need to hear you say it."

"Yes," I said, every nerve ending in my body tingling with anticipation. "Yes."

With one final clap of thunder, the skies opened.

Chapter 6

"My God, what happened to you?" Ari looked up at me from her seat at the table.

"I got caught in the storm," I said, my hair dripping onto my dress. "But listen." I dropped into the chair next to her. "I don't need a ride home."

"Oh?" One eyebrow cocked above an imperious gaze. "And why might that be?"

"That might be because I got invited up to Joe Lupo's room for a scrimmage."

"A *what*?"

I laughed. "A night of this-means-nothing fun and games so I can cross a few things off that bucket list. He seems very confident he can go where no man has gone before."

"Eeeep!" She clapped her hands. "This is amazing!"

"I know, but—God, Ari." I watched as Joe entered the ballroom—a minute behind me, as planned—and went directly to the bride and groom to say good night. "He's so hot. I'm scared I won't know what to do with a guy that hot."

"The same thing you do with any other guy." She stirred a hand in the air. "They all have the same parts."

"I know, but his parts are like...*supreme* parts. Highly sought-after, well-muscled, expensive, luxury parts."

She rolled her eyes. "Mabel, he's got a dick in his pants, not a Ferrari."

"You know what I mean! What if I panic and do the wrong thing? Or start panic-babbling? You know how I can't shut up when I get nervous. What if I get the hiccups? I've got bangxiety!"

"Listen to me." Ari shifted on her chair to face me, grimacing for a moment and placing a hand on her belly.

"Are you okay?" I asked, my chest filling with concern. "I don't have to go with Joe. I can come home with you in case you—"

"No." She pinned me with a stare. "You are going up to his hotel room for some fun, because you deserve it. You are not going to panic. You are not going to let your nerves take over your mouth. You are going to relax and enjoy every single second of tonight. This is not the kind of opportunity that comes along every day, Mabel."

"I know."

"So be safe, but also be reckless. Be wild." She grinned wickedly. "And remember every filthy detail because I will be asking you for all of them tomorrow. Now go."

"Going." I stood up. "Do I look like a drowned rat?"

"No. You look like a shimmering maid ready to be ravished by a rake."

"You read too much romance." Laughing, I leaned over and

hugged her. "Thanks for the pep talk."

"You're welcome." She sighed. "Someday I'll have wild sex again."

I covered my ears. "Good night, Ari."

"Good night, Mabel."

Without looking for Joe—we were trying to fly under the radar—I picked up my clutch and slipped out of the ballroom.

• • •

He joined me in the hallway a minute later. "All good?" he asked.

"Yes. I let Ari know I didn't need a ride home. Did you say goodbye to your friends?"

"Yeah. They gave me a bunch of shit about leaving early, but I just said I had a bad headache. I've had enough concussions that no one really questioned it." His gaze traveled over my body. "And I don't fucking care anyway. Ready to go?"

"Yes."

He took my hand and led me quickly down the stairs, through the lobby of the inn, and over to the elevators. Thankfully no one else was waiting, because the doors were not even closed behind him before he pinned me to the wall, cupped my jaw with one hand, and crushed his lips to mine. As the elevator took us up two flights, he slid his other hand up my ribs and covered one breast. My nipple was so hard it poked through the fabric of my dress. "I can't wait to get my mouth on you," he growled, teasing the stiff peak with his thumb. "I'm gonna make you come so hard."

I *believed* him. Not only because he was so confident, but just the touch of his thumb had heat coursing through me like TNT in my veins. I could only imagine what the rest of him could do.

Behind him, the elevator pinged and the doors opened. He grabbed me by the wrist and yanked me down the hall so fast I nearly tripped in my high heels. Stopping abruptly in front of room 308, he pulled the key from his wallet. It took him three frustrated tries to get the door unlocked, but once the green light flashed, he shoved it open, stood aside so I could go in first, and hung the Privacy Please sign on the handle.

Before it even slammed shut, his mouth was on mine again, hungry and demanding. I dropped my clutch to the floor. He shed his jacket.

Ari's words were in my head. *This is not the kind of opportunity that comes along every day. Be reckless. Be wild.*

I made up my mind that I was not going to be shy about what I wanted. I tugged at the knot in his tie and slipped it from his collar.

His palms skimmed over my shoulders, my back, my ass. He pulled me tight against him, and I felt the bulge in his pants, kicking up my excitement even higher. *I* was doing this to him. *I* was causing his body to heat up and get hard. *I* was the one he'd chosen to be with tonight. He could have left with any woman in that ballroom, but he wanted me, and he was making no secret about it.

"God, you smell so fucking good. I could swallow you whole." Bending down, he pressed his nose and mouth to the skin beneath my ear and inhaled, then swept his lips down my neck and across my collarbone. Reaching the notch at the base of my throat, he teased it with his tongue, sending that pulse of desire through me again. My core muscles clenched. My thighs were damp. My nipples tingled as his hands slid up my sides and rubbed them with his thumbs.

Trembling with excitement, I slid my hand down between us and stroked the hard length of his cock through his pants. He groaned, bringing his mouth back to mine, his kiss lush and insistent. Reaching behind me, he dragged down the zipper at my spine, and my dress fell to the floor.

Before I had a chance to be self-conscious, he swept me off my feet and carried me over to the bed, laying me across the foot of the mattress, my feet dangling off one side. Then he switched on the bedside lamp.

Surprised, I propped myself up on my elbows. "You want the light on?"

"The better to see you with, cupcake." His eyes drank me in from head to toe—I wore only my underwear and shoes—lingering on the scrap of black lace between my thighs. He licked his lips. "Is that okay?"

"Yes, it's just—I'm nervous now."

"Why?"

"For one thing, I'm naked and you're not."

"There's a reason for that." He leaned over me, bracing one hand by my shoulder and slipping one hand between my thighs. He caressed me gently with the side of his index finger.

"What—what's the reason?"

"I'm lining up the shot, and that takes precision." Bringing his head to my chest, he circled one nipple with his tongue. "Patience." He gave the tip a long lick before sucking gently. "Control."

My elbows collapsed, and I flung my arms over my head. He switched his attention to the other breast, and my back arched off the bed to meet his hungry mouth.

"This first part, see, it's all about you." He mimicked the circular motion of his tongue with his fingertips over my clit.

"That seems—unfair," I panted, opening my legs wider, desperate for him to touch me inside.

He slipped his fingers beneath the lace, keeping his touch slow and firm. "I promise, nothing gets me going like making the perfect shot. And if I get naked too soon, I might rush it. It's not about speed." He eased one finger inside me with an agonizing lack of haste. "It's about timing."

"Oh God, that feels good."

He closed his mouth over one aching nipple again, sucking harder this time as he added a second finger to the first. Somehow he was also using the heel of his hand against me, applying pressure and friction in just the right way. I felt the tension building at my core, need swelling between my thighs. He withdrew his fingers from me and rubbed my clit with wet fingertips in firm, hot little circles that had my abdominal muscles tightening and my vision going silver.

It was going to happen. It was actually going to happen. I was—

Then suddenly his mouth and hand were gone, and the mattress shifted like he'd gotten off the bed. For a fraction of a second, I was disappointed. Was this going to go the usual way?

Popping up on my elbows again, I expected to find him taking off his pants, but instead saw him drop to his knees by my feet, still dressed. He worked my skimpy black lace panties down my legs and tossed them aside, then tossed my legs over his shoulders. "I've been thinking about this all fucking night."

"You have?"

"Yes." He kissed each inner thigh. "From the moment I saw you by the window, all I could think about was getting your legs over my shoulders and fucking you with my tongue."

I watched in utter disbelief as the lower half of his handsome face disappeared between my legs and shivered as his tongue swept up the seam at my center. "Oh God," I whimpered as he did it again, and then again, long decadent strokes that ended at the top with a delectable little swirl across my clit. My head fell back, my eyelids fluttering closed as he worked his mouth on me, moaning with animal-like pleasure.

When he spoke, his voice was deep and raspy. "You taste so

fucking sweet. I can't get enough."

No one had ever made me feel so beautiful, so desired, so *delicious*. There was nothing polite or reserved about the way Joe was devouring me. His hands kneaded my thighs. He lifted my hips, driving his tongue inside me, making deep, growling sounds of ravenous delight. *Ravished*, I thought from the deepest reaches of my shattering mind. *I'm being ravished for the first time, and it feels so good.* My hands flattened on the bedding, then clutched at the comforter.

Oh God, please let this happen. Please let me know what it's like.

Then his fingers were inside me again, plunging deep to touch some secret place within that had the tension in my body spiraling tighter and higher all at once. He licked and sucked and flicked and swirled with his tongue while I writhed on the bed in front of him, until it was all too much and something in me unlocked, some wildness was unleashed, and my legs tensed behind his head and my core muscles closed around his hand and my clit fluttered against his tongue in wondrous, pulsing perfection. He moaned, the vibration of it carrying me to an even higher peak. I cried out with every crashing wave until they faded into the distance, leaving me wilted and panting.

Possibly dead. I wasn't sure.

When I could finally think straight, I slapped a hand over my mouth. "Sorry," I said, the words muffled behind my palm. "I was loud."

"Mabel Jane Buckley, you were fucking perfect."

Dragging myself up to a seated position, I braced my hands behind me. "You did it."

His grin was satisfied. His mouth still wet. "Cupcake, I'm just getting started." Wrapping his hands around my ankles, he untied the ribbons on my shoes—*with his teeth*. Then he stood up and removed the heels from my feet, dropping them to the floor. "Don't go anywhere."

"I don't think I could if I tried. Not that I would try."

He disappeared inside the bathroom and came out a moment later, tossing a condom on the nightstand before unbuckling his belt.

"Wait!" Regaining the use of my muscles, I jumped off the bed. Chances were good I might never get to undress another man with a body like his. I wanted to unwrap him like a candy bar. "Let me do it."

He laughed as I took off his belt, unbuttoned his shirt, and pushed it from his shoulders, my heart thumping harder with every article of clothing removed, every inch of bare skin revealed. He grabbed his undershirt from the back of the neck and whipped it over his head, revealing an upper body that rivaled any work of Italian art.

"Holy shit." I ran my hands over the muscles in his chest, the sculpted ridges of his abs, the curving bulges of his shoulders and biceps. His skin was warm and smooth. Without my platform heels on, I was a lot shorter than him—the top of my head would have fit neatly beneath his chin. I looked up at him. "Are you even real?"

His smile riled me up all over again. "Only one way to find out."

I quickly undid his pants and slipped my hand inside them, wrapping my fingers around his hot, hard cock. As I worked my hand up and down its length, I pressed my lips to his chest, teasing one nipple with my tongue. His cock thickened in my grip and he groaned, moving a hand between my thighs, where I was still warm and wet from his mouth. Soon he was thrusting into my fist.

"Jesus. I need to get inside you." Stepping back from me,

he ditched the rest of his clothes, pulled back the covers, and swooped me into his arms again. He lay me down with my head on the pillow this time and reached for the condom. Tearing open the wrapper, he rolled it on while I watched, realizing he was without a doubt the biggest guy I'd ever been with and hoping it wouldn't hurt so much that I couldn't enjoy it.

But even if I didn't have another orgasm, I'd had *one*, and that was something. If I had to fake a second or even a third, I could.

I shouldn't have worried.

A moment later, Joe was kneeling between my thighs, stroking my clit with the tip of his cock. Despite his obvious excitement, he didn't rush. My entire body was trembling with desire, with anticipation, with heat. In the light from the lamp, his skin was golden, his muscles a masterpiece of line and shadow. And his face—my God, that face. He probably left the light on all the time when he had sex just to remind women how lucky they were.

By the time he began to ease inside me, I was ready to beg for it. I grabbed his hips, pulling him closer. "Joe. Please."

"Please what?" he asked.

"Give me more. Give me everything."

He slid in deep, with a long, slow groan. "Fuck, you feel so good."

I couldn't speak—I held my breath as he stretched and filled me, willing my body to relax. I turned my face to the side because I didn't want him to see any pain there.

"Breathe," he whispered at my temple. "I'll go slow."

I closed my eyes. Colors danced behind my lids as he flexed his hips, his athletic body moving in slow, sinuous strokes that allowed me to feel every inch as a new sensation.

He was the biggest guy I'd ever been with, but he was also the most controlled, the most patient. I could sense the restraint in his muscles as he held himself back, making sure I was okay. Eventually, the tightness in my muscles eased, and my hips began to lift in tandem with his. I moved my hands to his ass and gripped his flesh.

Groaning, he began to move faster, thrust harder, drive deeper.

I buried my face in his chest and inhaled his scent—beneath the cologne there was something masculine that was just him, and it made me want to pull him closer. I dug my nails into his skin and my heels into the backs of his thighs.

That's when he started circling his hips with his cock buried deep, grinding his pelvic bone against me in a way that had my entire lower body humming like a live wire. It was the most intense pleasure I'd ever felt. Was this some kind of trick? Was there an internal switch he'd managed to flip? Was I actually going to have an orgasm *during sex*?

"Oh my God," I panted. "Oh my God, I'm gonna come."

"Fuck yes, you are." Reaching beneath my ass, he tilted my hips up to some magical geometric angle and thrust harder and faster, sending me to the brink of dissolution.

"Yes," I whimpered, my eyes squeezing shut. "Yes, *yes*, *yes*!" My volume rose with each helpless cry, until I was suspended at the edge of what I'd never known and always imagined. "Oh my God! Don't stop! Don't stop! Don't stop!"

And it happened—it actually *happened*.

All at once, I went careening over that cliff I'd only ever pretended to jump off, my body erupting in powerful, thunderous bursts that splintered me into a million pieces. I was still coming apart when Joe let go of my hips and changed his motion to long, hard, deep thrusts that jarred my bones. His ragged breaths became loud, primal grunts every time he rocked into me until finally his body tensed and I felt him grow even harder and thicker within me. With one final thrust, he buried himself deep, and I felt every throb of his climax, almost like it was my own. As the pulsing receded, he collapsed above me, and the beat of his heart knocked against my chest.

I'd never imagined it was possible to feel so close to another human being, let alone a stranger.

If the stars behind my eyes had been real, I might have made a wish.

Chapter 7

JOE

"How did you get that scar on your lip?"

"This?" I touched the decade-old scar with the tip of my tongue. "Took a puck to the face." I was stretched out on my back, while Mabel lay facing me on her side. Her head was propped on one hand, and she was studying me like I imagined her analyzing one of her buried treasures. She was so damn cute.

And she was a firecracker in bed—hot and fun and delightfully responsive. Whoever she'd been with before obviously had no idea what they were doing. And while I hoped she'd never date another clueless fuck again, I also hoped she'd never have anyone better than me.

I'm a selfish prick sometimes.

"A puck to the face?" Her nose wrinkled. "Ouch."

"It happens."

"Hockey seems like a *very* rough sport."

I chuckled. "It is definitely fueled by testosterone."

"There's so much fighting."

"Just part of the game."

"Do *you* fight a lot?"

I thought for a moment. "I don't like to start fights. But if you take a cheap shot at one of my teammates, I'm coming for you."

She laughed. "Is that what makes you a good player?"

"Not really. I mean, I play tough, but I'm a good player because I play hard. And I play smart. I always know where I'm supposed to be." I paused, giving her a little sideways grin. "Also, I know how to put the puck in the net."

Her lashes lowered as she smiled. "Yes. You do."

Fuck, that dimple. It did things to me.

"Come here," I said, pulling her on top of me. She came willingly, straddling my hips. Slipping a hand behind her neck, I pulled her head down and traced her strawberry lips with my tongue. "You have the sweetest mouth," I told her.

She smiled. "Thank you."

"And you smell so fucking good."

"Thank you."

"And you have beautiful legs." I ran my hands down her back and over her butt. "And a great ass."

She kissed me a little deeper, her tongue sweeping into my mouth. "You have a beautiful everything," she whispered. "Yesterday, when I was sitting next to you on the plane, I kept thinking about how hot you were."

"You hid it well. You barely even looked my way once you realized you weren't going to die."

"I was shy after that." She began to rock her hips over mine in a slow, undulating rhythm. My cock began to swell, and I reached between her legs, stroking her pussy until she was wet again. When I slipped a finger inside her, she rode my hand, circling her hips.

"You're not shy now," I said.

"No," she whispered, moving her mouth over my jaw and down my neck. "I'm not."

My jaw clenched, my breath coming faster as she rubbed her lips and tongue on this little spot below my ear that drove me crazy. How the fuck she could have known that was beyond me, but then she surprised me again when she brought one hand to my chest and played with my nipple, rubbing it with her fingertips, brushing it with the back of her knuckles, pinching it playfully. My fingers slipped out of her as she worked her mouth down my chest and teased the other nipple with her tongue, flicking it, sucking it, biting it gently—and then harder.

I groaned as she moved up again and began to grind against me, using my cock to give herself pleasure. Sliding my hands into her hair, I pulled her mouth to mine and kissed her hard and deep, thrusting beneath her rocking hips. After only a minute, I was trying so hard not to come, I wasn't sure I could last. "Wait," I told her, my body at the breaking point. "Just wait. Give me one minute."

Carefully, I lifted her off me and set her aside, then bolted into the bathroom to find another condom in my toiletry bag. I put it on right then and there—I was already close as fuck to exploding, and I did *not* take those kinds of chances.

Rushing back into the bedroom, I made a flying leap onto the bed, and she laughed as I sprawled out above her. Positioning my cock between her thighs, I crushed my mouth to hers, and the laughter turned into a moan.

"Oh God." Her hands clutched my back. "I never knew it could be this good. I never knew I could want this so much."

"What do you want?" I demanded, sliding in slow and deep.

"Tell me."

"I want—I want you to fuck me," she blurted, like her own words surprised her.

"Keep talking, cupcake." I spoke low in her ear. "Tell me every filthy little thing."

"I want your cock," she whispered. "I want you to make me come again."

"You want to come on my cock?" I growled, driving harder and faster at the angle I knew she liked.

"Yes—" She struggled to speak, her hands on my ass now, pulling me in deep. "Yes—and I want—to feel you—come with me—come with me—come with me—come—" Her words dissolved into one long sigh as she came undone beneath me. As her body contracted around me, I groaned long and hard, powering through an orgasm that thundered through my core and zipped along my limbs before ricocheting back again in hot, throbbing bursts.

And maybe it was because I hadn't had sex in months, maybe it was knowing I was the first guy to make her come like this, or maybe it was the thrill of a fucking hat trick—thank you very much—but it was the most intense climax I'd had in a long time. So intense that I didn't even want to move afterward.

Eventually, she tapped my back. "Joe?"

"Huh?"

"You're kinda heavy."

"Oh!" I lifted my chest off her. "Sorry."

"That's okay." She inhaled deeply. "I just needed a little air."

"Yeah. Me too." I ran a hand through my hair. My heart was beating ridiculously fast. "Be right back."

Inside the bathroom, I disposed of the condom and washed my hands. When I came out, she was sitting on the bed with the sheet pulled up to her waist. Her hair was a mess, her mouth was pink around the edges, and her eye makeup was smudged. She gave me a little smile that made her dimple appear. Somehow she managed to look innocent and sultry at the same time.

I had that urge again, the one that made me want to wrap her in my arms and keep her close until sunrise.

The fleeting thought brought me to my senses. "What time is it anyway?"

She looked at the clock on the bedside table. "Going on two."

"I should get you home," I said.

"Oh. Okay, sure." She sounded slightly surprised but popped right off the bed and began hunting around for her clothes.

"I have to get up early," I said, feeling like I owed her an explanation. "I want to get a workout in before the wedding party brunch. Also, I'm terrible to share a bed with. I take up all the space."

"Is that on your list of flaws?" Finding her underwear on the floor, she tugged it on.

It took me a second to realize she meant the list of boyfriend flaws I'd mentioned earlier. "Definitely. In fact, *hates to cuddle* might be number one on the list. Or maybe, *doesn't listen*. Or, *only loves hockey*."

She laughed as she scooped up her dress and purse, holding them in front of her chest as she hurried into the bathroom. "I just need a minute. Be right out."

Going over to my bag, I rooted around for something to wear and threw on jeans and a T-shirt. I was sitting at the end of the bed tying the laces on my sneakers when she came out of the bathroom. Her hair was smoother, her eye makeup was cleaned up, and she was wearing her dress, although she was holding it together in the back.

I rose to my feet. "Need me to zip you up?"

"Yes, please." She turned around. "Thank you."

After completing the task, I grabbed my wallet and car key. "Ready?"

"Yes." She located her shoes, picked them up, and let them dangle off her fingers. "But would it be awful to walk out of here in bare feet? These shoes are pretty, but they hurt."

"Tell you what—since I made you keep them on longer than necessary, I'll give you a piggyback ride out of here."

She giggled. "I did not mind keeping them on longer for you, since I couldn't even feel my feet at that point, but I'll take you up on that offer."

I turned around. "Hop on."

A moment later, she jumped onto my back, and I hooked my arms beneath her legs. Her arms looped around my neck. "Ready."

I carried her out of the room, down the hall, and onto the elevator. At that hour, no one was anywhere to be seen, not even at the front desk. Outside, the night air was warm and the pavement still wet. Mist blanketed my face and arms.

When we reached my SUV, I unlocked the doors, pulled open the passenger side, and managed to back her in without her feet ever touching the ground.

• • •

I pulled up in her driveway less than ten minutes later. It was a small white house, just one story, with a picket fence and a wide front porch. Exactly the kind of house I pictured her in.

"Thanks for bringing me home," she said. "I had fun."

"Me too. Need a lift to your door?"

"That's okay, I'm good from here." She unbuckled her seat belt. "It seems weird to say, 'It was nice meeting you' in this situation. But it was."

"It was," I agreed. "I'm very glad I caught that awful flight, and we lived to see today. That was an excellent scrimmage."

"Indeed." She laughed. "So who won?"

"Let's call it a tie."

"Good idea." Her laughter faded, and she put her hand on the door. "Well…good night."

"Good night." I didn't really trust myself not to get carried away if I touched her, so I kept my hands on the wheel.

She got out of the car and tiptoed across the grass to her front porch. A light came on above her front door. After unlocking it, she pushed it open and waved before disappearing inside.

As I drove off, I started to have second thoughts about not asking for her number.

Almost immediately, I shut them down. Sure, she was cute and fun and we'd had a good time tonight, but it's not like I was up in Michigan that often. And when I was, I was visiting my family, who lived almost two hours from here. Plus, asking for her number might have implied I was interested in more than just a good time now and then, and I didn't want to mislead her.

But later on, as I stretched out alone in my big bed, I caught a whiff of yellow cupcake.

And it made me wish she was still here beside me.

● ● ●

"Hey, Dad," I said at the dinner table the following night. "What was that story about the gangsters in your family tree?"

"Gangsters!" My twelve-year-old niece Claudia exchanged an excited look with her ten-year-old brother Benny. "I never knew we had gangsters in our family. Is that true, Papa?"

"That's the story my noni always told me." My dad reached over and cut up the chicken on six-year-old Gabrielle's plate.

"Don't gangsters, like, murder people?" Benny asked. "Are we actually related to a murderer?"

"Maybe," I said, winking at him.

"Joey Lupo!" My mother, who had just set a plate full of arancini on the table, sent me a furious look. "Don't say things like that."

"He wasn't a murderer," said my dad. But then he paused. "That I know of."

"So who was it?" Ellie, Gianni's wife, asked. "I don't think I've ever heard this story."

"It was my great-grandfather," my dad said. He looked at me from across the table. "The one you're named for. Giuseppe. But he also went by Joe."

"No shit," I said, impressed.

My mother, still arranging dishes to make room, sent me another scorching look. "Watch your mouth at the dinner table, please."

"Gigi, we've heard the word 'shit' before," Claudia informed her.

"I don't care," my mom said. "Is it too much to ask that Sunday dinner be free from profanity? Can't we at least pretend to be a nice, civilized family?"

My brother Paul burped loudly, which made the kids at the table burst out laughing before adding belches of their own.

"I don't think so, Coco," my dad said. "So just come sit down with the family we've got."

My mom sighed as she took the seat next to my dad. "We raised a pack of animals," she said.

He leaned over and kissed her cheek. "But they're our animals, cupcake."

Cupcake. I shifted in my chair.

"So Dad, it was your great-grandfather who was a gangster?" my sister Francesca asked. She piled food onto two plates, one for herself and one for her husband, Grant, who was walking their baby around the block in an effort to get her to stop crying. Apparently, she had colic and it had been a rough first month. Both Grant and Francesca looked exhausted—dark shadows under bloodshot eyes, pale faces, nonstop yawning. All reasons why it was better to be an uncle than a dad.

"Yes," my father said. "But I don't think he was a *gangster*. He was more of a bootlegger. As the story goes, it was his wife who got him involved."

"Seriously?" Ellie spread butter on a roll. "That's pretty cool. What was her name?"

"She was a little Irish spitfire everyone called Tiny," my dad said. "Five foot nothing with bright red hair. Evidently, her dad ran whiskey from Canada into Detroit during Prohibition, and she helped. They'd bring it across the river in the middle of the night."

I remembered what Mabel had said and thought how much she'd like this story. I wished I could tell her.

"My noni, who would have been her daughter-in-law, had lots of fun stories about her," said my dad.

"So she married one of their sons?" Gianni asked.

"Right."

"Their wedding photo is in the restaurant," my mother added.

"At Trattoria Lupo?" I tried to recall it and couldn't. "I've never noticed it."

"Me neither," Paul said.

"Wait, I've seen it," Alison chimed in excitedly. "Behind the hostess stand, right?"

"Yes," said my mom. "Nick's grandmother gave us a copy a long time ago."

"Oh! I've seen that photo too," said Ellie. "The black and white one! I've always wondered who it was." She turned to Gianni. "I asked you once, and you said you didn't know."

"I forgot." He shrugged.

My mother rolled her eyes. "Well, it's been there forever, and it's your family, and you all should know some of your history."

"Next time I'm in there, I'll look at it," I promised.

"My engagement ring is actually a replica of Tiny's ring," said my mom, holding out her hand. "It's got an art deco setting."

I glanced at the diamond ring I'd seen thousands of times but never really noticed. It did seem sort of old-fashioned, now that I was really looking at it.

"What made you ask about them?" my dad wondered.

I ate a bite of chicken piccata, its lemon flavor reminding me of kissing Mabel in the rain. "I was talking to this girl at the wedding last night who works at a museum, and she's doing some kind of exhibit about bootlegging. Wait, no—a fundraiser, not an exhibit. Anyway, she was telling me about these guys who ran whiskey from Canada, and it reminded me of your story."

"Was that the girl on the balcony?" Paul asked.

"Yes." I picked up my wine glass and took a drink.

"Ooooh, Joey took a girl out on the balcony," my sister teased. "How romantic."

"Who was it?" my mother asked. "Anyone I know?"

"Did you kiss her?" asked Claudia.

"Smoochy, smoochy," sang Gabrielle, followed by kissing noises.

Benny gagged and choked dramatically.

"No, Mom, no one you know." I gave Paul the stink eye, warning him he'd better not mention that I left with her last night. "She was just a girl I met, her name was Mabel, and that's enough about that."

"Mabel?" My mother smiled. "That's a sweet name."

It suits her, I thought. But I kept my mouth shut. My family was relentless about getting up in one another's personal business, and while I usually gave as much shit as I got, I didn't want Mabel talked about. Gianni knew her brother, and rumors spread quickly.

Despite the short amount of time we'd spent together, I felt protective of her.

Chapter 8

MABEL

ONE MONTH LATER

I stared in disbelief at two little pink lines.

No, I thought. It couldn't be right.

I'd only taken the test on a whim. To rule out *this* explanation for the extreme fatigue and dizzy spells I'd been experiencing over the last week or so. Because it couldn't be this.

I couldn't be pregnant.

I'd assumed it was stress. After the conference in Chicago, I'd thrown myself into planning the Bootleggers Ball fundraiser. The board of directors had loved the idea and suggested a gala in December, which didn't give me a ton of time to pull everything together—especially with classes starting soon—but I assured them I could manage it.

I spent the first two weeks of August doing research and working with a small committee of board members to plan an event splashy enough to draw big donors and entice them to support us. I contacted vendors, created a list of dream guests to reach out to personally, and begged a graphic artist I knew for help designing promotional materials for social media and posters.

I also prepped lesson plans and lectures for the two introductory anthropology courses I would teach this semester. And one day last week, I jumped out of bed at five a.m. after getting a call from Dash that Ari was in labor and could I please come stay with Wren while he took his wife to the hospital? I'd spent eighteen hours straight with the energetic little toddler, and she'd worn me right out.

I'd been so busy that I hadn't noticed a missed period. My cycle had never been perfectly regular, and I'd had some spotting at the end of July I'd assumed was just a light period because it had arrived kind of early.

And I hadn't had unprotected sex! Joe had worn a condom both times, hadn't he? I thought back on that night for the millionth time and felt certain that he had.

I hadn't forgotten a single detail.

The heaviness of that chest on mine, the roll of his hips above my body, the hitch of his breath as he moved inside me.

And the things he'd said. Oh God, those things he'd said to me.

I can't wait to get my mouth on you.

I'm gonna make you come so hard.

I could swallow you whole.

I can't get enough.

I need to get inside you.

Keep talking, cupcake. Tell me every filthy little thing.

And I had. I'd said things to him that made me blush when I

thought about them later. Things I'd never said to anyone. Things I'd never even *thought* about anyone.

But I wasn't sorry. And I must have gotten myself off to the memory of us tangled up in the sheets in his hotel room a dozen times since that night. It had been the most intense pleasure I'd ever known. Sometimes I looked up Joe's photos online and had to pinch myself that I'd actually spent those hours with him. It almost seemed like a dream.

But those two pink lines were real.

I stared at the stick on my bathroom counter for a full minute, then looked at my reflection in the mirror. I looked utterly bewildered. White as a ghost. My blue eyes—inherited from the mother I'd lost when I was too small to have memories of her—were full of fear. I wanted children, yes...but not now. Not like this. Not when I wasn't even in touch with the father, let alone not married to him.

I wasn't even dating him! Could I call us friends? I didn't even have his phone number. What on earth was I going to do, slide into his DMs and be like, *Hey, Joe, remember me? That woman who had a panic attack next to you on the plane and told you all the things she wanted to do before she died, like get married, have kids, and enjoy a one-night stand with a hot stranger? Turns out we might have crossed more than one thing off the list the next night.*

Tears filled my eyes. He was going to be upset. He was going to regret what we'd done. He was going to feel obligated to make offers out of pity—of money, of support, of apology. He didn't want a baby right now any more than I did. Maybe he never wanted one. Maybe this would ruin his life. Even if he never said those words to me, he might think them.

It was more than I could bear.

I took off my glasses, dropped my face into my hands, and wept.

• • •

"Oh, honey. Are you sure?" Ari looked at me from the rocking chair where she was nursing her baby, a little boy they'd named Truman. Dash had taken Wren to the park.

"I'm sure." Lying on the rug in the baby's room, I wiped the tears from beneath my eyes. "I took three home tests, and I saw my doctor."

"When?"

"Last week."

"You've known for a week and you didn't tell me?"

"I'm sorry." I reached over and put a hand on top of her foot. "I just didn't want to take anything away from this happy time in your life."

"Oh, Mabel." Ari's eyes filled, too. "Is it Joe Lupo's?"

I nodded, my throat tight. "Yes."

"You didn't use protection?"

"We did. A condom must have broken. If we learned anything from *Friends*, it was that condoms are only ninety-seven percent effective."

She laughed ruefully and shook her head. "Congratulations, you're in the top three percent. So how are you feeling?"

"Okay. At first, I was just dizzy and tired, but now the morning sickness has kicked in—although mine is worse in the evening."

"Yeah, it's different for everyone. But none of it's a party."

I sat up. "The physical stuff isn't even the worst of it. Not for me, anyway."

"God, Mabel. I feel responsible," she said, shifting Truman over her shoulder to burp him.

"What? Why?"

"Because I was egging you on, telling you to go be wild and

reckless." She patted the baby's plump little back. "I just never imagined this could happen."

"It's not your fault," I said firmly. "It's not anyone's fault. Listen, I've spent my entire adult life studying the history of humanity, and believe me when I tell you that things rarely go as planned. Volcanoes erupt and bury entire civilizations. Fires break out and burn down entire cities. Unsinkable ships lie at the bottom of the ocean." I inhaled and exhaled. "But life goes on. And a baby isn't a tragedy."

"What are you going to do?"

I lay back again and stared at the soft blue color on the ceiling. "I'm going to keep it."

"You are?"

"Yes." I placed both hands over my stomach. "I've considered all my options. I've spoken with my therapist. I've meditated and prayed and asked the universe for direction. I've thought long and hard about my life—past, present, and future. And I've made my decision."

"Mabel, this is so much."

"I know." I looked over at the airplane-and-cloud mobile hanging above the crib. "But I've always wanted kids. I want a family. This isn't exactly how I planned to start one, but it's the way it worked out. I'll be a single mom, at least for a while, just like my dad was a single dad. And Austin was a single dad."

My oldest brother had fourteen-year-old twins—my niece Adelaide and nephew Owen—who were the result of a California vacation fling. Since their mother hadn't been ready for children, Austin had offered to raise them on his own back in Cherry Tree Harbor. For a while, the three of them lived with my dad and me in the house where we'd all grown up.

Later, I'd been his summer nanny while I was home from college. But then, of course, there was the summer I'd been invited to work on a prestigious dig back east and Veronica had taken over my position…and they were now living happily ever after.

"You do have a great example in your dad and your brother," Ari said.

"I've been thinking about them both so much. About how my brother stepped up, even though he was only twenty-five and not ready to be a father, let alone a single dad. About what *our* dad taught us about love and family and showing up for one another, even when the worst possible things happen."

"Your family has been through a lot. It's made you all stronger. And so close."

"We didn't often say 'I love you' out loud. But I grew up knowing I was loved." I placed a hand on my belly. "I knew it just as surely as I know I'm supposed to love this baby with all my heart."

"Oh God, Mabel." Ari sniffled as she rose to her feet. "You can't do this to me. My postpartum emotions can't handle it." After placing Truman in the crib, she dropped onto the floor with me and lay back at my side. Took my other hand and clasped it in hers. "But I love your decision."

"You do?" Turning one cheek to the rug, I looked at her. "You don't think I'm crazy?"

"Not at all. And I'm here for you. We will *all* be here for you. This baby could not have chosen a better mom or a more wonderful, loving family."

I swallowed against the lump in my throat. "Thanks. I'm dreading telling my brothers."

"Take your time," she said. "My lips are sealed for now."

"Thanks. I'll do it soon, I just—" I swallowed again, but that lump refused to dissipate. "I need to tell Joe first."

"Do you know how to get in touch with him?"

"Nope."

"I could have Dash ask Gianni."

I shook my head vehemently. "No way. I don't want them speculating about why I need to get ahold of him. I'll figure out a way."

"Okay." She squeezed my hand. "Are you scared?"

"Yes," I said honestly. "I don't think he'll be a jerk about it, but honestly, I don't know him all that well. In fact, I barely know anything about him! Not his middle name or what college he went to or what he majored in or even what number he is on his hockey team." *Just what he looks like naked and sounds like in the dark.*

"Yeah, well, you guys didn't have a whole lot of time together. But from what I've heard about his family, I don't think he'll be a jerk. He'll probably want to do the right thing."

"I don't want that, either," I said, sitting up. "I don't want him to feel like he'll be forced to take care of me or something. I don't want to be anyone's obligation."

Ari sat up too. "But he'll want to take care of the baby, if he's a good guy."

"Maybe, but the one thing I *do* know about him is that his career is his priority. I don't plan to stand in his way. This pregnancy will not hold him back."

"Having a baby isn't easy," Ari said gently. "You're going to need support."

"I've got it," I insisted. "I have my family."

"You do have your family." She covered my hand with hers. "I'm just saying, if he offers to help you, don't be stubborn. He *is* the dad."

"I know." Softening, I rested my head onto her shoulder. "I think I'm just preparing myself for whatever the reaction might be. I'm putting up walls so I don't get hurt."

"Babe, you've got four older brothers who are going to lose their minds on this guy for getting you pregnant. If he does wrong by you on top of that, I don't care what kind of athlete he is, that guy's dead."

I laughed, even as tears slipped down my cheeks. "I don't want him dead. I just wish things were different. I wish we'd met in some romantic place, and he'd asked if he could see me again, and then we got to know each other and fell head over heels, and then he realized he wanted to spend the rest of his life with me, and then he got down on one knee and proposed, and then we had a beautiful wedding attended by everyone we love and I wouldn't even care if it rained that day because I knew we were meant to be, and then we'd move into our dream house right around the corner from you guys, and *then* we'd have a baby." I wiped my cheeks. "But that didn't happen. It was a meaningless one-night stand—not even a full night, because he drove me home after a few hours, since he doesn't like to share a bed."

"Are you serious?"

"Yes. He said he takes up all the space. And he hates to cuddle."

Ari shook her head. "You can't be with someone who hates to cuddle."

"I'm not *with* him. We are just two random strangers whose DNA is now percolating in my belly." I let my head flop back onto her shoulder.

She squeezed me again. "Everything is gonna be okay, Mabel."

"Tell me I'll still find the one, even with a baby."

"You absolutely will. Somewhere out there is a guy who's going to adore you *and* that little one. That's how you'll know he's the one. But first, you need to tell Joe he's gonna be a father."

• • •

In the end, I sent him a message on Instagram. I saw no other way to get through to him without asking a family member for help. It took me another week to work up the nerve to do it, and I must have typed and deleted a hundred different sentences. What I finally sent him was this:

> Hi, Joe. This is Mabel, from Cherry Tree Harbor. I have to come to Chicago next month, and I wondered if we could meet up? My timing is flexible. Let me know if you're around!

I'd decided that the pregnancy wasn't something I wanted to tell him about in a message, especially if he had an assistant handling his social media. If he turned down my idea about the in-person visit, I'd have to be a little more direct and ask him for his number, which I *really* didn't want to do.

Luckily, I didn't have to. It took him two days to answer me, but his reply was a relief.

> Hey Mabel. Good to hear from you. Sorry I didn't see your message sooner.

> Training camp starts mid-September. Would Labor Day weekend be okay? I know it's short notice, but I'm free that Saturday.

My heart started to race. That was this weekend. It was Monday—Saturday was just five days away. But I couldn't put it off any longer.

> Sure. How should I get in touch with you once I'm in town?

> Just call me.

The next message included his phone number, and I added it to my contacts before shooting him a quick text.

Hi, it's Mabel.

Cool, see you Saturday.

But he texted me the very next night.

So how have you been?

Good. You?

Good. Just getting ready for the season. Been
skating more.

You must be excited.

Yeah. Should be a good year.

I'll have to watch some games. What's your number?

Haha it's 19.

Thursday night he reached out again.

I meant to tell you, I asked my dad about that
relative who was the bootlegger.

Oh really? What did you find out?

Some cool stuff. Turns out, it was the great-
great-grandfather I was named after.

Giuseppe?

Yes. But he went by Joe too.

That's very cool.

My dad said he and his wife ran whiskey from
Canada into Detroit. They used to bring it over
in boats in the middle of the night.

Stop it, really?

That's what my dad's noni told him.

That's incredible!

It reminded me of you.

I stared at the screen while heat rushed my face. He hadn't just forgotten about me—that was good, right? While I was trying to decide how to respond, he texted again.

See you in a couple days.

I liked his final message and set my phone aside.

Then I ran to the bathroom and threw up.

• • •

Late Saturday afternoon, I checked into my hotel and sent Joe a text that I'd arrived in the city. He asked if I wanted to come over to his place and we could decide from there what we wanted to do, and I said that was fine. He sent me the address and let me know he'd leave my name at the desk so I could come right up.

I ate a handful of crackers to settle my stomach, cleaned up a little, and jumped in an Uber.

Joe's apartment was in a Gold Coast high-rise, and when I gave my name to the concierge, I was shown to the elevators. As I rode up to the sixteenth floor, I couldn't help thinking about the elevator ride up to his hotel room at The Pier Inn. His mouth and hands all over me. His voice in my ear. My stomach was just as jumpy this time around, although for a much different reason.

The doors opened and I walked down the hallway to his door. Taking a deep breath, I said a little prayer and knocked. When he pulled it open a moment later, I felt the air rush from my lungs. I'd forgotten how handsome he was.

"Mabel Jane Buckley." He opened his arms and moved forward to give me a hug, clasping me tightly to his chest. He smelled fresh and clean and masculine, and he felt slightly damp, like he'd just gotten out of the shower. "It's good to see you."

Closing my eyes, I allowed myself to be swallowed by his embrace, taking comfort in the solid warmth of his chest. "Hi."

After letting me go, he shut the door behind me. His eyes roamed over my blue floral skirt, the white T-shirt I'd tied at the waist, and my sneakers. "You look great."

"Thanks. So do you." He was barefoot and wore jeans and a plain black T-shirt that hugged his muscles.

He messed with his hair. "Sorry I'm a little wet, I just showered. Can I get you something to drink? Beer or glass of wine or something? I don't have champagne, but I think I have a bottle of white somewhere around here."

"Maybe just water?"

"Sure. Come on in." As we left the entryway and moved down a hall to the right, he swept an arm toward a bedroom on the left. "So, this is my place. Guest room there. Bathroom here." He gestured to an open door on the right, through which I saw shiny white marble with gray veins. The hall ended at a partially closed door, which he pushed open. "My bedroom."

I gave it a glance—king-sized bed, huge TV screen mounted on the opposite wall, massive windows with the blackout shades down.

He turned left again, leading me into a huge open space with a kitchen at one end and a living room at the other. The outer wall was a curved bank of floor-to-ceiling windows offering a stunning panoramic view of the city below and Lake Michigan beyond.

"Wow," I said. "What a view."

"Yeah, that's what sold me on this place. I like being able

to see the water." He went behind a marble-topped island and opened a stainless fridge. Pulling out a bottle of water, he handed it to me. "This okay?"

"Yes. Thank you." I uncapped it and took a few cold swallows, praying my nausea wouldn't hit while I was here.

"Have a seat." He grabbed a beer from the fridge and popped the cap off. "Tell me how things are going at the Cherry Tree Harbor Historical Society."

I went over to one of two navy blue couches that met in an L shape and perched on the edge of the cushion. "Pretty good."

He dropped down next to me, leaning back with casual ease. It struck me how unsuspecting he was. He had no idea I was about to lob a grenade in his direction.

I quickly took another sip of water.

"I was glad to get your text," he said.

Not for long he wasn't.

He smiled, his blue eyes twinkling. "I had a lot of fun that night we hung out together."

"Me too. That's…" I dug my thumbnail beneath the label on the water bottle. "That's kind of why I'm here."

He chuckled. "You look nervous."

"I am."

"You don't have to be nervous with me, Mabel." He gave my shoulder a playful poke. "We don't have to start all over again. I already put the puck in the net, remember?"

"That's the thing," I said. "The puck sort of—*stayed* in the net."

He cocked his head but still wore a smile. "Huh?"

I set my water bottle on the coffee table and placed my hands on my stomach. "I'm pregnant, Joe. I got pregnant that night."

Chapter 9

My face was immobile, like my smile had been set in cement. "Sorry, what?"

"I'm pregnant."

I looked around, like this might all be an elaborate setup. A practical joke. Were my brothers about to jump out and laugh their asses off at me? I had to admit, this would be a good prank.

But the room remained silent.

"Is this—are you—sorry." I shook my head and stared at Mabel's stomach. "Did you say *pregnant*?"

"Yes." She took a breath. "I know this is a shock."

"From that *one night*?"

"Yes."

"But it was just a scrimmage," I insisted. "It wasn't supposed to count."

She laughed nervously. "I don't think all the players got that message."

I jumped off the couch and backed up, putting distance between us, although it was a little too late for that. "How did this happen? I wore condoms!"

"Yes, well...turns out, there were some elite athletes in the game that sort of breached the defensive line. And then one of them stayed to celebrate the victory."

The victory? This wasn't a victory. This was a nightmare!

"Did I put it on wrong?" I racked my brain, trying to remember if I'd been in such a rush that I'd skipped some critical step.

"No. It just...failed, Joe. It can happen."

"Not to me, it can't!"

"Look, don't panic, okay? I'm not here to make any demands. You don't have to change your life."

I looked at her and squinted, like she wasn't in focus. "Huh?"

"You can still be who you are. I don't expect you to drop everything and be a dad."

A dad? What was she talking about? I couldn't be a dad. My *dad* was a dad.

I was a hockey player. That's all I knew how to be.

My brothers were dads, but they were different than me. Gianni was married to the only woman who'd ever put up with his bullshit, and he'd always worshipped her. Although, now that I thought about it, Ellie had gotten pregnant before they were married. Was there some sort of curse on the Lupo men?

But Gianni and Ellie were always going to be together! They'd been getting under each other's skin since childhood, thrown together constantly because our moms were best friends. They'd gone to high school together. He was a chef and he ran the restaurant at her family's winery. She was a wine expert and ran the tasting room. They'd been made for each other.

Paul had always known he wanted a family, and Alison had been there all along. He was a lawyer, and she was an accountant. They both liked rock climbing and jigsaw puzzles. They made perfect sense.

Mabel and I were polar opposites and near strangers. We didn't even live in the same city. We'd spent less than twenty-four hours together.

She was going to have my baby?

I don't want this, I thought like a selfish prick. *I don't fucking want this.*

"Joe? Are you okay?" Mabel was looking at me with worried eyes, but I couldn't answer her.

The room had started to spin like I was on a carnival ride. I could even hear the creepy organ music, wavering like a warped record. I swayed on my feet as the edges of my vision blurred. As the edges of my life frayed. The beer slipped from my grip and hit the floor, and my knees began to buckle.

"Joe!" Mabel stood up.

I backed up until the backs of my legs hit another piece of furniture—a chair—and I dropped into it. I couldn't speak. Couldn't think. Couldn't breathe. My eyes closed.

What the fuck?

Her announcement sank into my head like a stone reaching the bottom of the lake. *I'm pregnant.*

I'm not sure how much time passed while I wished with all my might that this wasn't happening. That I'd inadvertently slipped through a portal to an alternate dimension, but I'd find my way out any moment now, and things would go back to normal.

But when my eyelids went up, I was still sitting in the chair, and Mabel was on her hands and knees, mopping up the beer I'd spilled on the rug.

It brought me to my senses.

"Let me do that." I got off the chair and took over, sopping up the mess with a towel she must have found in the kitchen while I was catatonic.

She sat back on her heels and adjusted her glasses. "Are you okay?"

"Yes. No. I'm…in shock."

"I was too, when I first found out."

"How long have you known?"

"A couple weeks."

"And it's definitely for sure in there?" I looked at her stomach, which appeared suspiciously flat.

"It's definitely for sure in there, but it's only the size of a pea. You can't see it yet."

"You've seen a doctor?"

"Yes. I'm almost eight weeks along."

I cocked my head. "But the wedding wasn't that long ago."

"Pregnancy math is weird," she said. "It starts from the date of the last period, not the date of conception."

"Oh." Jesus, I knew *nothing* about this stuff.

Mabel hugged herself. "It's real, Joe. I know it's hard to believe, but it's real."

I went back to mopping up the spill, like a stain on the rug was my biggest problem at the moment. I knew she was scared, and instinctively, I wanted to reassure her. But dammit—I was so out of my element. I felt lost.

"Say something," she begged.

I knew what I was supposed to say. What a better man would say—or ask. But the words weren't coming.

"Give me a minute," I said instead.

She rose to her feet and sat on the couch again, while I went over to the kitchen, rinsed the towel, and set it aside. Wiping my hands on my jeans, I came back to the couch and sat down next to her.

"Sorry. I should have asked this sooner," I said. "Are *you* okay?"

"Yes." She nodded, but then she promptly burst into tears.

I got up again, found a box of tissues, and set it on the coffee table.

"I'm sorry," she said, removing her glasses. "I've never been a big crier, but my emotions are all over the place."

"Don't apologize." I lowered myself to the couch again. My emotions were all over the place too—I was furious the condom had failed, terrified of the future, guilty as fuck for putting her in this situation. And her tears were killing me. Reaching for her, I pulled her into my arms. "Hey. Come here."

She wept against my chest for a minute, but then pulled herself together. "Oh God, your shirt. I made a mess of it."

I looked down at the wet splotches. "I don't care. The shirt can be washed. We've got bigger issues than laundry."

She plucked a tissue from the box. "True."

I steeled myself for the answer to my next question. "Have you decided what you want to do?"

"Yes." She blew her nose and took a breath. "I'm going to have the baby. And I'm going to keep it."

"Okay." My stomach lurched. "Where do you want to live?"

"In Cherry Tree Harbor, where my family is."

"Do you think we—I mean, should we get—" The last word stuck in my throat.

"No," she said firmly. "I know what you're going to ask, and the answer is absolutely not. Times have changed. People don't have to be married to have a baby. That's not what I want. And I know it's not what you want."

"Okay." Not gonna lie, I breathed easier. Being a dad was

one thing. Being a husband was another. One sucker punch was enough. "I just feel like such an asshole, Mabel. I don't know what to say except I'm sorry."

"You're not an asshole. You didn't do anything wrong." She put a hand on my leg. "Neither of us wanted this, Joe. And I know how focused you are on your career right now. It's okay—this won't get in the way of your dreams."

"What about your dreams? I don't even know what they are."

She sat up a little taller. "To be honest, I've achieved a lot of my professional goals already. I came back home to focus on family, and while this definitely wasn't Plan A to start my own, it's what happened. Maybe there's a reason."

My eyes closed. I couldn't see any good reason for this.

She took her hand off me. "I'm not here to put pressure on you or trap you into anything, Joe. If you don't want to be involved, I don't have to name you as the father. I can just—"

"What? Fuck that." Incensed, I opened my eyes and shifted to face her on the couch. "I'm not going to be some deadbeat dad, Mabel. I want to be involved. I want my kid to know me."

Her eyes filled, and she burst into tears again.

Confused, I ruffled my damp hair. "Did I say the wrong thing?"

"No." She reached for another tissue. "I was just so scared about your reaction."

"What did you think I'd do?"

"I wasn't sure. I mean, we hardly know each other. What if you didn't believe me that the baby is yours? Or what if you didn't want me to have it? Or what if you just didn't care at all and told me to get lost?"

"I never would have done any of those things." But I couldn't blame her for being afraid—she was right. We hardly knew each other.

"I was trying to be prepared for any reaction, but the entire drive here, I was—"

"Wait, you drove here?" I interrupted. "By yourself?"

"Yes."

"How long did it take you?"

"About seven hours. I stopped a couple times."

I didn't like thinking about her alone on the road for so long. What if she'd gotten a flat tire or had an emergency? "I would have flown you down."

She shook her head. "I didn't want to tell you about the baby over the phone, and anyway, I couldn't bring myself to get on a plane. My anxiety was off the charts. It's not just me I have to worry about anymore, you know?"

My chest ached with an unfamiliar tightness.

"Joe, there's something you should know about me." She stopped and considered. "Well, there are probably a lot of things you should know about me, but I'll start with this one thing, because it has shaped me in so many ways."

I leaned one elbow on the back of the couch, listening.

"My mom died when I was very small. She had cancer, and it took her really quickly." She shredded the tissues in her hand as she talked.

"I'm sorry," I said, the ache in my chest deepening. My mom had had a brush with cancer about a dozen years ago, but thankfully, she'd beaten it and remained in remission. But it had been the worst time of my life. "That must have been hard, growing up without your mom."

"It was. But my dad was amazing, and I had my brothers too. And there were aunts and uncles and lots of family friends around—people stepped up and pitched in." She sniffed, giving me a tearful smile. "But losing her like that left me with this awareness that life is fragile and precious. That you can never take anything for granted. That keeping the people you love safe isn't always possible—but you try. You do the best you can." She took a deep breath. "So I drove here instead of getting on a plane."

Her fear of flying made even more sense to me now. It wasn't just about some fake fifth grader fortune-teller. "I understand."

"But I think the loss of her also gave me an appreciation for life," she went on, her tone growing more hopeful. "And my dad taught us all that while it's unpredictable, it's still joyful. I had a wonderful childhood."

"I have a great dad too," I said, wondering what he was going to say about this. "He always believed in me. So did my mom."

"Maybe I can meet them sometime."

"Sure." A sharp pain shot between my temples, and I rubbed them with my thumb and forefinger. "So what's next?"

"I'm going to tell my family."

"Okay." I pictured her four menacing brothers coming at me on the ice like two pairs of defensemen, ready to take me out. I'd deserve it.

"And then I'm just going to continue working and teaching, but I've already let the college know I won't be back second semester. The baby is due in April, and I'll need some time to prepare."

"Will you stay in your house?"

"Yes. There's plenty of room for me and a baby there. And it's close to my dad and his wife—he's remarried now—and not too far from my other siblings."

"We should probably talk about finances," I said. "I want to support you."

"We can work all that out later." She reached for her water bottle and took a sip. "For now, I think we just need to get used to the idea…and maybe get to know each other."

"Okay." My stomach growled then, a long, deep groan.

"Whoa." She laughed. "Are you hungry?"

"I guess. What about you?"

"My stomach is a little off at this time of day, but I should eat dinner eventually."

"Do you want to go out?" I saw her hesitate at the idea, and to be honest, I didn't really feel like going to a restaurant around here either. I'd be recognized, and the internet might gossip about me being seen with a date. "Or we could just stay here. Get takeout. Or I could cook."

She shrank back a little, her eyebrows rising. "You cook?"

"My dad taught me how to make a few things. Do you like spaghetti?"

"Yes."

"Perfect. It's settled."

She followed me to the kitchen. "Can I help?"

"Nope," I said, going to the freezer to pull out some ground beef for the Bolognese. "Just grab a counter stool and talk to me."

Laughing, she slid onto a stool and propped her elbows on the marble island. "That I can do. Talking is my specialty."

• • •

I made us pasta and salad and garlic bread, and she ate some of everything with no complaints about carbs or gluten. We talked about the family recipes, the fundraiser she was organizing, the upcoming hockey season, each other's siblings and their kids. I made an effort to pay attention to names, although she had a pretty big family, so it was hard to remember them all.

She had a lot of questions for me. "What's your middle name?"

"Thomas. It's my mother's maiden name."

"Where did you go to college?"

"Notre Dame."

"What did you study?"

"Business."

We didn't talk much about the baby or how this was going to work, but I was glad for that. I needed some time to process.

Afterward, she offered to do the dishes and help clean up the kitchen, but I could see how tired she was and told her I'd handle it.

"Thanks," she said, yawning as I walked her to the door. "That long drive wore me out."

"I'm tired too, and I didn't even make that drive."

"Well, today was a lot—for *both* of us." At the door, she faced me with a serious expression. "Thanks for being so understanding."

I grimaced. "I'm not sure you should be thanking me for anything."

"But I feel grateful. You could have turned out to be a big jerk."

"I've still got time."

She laughed. "True. Hey, speaking of time, I have an ultrasound scheduled for next week. You don't have to be there or anything, but I wanted to let you know."

"Yeah, I'm not sure I could get away, with training camp starting."

"It's okay." Her shoulders rose. "Like I said, I don't expect you to change your life around. I know your priority is your career right now. I'm just in a different place."

"I should thank *you* for being so understanding," I told her. "You could have come in here with a list of demands."

She shook her head. "Not my style."

"I'm grateful." I glanced over my shoulder into the guest

room. "Hey, I should have offered this before, but do you want to stay here tonight?"

"No," she said without hesitation. "I already booked a room, and my car is parked in the hotel garage. Plus..." She looked down at her phone in her hand. "Plus, I think it's best if we don't confuse things."

"Confuse things?"

She chewed her bottom lip. "I just think this will work better if we stay really clear on the boundaries. It would be bad for everyone involved if things got—complicated between us."

I nodded, knowing she was right, glad at least one of us was this level-headed. "Can I at least pay for your room and the parking?"

"Maybe next time," she said with a smile.

"Okay. Well...call me, I guess?"

"I will. I have your number now." She wagged her phone.

I laughed. "Right."

She opened one arm and rose up on tiptoe, and I gave her a hug, the most impersonal one yet. Our lower bodies didn't even touch. "Good night," she said. "Thanks for dinner."

"You're welcome. Have a safe trip home." Letting her go, I pulled the door open. "Take care of yourself, Mabel."

"I will." With a final wave, she walked out.

I watched her walk down the hall, then shut the door behind her and leaned my forehead against it. Thumped it a few times.

What. The. Fuck.

I was going to be a father.

• • •

For hours that night, I lay in bed, stretched out and staring at the ceiling. I was tired, but I couldn't sleep. So much was running through my mind.

When I'd gotten Mabel's message on Instagram, I'd been excited about seeing her again. Since Footsie's wedding, I'd thought about her a lot—mostly in the shower with my dick in my hand—and every time, I regretted not getting her number. Not because I wanted to date her—or have a baby with her, for fuck's sake—but I'd had such a good time that night. I thought it would be worth reaching out next time I went home to see if she might like to play another scrimmage.

Except that it hadn't turned out to be a meaningless practice matchup at all. At some point, I'd gotten her pregnant.

I remembered how intense the sex had been, how hard I'd come, especially that second time. It almost didn't surprise me that my stuff had busted right through the condom.

There were some elite athletes in the game that sort of breached the defensive line.

For a half second, I was like *fuck yes, there were elite athletes in the game*, but I stopped short of celebrating my genetic prowess. I hadn't scored this goal on purpose. It was an accidental shot, a wild bounce of the puck. It shouldn't count, but it did.

I remembered how much shit I'd given Gianni after he'd gotten Ellie pregnant. God, he was going to give it right back, and I'd have to take it. My mom would be sad. My dad would be upset. Neither of them would understand that this wasn't my fault—I hadn't been irresponsible. It was just bad luck.

And I couldn't do what Gianni had done. I wasn't going to marry Mabel or live with her or be there every day. I just couldn't. And she didn't want me to! She hadn't even wanted to stay the night in my guest room. She wanted to keep things casual and friendly between us. Almost professional. Boundaries in place.

Which was fine with me.

I wasn't going to be a dad like my father and brothers were. Hands on, there all the time, twenty-four/seven dads. It just wouldn't look like that for me, and everyone would have to deal with it. I'd be supportive, but my priority was still hockey. I'd be better able to support them with a successful career, right? First as a player and then as a coach or maybe a commentator? Focusing on the game was best for everybody.

But I tossed and turned for several more hours and finally fell asleep toward dawn. When my alarm went off for the morning skate, I reached for my phone, hit stop, and set it aside.

Then I picked it up again and sent Mabel a message.

> Hey, can you send me the date and time for the ultrasound appointment? Thanks.

Chapter 10

MABEL

"So? How did it go?" Even over Bluetooth, I could hear the anxiety in Ari's voice.

"It went fine," I said, cruising along I-94, Chicago in my rearview. "Maybe even better than fine. I didn't even get the hiccups."

"Tell me everything! Was he shocked?"

"Definitely," I said, recalling the dumbfounded expression on his face and his insistence that it had only been a scrimmage and wasn't supposed to count. "It took him a little time to accept the news."

"But he didn't question whether it was his or anything?"

"Nope. Not at all. He just seemed in denial for a bit, then really sorry, and finally kind of resigned to it, I guess."

"How about when you told him you're going to have it and

raise it on your own?"

"He didn't argue. He said he wanted to be supportive."

"Wow. So what does that look like?"

"I'm not sure yet," I said, signaling and checking my blind spot before changing lanes. "I think he means financially, but he also said he wanted to be involved. That was his word—*involved*. We had dinner at his apartment and talked for a couple hours, but we didn't really make any firm plans."

"What's his apartment like?"

"Gorgeous. I mean, it's kind of sparsely decorated, like no art or anything. But almost an entire wall is windows overlooking Chicago and Lake Michigan, so I guess that's the art."

"Is it like a man cave? Like beat-up furniture and takeout containers everywhere? Or is it like playboy cool, all chrome and leather and mirrors over his bed?"

I laughed. "Neither. His couches were comfortable and navy blue, and he had a couple beige chairs. Bathroom was white marble. I was not in his bedroom, so I cannot tell you if there were mirrors, but he has a couple huge TVs. Nice kitchen."

"Sounds like an above-average bachelor pad. So did you order in?"

"No, actually, he cooked dinner for us."

"Really? What did he make?"

"Spaghetti. It was really good. He said it was his family's meat sauce recipe."

"He loves giving you the family meat sauce, doesn't he?"

I laughed. "Very funny."

"Sorry. Couldn't resist. Well, it sounds like it went as well as you could have hoped, right?"

"I think so." I recalled sitting across from him, watching him cook, the easy way he moved around in the kitchen, the things he said about his family, the excited way he talked about hockey.

He'd also made an effort to ask about my job and my family. "It was nice getting to know him a little better."

"So is there any chance the two of you might…" Her voice trailed off on a hopeful note.

"No," I said firmly. "No chance."

"You sound very sure about that."

"I am. He seems like a good guy, and he's hotter than the business end of a blowtorch, but he is *not* for me. He's not for anybody right now. The love of his life is hockey. The love of my life is gonna be this baby." I paused. "Which is why when he asked if I wanted to stay the night, I said no."

"He asked you to stay the night?" Ari's voice rose to a high pitch.

"In the guest bedroom."

"Oh." Her tone said *womp womp*. "Why'd you say no to that? You could have saved money on a hotel room."

"I'd already checked into my hotel room, but besides, I don't want to blur the lines. We're getting to know each other better so we can amicably co-parent. That's all I want."

"God, you're so logical! I'd have been like, 'Of course I'll stay over, and just so you know, the bedroom door will be open.'"

I laughed. "I won't deny that I find him incredibly attractive. But I have to rise above it. Number one, so I don't get hurt. Number two, so this kid doesn't end up with a mom and dad who can't be in the same room together or have nothing nice to say about each other. I don't need him to be my boyfriend—I just want him to keep his word about being involved in this baby's life. That's more important than my crush on him."

Another sigh. "Again. You're so darn reasonable."

"I'm talking a big game," I admitted. "Underneath the words, my emotions are all over the place. I still have whiplash. I'm scared that I have no idea what I'm doing. But I know it's right."

"Sometimes, you just have to go with your gut. And I'm really glad he was supportive."

"This morning, he texted me asking when and where my ultrasound appointment is."

She gasped. "Is he coming?"

"He can't. Training camp starts next week. But he said he'd like the information anyway, so he can remember to ask me about it, and I seriously almost cried. It just helps knowing I won't be totally in this alone."

"When will you tell your family?"

"Tomorrow, I think." The whole Buckley clan was gathering at my dad's house for a Labor Day barbecue. "I'm nervous."

"You'll be fine. They're going to be supportive."

"I know they will eventually, but I just hope my brothers don't go all caveman and start slapping their fists into their palms or acting like Joe took advantage of their innocent baby sister."

Ari laughed. "Yeah, they might act a little like that." In the background, I heard Truman start to fuss.

"I'll let you go," I told her. "Just promise me you'll be on my side tomorrow."

"Tomorrow and always," she said. "Drive safely."

• • •

The following day, I joined all my siblings and their families over at the home where we'd grown up. It was a gorgeous sunny day, the temperature hovering right around seventy-five degrees, a breeze rustling the leaves of the giant maple tree in our backyard.

Austin and my dad were at the grill. Xander, Devlin, and

Dashiel were playing T-ball on the lawn with any of the nieces or nephews who could swing a bat and run the bases. Austin's wife Veronica and Devlin's wife Lexi were watching the smaller ones splash around in a plastic baby pool, and Ari and I were sitting at the umbrella table with Xander's wife Kelly and her mom, Julia, who had married my dad a couple years ago. Nearby, baby Truman slept in his buggy in the shade.

It was an idyllic afternoon, and I was surrounded by love, but my stomach was uneasy.

I kept trying to talk myself into breaking the news to one family member or another, but I never quite worked up the nerve. Finally, when all the adults were squeezed in around the umbrella table and the kids were all set up at the little picnic tables my dad had purchased to accommodate all his grandkids, Ari nudged me with her foot.

I put my hamburger down without ever taking a bite from it. "So I have some news," I said.

Nobody stopped eating. Xander asked Veronica to pass him the mustard. Dashiel told Devlin to stop elbowing him.

"I'm not doing it on purpose, I'm just a lefty," Devlin said.

"Can someone pass the potato salad?" my dad asked.

"What's the news, Mabel?" Ari asked loudly.

"I'm pregnant."

Silence. Suddenly ten pairs of eyes were on me. The bowl of potato salad hovered above the table in my dad's hand.

"You're what now?" Veronica asked.

"I'm pregnant." I touched my stomach. "I know it's a bit of a surprise. It wasn't, um, planned."

No one spoke. I looked helplessly at Ari.

"Well, I love surprises," she said brightly. "And if you have a boy, he and Truman will be cousins *and* best friends! Even if it's a girl, I bet they'll be best friends!"

I gave her a grateful smile.

"But—who—I mean—well!" My dad laughed nervously, setting the potato salad down. "This is certainly an interesting turn of events."

"Who's the father?" demanded Devlin, always one to get down to business.

"The father is someone I met at a wedding in July. We sort of…hung out together that night, but we're not dating. He lives in Chicago."

"What's his name?" Kelly asked.

This was the part I'd been dreading. "Joe Lupo."

"Joe Lupo?" Austin repeated.

"Not Joe Lupo, the hockey player," said Dashiel, his head cocked and his eyes narrowed.

"Yes. That Joe Lupo."

More silence. Someone growled—I think it was Austin. Xander cracked his knuckles.

"There's no need to be upset," I said calmly. "I've spoken to Joe, and we have an understanding."

"He's gonna understand my fist in his—"

"Xander, that's not going to be necessary." I met his dark, angry eyes. "We're good."

Veronica's jaw was still hanging open, but when I met her eyes, she understood the silent plea for help. "Wow! Congratulations, Mabel! You're going to be an amazing mom."

"Thanks." I smiled at her. "Now that the shock is wearing off, I'm getting a little more excited."

"So you're due in, what, April?" asked Lexi.

"Yes." Then I looked at Kelly, who was also pregnant, due in a couple months. "I'm sure I'll be coming to all of you for advice."

Kelly smiled warmly. "We'll be here to give it. I'm happy for you, Mabel."

"Well, I think this is wonderful," Julia said. "There's certainly nothing George and I love more than grandchildren, so adding one more to the bunch is the best gift anyone could give us."

My father recovered enough to nod. "That's right. I feel like the luckiest guy in the world right now. Congratulations, honey."

I smiled at him, my eyes filling with grateful tears. "Thanks, Dad."

• • •

By evening, the text thread I had with my sisters-in-law had blown up.

Veronica
OMFG JOE LUPO

Kelly
I KNOW!!!!

Lexi
MABEL! GET IN HERE AND TELL US EVERYTHING.

Kelly
Ari, did you know about this?

Ari
Yes, but I was sworn to secrecy.

Veronica
Austin keeps growling.

Kelly
Xander still wants to beat him up.

Lexi

Devlin is trying very hard to be happy about it,
but I know he looks at Mabel and sees a kid in
pigtails.

Ari

Dash is taking it pretty well. He says the Lupo
family is really great.

Veronica

Have you met them yet, Mabel?

> No. I'm not sure when that's going to happen.
> He needs to tell them first.

Kelly

And you need to tell us ALL THE THINGS.

> Honestly, it's a tale as old as time, you guys. I
> went to a wedding, got a little tipsy on champagne,
> and hooked up with a hot groomsman.

Lexi

Who happens to be a hotshot in the NHL.

Kelly

He shoots, he scores!

Veronica

He's got that high stick action!

> Hahaha.

Veronica

Sorry, Mabel! We shouldn't make jokes. Are you
feeling okay?

Yes. I'm fine, just a little morning sickness, and I don't even mind the jokes. If I couldn't laugh about this, I'd lose my mind.

Lexi
So he was supportive when you told him?

Yes. Shocked and upset, but supportive. I just hope my brothers don't take his head off when they meet him.

Kelly
Your brothers will come around. Xander loves hockey. Once he gets over the stupid NO ONE PUTS HIS HANDS ON MY LITTLE SISTER thing, I'm sure he'll be fine.

Veronica
Austin has NO ROOM to talk. The same thing happened to him with the twins. And everything was fine.

Ari
I keep telling her she's going to be a great mom. And she's not alone.

Kelly
^^^THIS

Lexi
100%

Veronica
Buckley women FTW

Thanks, guys. Love you.

Later that evening, I also got a text from Julia.

Hello, sweetie. I have been thinking about you nonstop. I know you have your dad and your brothers and all your wonderful sisters-in-law, but if I can be a comfort to you, don't hesitate to reach out. I know I am not your mom, but please know that I am here for you, should you need anything. A hand to hold, a shoulder to cry on, a cheerleader to tell you you're doing great. Because there's no doubt in my mind that you will. You are smart, strong, caring, and patient. We love you.

A lump formed in my throat, and I closed my eyes, giving myself a minute to deal with all the feelings whirling through me like a tornado.

Julia, thank you so much for the kind words. I know I will be reaching out to you for all those things. I appreciate you more than you know, especially because you make my dad so happy. I hope I find what you have someday.

Darling Mabel, I'm sure you will. Love often takes its time but is always worth the wait.

I hearted her message, hoping she was right.

• • •

My ultrasound appointment was on Wednesday afternoon at three o'clock. Ari had offered to meet me there, but I told her I didn't mind going on my own.

"Are you sure?" she asked over the phone. "I can put real clothes on, jump in the car, and be there in ten minutes. Dash is here, and he can stay with Wren and Truman."

"I'm sure," I said. "Enjoy your family time. I'll send you the picture."

"You better." She paused. "Have you heard from Joe?"

"No," I admitted. "Not a word."

"What the hell? I thought he was going to be involved."

"I think he meant with the kid, not necessarily with the pregnancy."

"Still. He could at least check in with you."

"It's only been four days, Ari. He's probably still processing it. And training camp is starting, so he's really busy." But even as I made excuses for him, I tamped down my own disappointment. "Look, if this is how it's going to be, I'd rather know it now."

"Maybe we should have let Xander punch him."

"No," I said as I pulled into a parking spot at the doctor's office. "You can't punch someone for being busy. I dropped this bombshell on him out of nowhere. He's in the NHL. His schedule really isn't negotiable."

"He can't find the time to send a text asking how you're doing?" she asked testily.

I had no answer for that. "Look, I'm here, so I have to go. I'll call you afterward."

We said goodbye, and I dropped my phone in my bag as I entered the building. After signing in, I waited in the lobby, trying not to be nervous. There was a lot that could still go wrong so early in a pregnancy, and although I'd tried to stay off the internet the last few days, I'd unwisely searched a few things. The longer I sat there, the more my anxiety spiked, and I started to regret telling Ari I didn't need her here. In the future, I'd bring her or maybe Julia along. It would be nice to have a hand to hold.

A grandmotherly nurse appeared in the doorway. Her name tag said June. "Mabel Buckley?"

I stood up. "Yes, that's me."

June smiled. "Right this way."

After being shown to a room, I was instructed to get undressed and drape the sheet over my lower body. The tech would be in momentarily.

I slipped out of my flats, pulled off my work pants and underwear, and climbed onto the table, spreading the paper sheet over me. After a couple minutes, there was a knock on the door. "I'm ready," I called. "Come in."

Expecting the tech, I was surprised when June poked her head into the room. "Just me," she said. "There's a man here who says he's the father and wants to know if it's okay if he comes back."

My jaw dropped. "He's here?"

She smiled, her eyes twinkling. "Well, someone's here. Big guy? Dark hair? Quite handsome?"

"Yes," I said in disbelief. "That sounds like him. His name is Joe Lupo."

June nodded happily. "That's what he said. Okay to bring him back?"

"I—um—sure."

She shut the door again and I sat there, dumbfounded. Joe was here?

Hiccup!

My heartbeat tripped over itself again and again and again. My hands fisted in the paper sheet. When the knock sounded on the door again, I frantically rearranged it, trying to cover as much of myself as possible, which—given the circumstances—made little sense. This man had already seen me completely naked in a hotel room.

But somehow I was more vulnerable here and now.

"Come in," I called weakly.

The door opened.

Hiccup!

Chapter 11

JOE

I still hadn't wrapped my brain around the idea that I was going to be a father.

After brooding about it for forty-eight hours, I'd finally broken down and messaged my brother Gianni Monday night.

> Got a minute?

Sure, what's up?

> Can I call you?

Give me a few and I'll call you. Getting the kids to bed.

My phone vibrated about fifteen minutes later, and I flopped back on the couch before taking the call.

"Hey."

"Hey. Everything okay?"

"Yes. No." I exhaled. "I need advice."

"Quit trying to score from the blue line."

"It's not about hockey."

He laughed. "There's something else in your life besides hockey?"

"There is now."

"Sounds kinda serious."

"It is." I leaned forward, one elbow on my knee, and pinched the bridge of my nose. "I got someone pregnant."

Silence. "Courtney?"

"Not Courtney."

"Who?"

"This girl named Mabel Buckley. It was a one-time thing the night of Footsie's wedding."

"So you did more than just take her out onto the balcony."

"Yeah."

My older brother exhaled. "Well, first I'm going to say what you said to me when I told you Ellie was pregnant."

"What did I say?"

"You said *dude*. That was it. A one-word text."

"Yeah, well, the rest of the thought was, 'Dude, how could you be so fucking stupid?' But now I know."

"Now you know. So what happened?"

"Condom broke."

"Damn. So she got in touch with you?"

"Yeah. She drove down here over the weekend to tell me. She lives in Cherry Tree Harbor."

"Is she related to Dashiel Buckley?"

"His sister. He probably wants to kick my ass right about now."

"Nah, he's not the type." Gianni paused. "How does *she* feel?"

"She's okay. She wants to have the baby and raise it on her

own up there where all her family and friends are. She said she doesn't expect anything from me."

Silence. "Not how Courtney would have reacted."

"Nope."

"So how do *you* feel?"

"I don't know. It's like—" I got off the couch and wandered over to the windows, where darkness pressed against the glass. "I was really glad when she didn't get mad or start issuing demands, but when she said I didn't have to be involved, it kinda felt like a punch in the gut."

"You want to be involved?"

"I don't *want* any of this, but if she's going to give birth to my kid, I want him to know who his dad is."

"So he gets your name and that's it?"

"I didn't say that," I said defensively. "I'm going to help support them. I'm not abandoning them."

"You better not. Otherwise you won't have to worry about Dashiel kicking your ass, because it will be Dad coming after you. I remember how he came at me when Ellie and I weren't sure what we wanted to do. He's big on taking responsibility. Family first and all that."

"But you guys were different," I argued. "You were friends. I barely know Mabel. And she said flat out she doesn't want to get married."

"Ellie said the same thing."

"You guys were *different*," I repeated. "Mabel and I are not going to be together. And Dad will just have to get used to it."

"Okay, so what advice do you want from me? Sounds like you've already decided how you're going to handle this."

"I don't know." I rolled my shoulders, trying to ease some of the tension in my neck. "Tell me how to be an accidental dad, I guess."

"You just show up, Joey. That's what you do. You show up."

I looked out at the city, glittering at my feet. "But I'm not even there. I *can't* be there. My life and career are here, and it requires all my time and energy. I'm at the top of my game right now, and I need to stay there. I've worked too hard to let it all just fizzle out."

"So show up when you can. Let her know she's not alone. You can't be that guy who just sends a check. That guy's an asshole."

"He is," I agreed through a clenched jaw.

"And you're a cocky son of a bitch, but you're not an asshole."

"Thanks." Maybe that was why I called him. I needed someone to tell me I wasn't the bad guy.

Gianni was quiet for a moment. "You'll figure it out, Joe. I did. And you know what? Once that baby is born, you won't believe there was ever a time you didn't want to be a father."

I thought about that but still wasn't sure he was right. "There's this ultrasound appointment coming up. Do you think I should go?"

"If you can. I remember Ellie's first one. I was scared shitless. And I felt like I didn't belong there, like I wasn't sure what my place was. But that was when it really hit me—I was going to be a father. Everything changed for me that day."

But I didn't *want* anything to change. That was the problem. I closed my eyes and swallowed hard.

"And Joe?"

"Yeah?"

"Take a video. You'll want it later."

I would?

I couldn't imagine why I'd want to record an ultrasound—wasn't it just a sort of livestream of Mabel's uterus?—but I decided to go to the appointment, if I could make it work with my schedule. If Gianni had done it, I could do it.

I wasn't about to be bested by my brother.

But *scared shitless* was spot-on. As I opened the door to the room where Mabel was waiting, I was sweating buckets. My stomach was churning. My mind knew I was doing the right thing, but my gut was telling me to run in the other direction.

Mabel took one look at me over her shoulder and hiccuped.

I couldn't help smiling. "Uh-oh. I didn't bring a lemon with me."

She laughed nervously. "Hey. This is a surprise."

I entered the room, closing the door behind me. "Sorry. I wasn't sure I could make it, so I didn't want to say anything ahead of time."

"That's okay. I'm glad you're here."

I stood awkwardly by the door, uncertain if I was supposed to sit in the little chair by the counter or remain on my feet. I felt vaguely in trouble, like I'd been sent to the principal's office to hear about the consequences of my reckless behavior. My eyes wandered to the screen on the other side of the examination table Mabel was on. "Should I—"

Two quick raps on the door interrupted our conversation. "Ready?" called a female voice from the hall.

"Yes!" Mabel called out.

I jumped out of the way as the door opened.

"Hi Mabel," said the woman who entered. She reminded me a little of my mom, and I felt guilty that this stranger knew about my kid before my mother did. "I'm Catherine. I'll be doing your ultrasound today." After dimming the lights, she turned to me and smiled. "Is this Dad?"

Christ. I was Dad.

"Yes," I said, my voice barely audible.

Mabel hiccuped.

"Perfect. You can stand right there by her side," Catherine said, moving to the foot of the table. "Okay, Mabel, I'll have you lie back and put your feet in here…"

While Catherine arranged Mabel's lower body and fiddled around beneath the paper sheet, I took a step closer to her. "Is this okay?"

"Of course." She smiled, but I detected the worry behind it and moved even closer.

I wasn't sure where to put my hands, so I folded them in front of my crotch.

"Okay, this gel will be a little cold, sorry," Catherine said, her hand disappearing under the sheet with some kind of wand that looked like a microphone.

Mabel's hands were clenching and unclenching at her sides. Instinctively, I took one and held it in both of mine. It was cold. "Are you nervous?"

She nodded, her blue eyes wide. The smile and the hiccups had disappeared.

"Okay, are you ready to see your baby?" Catherine asked.

Neither of us answered, but we both looked at the monitor.

Fuzzy, ghostly shapes that reminded me of jellyfish blobbed around on the screen.

"There we are…" Catherine moved her arm and clicked a few buttons on her console. "Okay, this pregnancy looks just beautiful. There's the yolk sac," she said, indicating what looked like a small glow ring. "And there's the embryo."

"That's the baby?" I asked. My puck in the net looked like a small frog to me.

"Yes. This is the baby's head, and that's his little butt." A dotted line appeared on the screen, and she clicked some more buttons. "You can see arm and leg buds have formed, and everything looks just perfect."

I exhaled with relief—I hadn't even realized I'd been scared. Mabel squeezed my hand, and I held hers even tighter.

"And now..." Catherine moved her arm again. "See that flickering in the center there? That's your baby's heartbeat."

My chest grew tight. How was it possible to see something so small? Hadn't Mabel said the baby was only the size of a pea? "It is?"

"Yes. Let's have a listen, shall we?"

More clicks, and then suddenly I could hear it—this wild little galloping that made my own heart feel like it had just been given a jolt of electricity.

"Doesn't that sound nice?" Catherine asked. "It's at one-sixty-nine, which is perfect."

Stop talking! I almost yelled. I just wanted to hear that sound. Suddenly I realized why Gianni had suggested recording this moment.

But Catherine moved on before I could ask permission to take a video, taking more measurements and chatting with Mabel about her cervix, which I tried not to hear. When it sounded like she was about done, I spoke up.

"Would it be possible to get the heartbeat once more?" I asked. "I'd like to take a video, if that's okay."

"Sure." Catherine tapped some buttons, and the little flicker appeared again, along with the graph on the bottom and that quick fluttering sound.

"You want to take a video?" Mabel looked up at me in surprise as I pulled out my phone.

"Yes. Is that okay with you?"

"Yes, I'm just—" She smiled. "Yes. It's fine. I'd like to have it too."

"I'll send it to you." I aimed my camera at the screen and hit record, my own pulse accelerating as I captured that tiny beating heart.

A feeling I couldn't explain engulfed me like a tidal wave.

• • •

Outside, I walked Mabel to her car.

"Are you missing training camp?" she asked.

"No. I caught a flight after practice this morning. Rented a car at the airport and shot up here."

"When do you go back?"

"Really early tomorrow." I paused. "I thought maybe after this, I'd drive down and tell my parents."

"Oh." She glanced up at me. "Are you nervous?"

"Yes and no. I mean, I'm not the first Lupo brother to find myself in this situation—this happened to Gianni too."

"Really?"

"Yes, but it was a while ago." I ran a hand through my hair. "My niece Claudia is twelve now."

"So they got married?"

"Yes. But they were... Their situation was different."

She nodded in understanding and gestured toward an older-model, two-door Kia. "This is me." It reminded me of what she'd said about being so practical she'd never know what a new car smelled like.

I stuck my hands in my pockets while she unlocked the doors. "Thanks for letting me come today."

"Of course," she said. "Good luck with your family. I told mine on Monday."

"How did it go?"

"Pretty good, I think," she said in a way that made me think she wasn't being 100 percent truthful. "I mean, they were all surprised, but once they heard me talk about it, I think they started to accept the news."

"Did you tell them who the father is?"

She nodded. "I did, yes."

"Do they hate me?"

"No!" she said a little too quickly. "No, of course not."

"I don't believe you. If some guy got my little sister pregnant like this, I'd want to fucking punch him."

"There may have been some mention of punching," she admitted. "But I talked them all down."

"Thanks."

"I'm really glad you were here today, Joe."

"Me too. That heartbeat thing was crazy. I had no idea we'd be able to see it, let alone hear it."

She laughed. "It *was* crazy. Made it so real. Not that the morning sickness and body aches and extreme fatigue weren't real enough, but this was on another level."

I looked at her stomach. "It's kind of weird how uneven the whole thing is. I never thought about this before, but the woman really has to do all the work, doesn't she? Like, the guy's part is over so fast and then we just get to sit back and watch. The mom has to, like, *grow* the human. And then get it out."

Mabel's expression was wryly amused. "Yes. It does seem a bit uneven."

I wanted there to be more I could do, but what the fuck was there? "Hey, are you hungry?"

She shrugged. "A little. This is usually when my morning sickness kicks in, but it's actually not bad today."

"Want to get something to eat before I head down to see my parents?"

"Okay. What are you in the mood for?"

"You choose," I said. "What's your favorite place in town?"

"Do you like diner food?"

"Definitely."

She grinned. "Let's go to Moe's."

• • •

Twenty minutes later, I was seated across from her in a booth at Moe's Diner, a retro-style place complete with black-and-white tiles on the floor, a long chrome-edged counter with red-vinyl-topped stools, and a jukebox in the corner.

"This is Ari's family's place," Mabel said as I looked over the menu. "Ari ran it for a while, but now that she has kids, she's not here as much. I pretty much grew up here."

"So what should I get?"

"Well, you can't miss with any of the burgers here, but the specials are always delicious too."

"I'll go for tried and true." I set the menu aside. "The sign in the window promised the best burger in town."

She smiled. "It's the truth."

We put in our order, and while we waited for our food, I asked Mabel more about growing up here, where she'd gone to school, what she did on the weekends. I told her to quiz me on her brothers' names and got all of them right, but mixed up their wives and totally flubbed with her nieces and nephews.

"That's all right," she said, laughing as she poked her straw into her iced tea. "There are a lot of them."

Of course, she remembered the names of my parents, all my siblings, their spouses, and their children—even their ages—which she shrugged off.

"I just have a good memory," she said.

"Have you thought about what you'll name *this* baby?" I asked.

"Not really. I figured I'd wait and see if it's a boy or girl first."

"When do you find out?"

"At the next ultrasound."

I nodded. "When will that be?"

"Around twenty weeks, so halfway through. Which would be around Thanksgiving."

Thanksgiving. The season would be in full swing, and there was no way I'd get time off to shoot up here. "I probably won't be able to make that one," I said apologetically.

"It's okay. I don't expect you to."

"Maybe you could take a video for me."

She smiled. "I will."

Our food arrived, and everything looked fantastic. I polished off my burger and fries in minutes. "Well, you were right," I said, laying my napkin on my empty plate. "The sign didn't lie."

Her eyes sparkled as she ate a spoonful of her soup. "Told ya."

I sat back and looked around. The diner wasn't too busy at this hour—it was only about five o'clock—and most of the customers were older. A few old-timers seated at the counter kept turning around to look at us, and I wondered if maybe they were hockey fans. But the way they kept pinching up their faces, their eyes going beady beneath their brows, made me think again.

"You know those guys at the counter?"

She glanced over her shoulder. "Oh," she said. "Yes. Those are friends of my dad's. Gus and Larry."

"They're giving me the stink eye."

She set down her spoon and picked up her iced tea. "Just probably wondering who you are, since they know everyone in this town. I've known them all my life. Larry's a barber—and the town grump—and Gus is a retired mail carrier."

"Is it possible they've heard about…"

She looked dubious. "I doubt it. I just told my family on Monday, but then again, this is a very small town. News spreads fast."

"They're definitely looking at me like I've done something offensive."

She laughed. "Ignore them. They're harmless." Patting her

stomach, she said, "I think that's all I have room for. Let's get the check. You probably want to get on the road, huh?"

"I should." But in all honesty, I *didn't* really want to. I wished I had more time with her. I'd ask to see the house where she grew up and where she worked and maybe where our kid might attend school. Was there an ice rink around?

"I'll be right back," she said. "I need to use the bathroom."

While she was gone, I paid the bill and tipped the server. When she returned to the table, she looked surprised. "Hey, I was going to treat you, since you cooked last time."

"Too late." I slid out from the booth. "Ready to go?"

"Yes. Thanks for dinner."

"You're welcome." I kept my head down as we went outside, avoiding the scrutiny of Gus and Larry. I could stare down any menacing six-foot-plus forward at a face-off, but for some reason, I could not bring myself to make eye contact with those two old geezers.

Outside, we walked down the block toward my car. We'd dropped hers off at her house on the way over. "If you like ice cream, that's the best place to get it," she said, pointing to an old-fashioned storefront with a sign that said THE SWEET SHOPPE. "That's probably where I'll be eating my pickles and salted caramel vanilla."

I laughed. "That sounds terrible."

She pointed a finger at me. "Don't judge."

We passed a coffee shop she said she frequented, a gift boutique owned by an aunt, and a wine bar called Lush, which she looked at and sighed. "That is where I used to sip sparkling rosé on the patio, but those days are gone for a while."

Again, it hit me that she was required to make all the physical sacrifices and bear all the weight—literally and figuratively—of this pregnancy. "Mabel," I said as we started walking again. "I wish there was more I could do for you."

She glanced at me in surprise. "Like what?"

"I don't know. I'm going to send you some money right away, and then set up monthly payments, but I feel so guilty I can't do more."

"Don't," she said, looking straight ahead again. "I'm grateful for the financial help, but other than that, I'm fine, Joe. I'm even getting excited. When I saw that little heartbeat today, it just reinforced my decision. I want this baby, and I'll be a good mom."

"I know you will," I said quickly. "I wish I felt the same way about myself as a dad."

"I have confidence in you."

"You do?"

"Sure. Look how you rose to the challenge of putting the puck in the net," she pointed out, elbowing me in the side. "Nailed it. You're obviously an overachiever."

"Very funny," I said as she laughed at me. "I wish my parents would see it that way, but I have a feeling they won't."

"Are you really nervous about telling them?" she asked as we reached my rented SUV.

"A little," I confessed. "I'm a grown man, but I still care what my mom and dad think of me. I've always looked up to my dad, and I hate the thought that this will lower his opinion of me. And my mom is going to cry, I guarantee it."

"Because she'll be upset?"

"Because she'll think this baby will not be in her life."

Mabel thought for a moment, chewing on her bottom lip. "What if I came with you to tell them?"

I blinked. "You'd do that?"

"I could, if you thought it would help. Maybe we can sort of reassure them that this was no one's fault and we're going to co-parent the best we can. And I will make it clear they are welcome to be part of this baby's life—in fact, I'd love that."

"They'd love that too." Impulsively, I threw my arms around her, lifting her right off her feet. "Thank you."

"Of course." She seemed a little flustered as I set her down. "The only problem is, I have to be at work tomorrow, and you have to be on an early flight. So why don't I follow you down to Traverse City in my own car? That way you don't have to drive me back."

"Fuck that." I shook my head. "I will drive you back tonight. It's the least I can do."

Chapter 12

*O*n the drive down to Traverse City, Joe and I worked out a tentative plan for his financial support during the pregnancy and once the baby was born. He was more than generous, offering to cover not only my mortgage and medical care, but additional funds to cover living expenses. I knew not every man in his situation would respond the way he had, and it made me even more curious about his parents. They'd obviously raised him well.

"Tell me more about your mom and dad," I said.

"Well, my mom, Coco, used to be a wedding planner, but now she works at the restaurant with my dad. She's the best. My brothers and I put her through so much hell growing up, it's a miracle she didn't lose her mind. She's definitely going to try to feed you. What she loves most in the world is taking care of people."

"What about your dad?"

"What my dad loves most in the world is my mom."

"Awww."

"I mean, he loves his kids too, but he's crazy about my mom. Family is everything to him. When we were growing up, he never missed a game, a school play, a swim meet..." Joe's voice trailed off, and he was silent for a moment. Was he thinking about what kind of father he'd be? "But his restaurant is important to him too. And he loves cooking at home. Both my parents do. We had great big Sunday dinners, always."

"I'm looking forward to meeting them." I chewed my lip. "Are they going to think I'm..." I wasn't sure how to finish the question. Careless? Stupid? A hockey fangirl who did this on purpose?

"They're going to like you. I promise." He grimaced. "They might be upset with me, but they will not blame you."

"I just don't want them to think I'm...looking for anything from you."

"Mabel. Don't." He shook his head and glanced over at me. "They will not look down on you or think you're some kind of puck bunny gold digger. I promise you—they are not like that."

"But puckbunnygolddigger225 is my Instagram handle. They might get suspicious."

He burst out laughing, and the sound made me happy.

"So did you always know you wanted to play professional hockey?" I asked.

"Oh yeah. When I was a kid, I used to lie awake at night and imagine the arenas I'd play in, the games I'd win, the goals I'd score. I'd dream about flying down the ice on a breakaway, outsmarting the goalie, flipping the puck into the back of the net. I'd imagine what it would feel like to lift the Stanley Cup."

I smiled. "And you never doubted you'd get there?"

"I mean, everyone has doubts now and then. But I'm very determined when I set my mind to something."

"I know this about you."

He gave me a sly grin from the corner of his mouth along with a sideways glance. "I guess you do."

"Does the pressure ever get to you?"

He shrugged. "Sometimes. But it's part of the deal."

We arrived at their house around seven-thirty and walked in the back door, entering a large, homey kitchen done in cozy earth tones. A woman with shoulder-length dark hair stood at the sink, her back to us. When she heard the door open, she turned around, and her face lit up with joyful surprise.

"Joey Lupo! What are you doing here?" She quickly shut off the faucet, dried her hands, and raced over for a hug.

"Surprise," he said, bending down to embrace her.

"I wish you'd have told me you were coming! I'd have held dinner for you."

"That's okay, we already ate." He turned to me. "Mom, I'd like to introduce you to someone. This is Mabel. Mabel, this is my mom."

I smiled at her. "It's nice to meet you, Mrs. Lupo."

"Please. Call me Coco." She smiled warmly at me as she shook my hand. I saw where Joe had inherited the wide-set blue eyes, thick black lashes, and beautiful golden skin.

A man entered the kitchen, and I immediately knew it was Joe's father. They were built the same, with wide shoulders and tapered waists, and the nose and mouth were nearly identical to his. Mr. Lupo's hair was salt and pepper, and his face had the creases of a happy life, but he was still handsome. He wore a navy blue T-shirt that said BAYSIDE SPORTS, and his muscular forearms were covered with tattoos, which surprised me.

"Hey, I thought I heard your voice," he said to Joe with a grin that matched his son's.

"Hey, Dad." Joe engulfed his father in a hug, and they thumped each other on the back.

"This is a nice surprise," his father said. "What are you doing up this way?"

"I'll get to that in a minute. Let me introduce you to someone." He gestured to me, and I held out my hand. "This is my friend Mabel."

"It's nice to meet you," I said.

"I'm Nick," he replied. His hand was big and his grip strong, just like Joe's. "Nice to meet you too. What can we get for you? Something to drink? Are you hungry?"

"Nothing for me, thank you."

"You have to have something," Coco insisted, going to the fridge and pulling it open. "I've got meatballs. Or chicken and rice. Or maybe some chilled gazpacho?"

I laughed, remembering what Joe had told me about his mom. "No, thank you."

"Glass of wine?" his father asked. "Cold beer? Sparkling water?"

"Water would be nice," I said.

"Joe?"

"Nothing for me, thanks. Did we interrupt your dinner?"

"No, we ate a little early tonight."

Coco brought me a chilled bottle of Pellegrino. "Here you are, darling."

"Thank you." I smiled, meeting her eyes, which looked full of hope. I wondered if she thought I was Joe's new girlfriend.

"So, Mom, Dad, do you have a few minutes?" Joe asked, the worried look back on his face. "We'd like to talk to you."

"Of course. Why don't we go sit down?" Coco led the way past the large kitchen island to a plump, L-shaped sectional in front of a stone fireplace. She gestured toward one end of the couch, and I sat down. Joe lowered himself to my side, and his parents sat on the adjacent section.

"So," Joe began, wiping his hands on the knees of his light brown pants. "We've got something to tell you."

Nick suddenly appeared uneasy, but Coco smiled at us. "Yes?"

"Mabel is pregnant."

Nick cleared his throat. "Does that mean what I think it means?" he asked his son.

"Yes," Joe said, color rising in his face. "I'm the father."

"Oh." The smile faded from Coco's face and she put her hands to her cheeks. "Oh, my. This is—this is a surprise."

"For us too," I said, attempting a laugh that quickly died out.

"I'm a little confused. Is this—is this the Mabel you just met at the wedding?" Joe's mom asked him. "The one you mentioned at dinner afterward?"

"Yes," he said.

I stared at him in disbelief. He'd mentioned me to his parents?

Nick tipped his head into his hand and rubbed his temples with a thumb and forefinger.

Joe seemed lost for words, so I decided to step in.

"Actually, we met because we sat next to each other on the flight here from Chicago," I said. "We had to fly through a thunderstorm, and I was terrified. Joe held my hand and kept me calm."

"That's very sweet," said Coco distractedly, looking at her son. "So then you invited her to the wedding?"

"No, that was a coincidence." Joe glanced at me. "She was a guest, and we recognized each other."

"Mabel, do you live in Chicago?" Nick asked.

I shook my head. "I live in Cherry Tree Harbor. About an

hour and a half from here."

"I see." He regarded his son. "So how is this going to work?"

"Mabel would like to raise the baby in her hometown, where she has friends and family to support her."

Nick folded his arms over his chest. "And what about you? Why aren't you supporting her?"

"I will," Joe said defensively. "Of course I will."

"From two states away?"

"I play for Chicago, Dad." Joe's tone was defensive. "That's where I have to live."

"And I'd prefer to stay in Cherry Tree Harbor," I said quickly. "I don't know anyone in Chicago, and Joe would be gone all the time. It doesn't really make sense for me to move, since we're not, you know, *together*."

"But Joey, how often will you see the baby?" Coco leaned forward, her brow etched with concern.

"As much as I can, Mom." He sat up taller. "I'm not going to be some deadbeat dad. I just have to focus on hockey right now."

Nick's face wore some displeasure. "Maybe you should have thought about that before you—never mind." Closing his eyes briefly, he exhaled.

"This isn't Joe's fault," I said. "I don't want you to think he wasn't careful, because he was. And while neither of us asked for this, I'm at a point in my life where I'd like to start a family. So this baby isn't exactly unwanted. It was just unexpected."

When Nick looked at me, his gaze had softened. "Mabel, I hope my son has been a gentleman."

"He has," I assured them. "Really, he has. He's being very generous with his support. He even flew all the way up here to go to my ultrasound appointment this afternoon."

"Did you really?" Coco clasped her hands at her chest. "Did you get a picture?"

"Yes, but we have something even better than that." I nudged Joe with my leg. "Show them the video."

He stood up and pulled his phone from his pocket as he walked around the back of the couch where his parents sat. Leaning forward, he played them the video, and I watched as their faces softened. Coco put a hand over her heart, her eyes tearing up. "Oh," she said. "That sweet little thing. Listen to that heart just beating away. When are you due, Mabel?"

"April 23rd."

"Playoff season," said Joe to no one in particular.

"If you need anything, Mabel, you come to us," Nick said gruffly, his eyes still on the screen.

"I will," I said. "And both of you will be welcome to see the baby any time you want. Family is the most important thing in the world."

"We feel the same," Nick said.

Coco rose from the couch and held her arms out to me, and I stood up to embrace her. "It's going to be okay," she murmured, rubbing my back. "We're here for you."

I wanted to thank her, but my throat had grown painfully tight. Her hug felt so good, so maternal, so soothing. She smelled like fabric softener and something vaguely floral. I fought back tears, because I didn't want them to think I was upset or scared.

"Can I ask for your mom's email or number, Mabel? I'd love to send her a little note," said Coco.

"My mom passed away when I was two," I told her, "but I'd be happy to give you my dad's email. He raised me. And he's recently remarried to a lovely woman named Julia—I can give you both emails."

Coco's eyes were shining as she nodded. "That would be wonderful." Then she swept me up into her arms once more, holding me even tighter. When she finally let me go, Nick was there with his arms open, and I let myself be scooped up against his warm, solid chest.

Releasing me, Nick kissed my cheek. "This is your home now too," he said. "Come see us anytime. You're family."

"Thank you," I said. "I appreciate that."

I caught Joe's eye, and he smiled at me, telegraphing a silent message. *See? I told you it would be okay. They already love you.*

My heartbeat quickened.

• • •

We stayed a little while longer—Coco and Nick *insisted* I eat a little something, so I said yes to some homemade cookies and herbal tea. I answered a lot of questions about my family, my job at the historical society, my travels over the course of my career, and my favorite kinds of foods. Coco took notes on everything, which made me laugh.

Finally, Joe said we'd better get going, so we said our goodbyes. His parents came out to the driveway and waved us off, Coco blowing kisses and Nick giving a wave, one arm wrapped around his wife. As Joe backed out, I watched Nick pull Coco close and kiss her forehead.

"Your parents are wonderful," I said as we got on the road. "And they seem so happy together. How long have they been married?"

"Like thirty-five years or something?"

"Wow. That's incredible. They're still so in love."

"Yeah. I used to hate it as a kid. They were so embarrassing. Always touching each other."

I laughed. "But it's sweet. I hope I have that someday, don't you?"

He shrugged. "I haven't thought about it much."

I remembered how he'd scoffed at wedding traditions and

figured he wasn't much of a romantic. Funny, given how romantic his parents were.

We got on the highway, and I dozed off, the fatigue of the day settling deep in my bones. Joe had to wake me up. "Hey." He tapped my leg gently. "Home sweet home."

"Oh." I picked up my head, pain shooting through my neck because it had been at an odd angle for over an hour. "God, did I sleep the whole way?"

"Yes."

"I'm sorry."

"Don't worry about it. You need the rest." He yawned. "And it's late."

I checked the clock—it was after eleven. "It is late. I feel bad you have to drive all the way home now. What time is your flight?"

"Six. But I have to return the rental car first."

"Do you want to stay here? Then just get up early and go?"

He hesitated. "I do have my stuff with me. Do you have an extra bedroom?"

"Yes, but it's set up as an office right now. My couch is super comfortable, though. I fall asleep on it all the time."

While he was considering the offer, he yawned again. "Fuck. I didn't realize how tired I was."

"Just crash here," I said, unbuckling my seat belt. "Otherwise I'll be worried about you on the road tonight, and I won't sleep, and then you'll have that on your conscience."

"Are you sure this doesn't break any rules?"

"I'm positive. We're friends, right? And it's totally cool with me if a friend wants to crash on my couch." I held up the plastic container Coco had given me. "Especially when that friend's mom sent me home with cookies."

He turned off the engine. "Okay. Then I'll stay."

We got out of the car, and Joe grabbed his bag from the back seat. My heart, which clearly had not gotten the message that this was a platonic sleepover, sent out frantic beats that pulsed in other places.

My cat greeted us in the front hallway, and Joe knelt down to pet her. "Hi, Cleo."

"She likes you," I said as Cleo purred.

"Most girls do."

I groaned. "That is totally something one of my brothers would say."

He laughed, his knees cracking as he rose. "Can I use your bathroom real quick?"

"Sure. It's right in there." I pointed down the hall. "Clean towels are in the closet if you need one."

While Joe was in the bathroom, I spread a sheet and blanket on the couch and retrieved a pillow from my bedroom. As I laid it at one end of the couch, I found myself wishing he could just crawl into bed with me.

But I knew what would happen if he did.

And since he didn't like sharing a bed, he'd probably still come out here and sleep on the couch, and I'd feel even worse about myself.

Just say good night and go to your room.

I was just putting a bottle of water on the coffee table when he entered the room. "Thanks for all this," he said, dropping his bag on the rug. "I hope it's not too much trouble."

"No trouble at all," I said. "Can I get you anything else?"

"I think I'm good." He met my eyes. "I'm not going to wake you when I leave. It will be crazy early."

"Okay."

"And I'm not sure when I can get back up here once training camp starts."

I was already shaking my head. "Don't worry about it. I'm really glad you were able to come to the appointment today."

"Me too." His crooked grin appeared. "I had no idea what to expect, and I was scared shitless."

"I could tell." I laughed. "But you got through it."

"I did. And I really appreciate you coming to my parents' house with me. I know they appreciated it too."

"Of course. Your dad didn't even seem too mad about it."

"I'll probably get an earful once he gets me alone, but I guess that's his prerogative as my dad."

"He just wants to make sure you're doing right by me and the baby," I said. "And you are."

He dropped his chin to his chest, rubbing the back of his neck. "Mabel, I know we didn't ask for this. But I just want to say that if I have to go through this with someone, I'm glad it's with you—if that makes sense."

"It does. I had the same thought earlier. A lot of guys in your position would not have handled this the way you are. We'll make a good team."

"I hope this baby has your memory and your intelligence and that dimple in your smile."

I laughed as heat rushed my face. "And I hope it has your athletic ability and your discipline and those eyelashes."

He grinned, dropping his hand. "Think it's a boy or a girl?"

"No idea."

"Do you hope it's one or the other?"

"No," I said honestly. "Do you?"

He paused. "I'll definitely be more nervous if it's a girl."

"Why?"

"I don't know. With a boy, I just feel like I'll know better what to do. A girl seems so much more—I don't know. Fragile. Am I an asshole for saying that? Fuck. I don't mean to be sexist."

He looked so worried I had to laugh.

"You're not an asshole. I want us to be able to be honest with each other. And you'd be a great girl dad, Joe. You have nothing to worry about either way."

"Thanks." He took a step toward me and tugged my arm. "Come here."

I went into his embrace, and he held me tightly against his chest, his chin resting on the top of my head. Against my ear, I could hear his heartbeat, and it reminded me of the baby's.

Our baby's.

Closing my eyes, I let myself be swept away by the warmth of his body, the scent of his skin, the belief that he would be there for me, even if he didn't love me.

"You have nothing to worry about either. I won't let you down," he said quietly but firmly. "Or the baby. I promise."

"Okay." I stayed right where I was, my arms looped around his strong torso. I just needed another thirty seconds of this.

"I should say good night." But he didn't let me go.

"Me too." Leaning back from the waist, I looked up at him.

His eyes were on my lips. He swallowed, his Adam's apple bobbing in his throat. Then he kissed my forehead and released me. "Good night."

"Night," I whispered. Then I spun on my heel and rushed into my bedroom, closing the door behind me.

By the time I woke up the next morning, he was gone.

• • •

Later that night, he texted me.

Hey. Thank you again for letting me crash on your couch.

You're welcome. Anytime.

Keep me posted on everything, okay?

                                        I will.

Take really good care of yourself.

                                        I will.

And let me know if there is anything you need.

Like ice cream and pickles.

                    Actually I'd rather have ice cream and
                                        potato chips.

It would be on your doorstep as fast as I
could make it happen.

                                Haha, thanks.

But what I thought was, *Don't be too sweet to me, Joe. This only works if I can keep my feelings for you from ballooning out of control. Be kind, be sensitive, be generous. But don't take care of me like I belong to you.*

It felt too good, being his.

Chapter 13

MABEL

"*O*h, Mabel." Ari's eyes misted over as she watched the video from my ultrasound. "So sweet."

"I know. I still can't believe it." I set the phone down on the table on her shady patio, where we were sitting with cold drinks late Saturday morning. Truman and Wren were napping upstairs, and Dash was running errands.

"And Joe is the one who asked to record it?"

"Yes." I'd told her all about his surprise appearance at the doctor's office. "I didn't think anything else could shock me at this point, but that did it."

"Tell me about meeting his parents. Was it weird?"

"It was a little uncomfortable at first, but they're so great. His mom has already reached out. She wants to drive up sometime this fall and have lunch with me, my dad, and Julia."

"Have you heard from Joe since he went back?"

"A couple times. Mostly just about setting up the automatic payments to my bank account from his. He's being really generous."

"Good. He can afford it." She picked up the iced maple Frappuccino I'd brought her and sipped. "Anything new between the two of you?"

"Nope."

"You mentioned he stayed the night at your house."

"On the couch. It was late."

"Still. It's not like he couldn't afford a hotel room," she said suggestively.

"Ari, stop it. We're friends. I offered to let him sleep on the couch so he didn't have to drive all the way back down to his parents' house. He'd already been on the road so much that day."

Her eyebrows rose as she sucked on the straw. "And he stayed on the couch the entire time?"

"Yes. Then left in the morning without even waking me."

She sighed as she set the plastic cup down. "That is not romantic at all."

"Because *we* are not romantic at all. Although," I said, swirling the ice around in my matcha latte, "he did give me a very nice hug before saying good night."

"That's it? A hug?"

"Yes. And a kiss on the forehead."

"He's a regular Boy Scout now," she said with a giggle.

"Listen, I'm glad. If he'd tried things with me, I don't know that I'd have the willpower to say no. And by respecting my boundaries, he's proving that he's a good guy. That's important to me. We're talking about the father of my child."

"I get it, and I'm glad he's turning out to be a gentleman. I'm just a romance junkie, and I like it when things get spicy."

"Well, you'll have to find another story to get invested in, because this one stays sweet."

At least, it did in real life. In my fantasies of Joe, which I entertained almost every night, usually with a toy that required batteries, it was a five-alarm fire.

But that was my little secret.

"Did you guys talk about dating other people?" Ari asked.

"No, it never came up. He actually told me at the wedding he's just coming off a bad relationship and isn't looking to date anyone. He claims he's a bad boyfriend."

"How would you feel if he did date someone?"

I shrugged. "Not much I could do about it. And it's bound to happen sooner or later. I don't want this baby to mean the two of us have to stay single forever."

"Just out of curiosity, would you date someone while you were pregnant?"

"I don't think so. It would be weird." I sipped my drink again. "But I tell you what, now that I know what good sex is, I am never settling for less."

"*Good.* You shouldn't."

"I just hope somewhere out there is a guy who can put the puck in the net as well as Joe Lupo."

Ari laughed. "It was that good, huh?"

I closed my eyes and shivered. "It was that good."

"Well, I don't care what you say, I'm not giving up hope on the two of you. Having a baby together might make him rethink his priorities."

"No, Ari. No." I shook my head. "I don't want that. I never want to wonder if he's with me just because I got pregnant. And I never, ever, *ever* want him to resent either me or the baby for slowing down or putting an end to his hockey career."

"Maybe he could have both," Ari suggested. "Dash and I make it work with his acting career."

"You guys are different. You knew each other, had history together—and you fell in love *before* you had children. You never had to worry about why he chose you. It's not the same for me. Forget it."

Ari pouted. "Fine, but only because he hates to cuddle."

"Who hates to cuddle?" Dash came out the sliding screen door onto the patio, dropping a kiss on Ari's head before taking the chair next to her.

"Joe Lupo," she said.

I tried to defend him. "He doesn't really hate to cuddle, he just doesn't like to share a bed."

Dash made a face at me. "So did you get pregnant in the back seat of his car?"

"Oh Jesus. I'm leaving." I slid my chair from the table and stood. "I have to open the historical society at noon. We always have good foot traffic on a Saturday, so I don't want to be late."

"Maybe we'll put the kids in the stroller and walk into town," Ari said. "We'll poke our heads in and say hi."

"Sounds great. Bye guys." Giving them a wave, I hurried down the driveway toward my car, which was parked on the street. I had plenty of time, but I had no desire to talk any more about Joe Lupo, cuddling, or where I got pregnant.

And as for any hope that Joe and I would get together, the sooner Ari gave it up, the better. I knew she just wanted me to be as happy as she was, but not everyone's path to love and marriage and family was a straight line.

Some people just got lucky.

• • •

Summer turned to fall, setting the trees ablaze with color. I admired them on the power walks I now took every evening, since I lacked the energy to run or even jog.

Cherry Tree Harbor's tourist season remained in full swing, but families with children were replaced by couples or groups of friends who ventured north for hikes and leaf peeping. This was also a crowd who appreciated architectural history, so we stayed busy at the historical society with the Painted Lady Showcase, a guided walking tour of local Victorian homes that had been restored to their original exterior colors.

Classes at the community college began, which occupied my Tuesday and Thursday evenings and much of my weekend for planning or grading.

Deposits started showing up in my bank account. I started to make lists of things I needed to do at home, such as turn my office into a nursery, and big items I'd need to purchase, such as a car seat and stroller and crib. I spent an hour in my local bookshop looking at books on pregnancy and parenting, and bought several to take home. I even purchased one for first-time fathers thinking I'd send it to Joe, since he seemed nervous about being a dad, but by the time I got home, I lost my nerve. I set it on the coffee table in the living room with mine, figuring maybe I'd mail it in a month or two.

And finally, hockey season began.

I texted Joe asking how I could watch his games.

You want to watch my games?

Yes!

My guess is that your network will carry only Detroit, so you'll probably need a subscription service to stream Chicago's games.

How do I go about getting that?

I'll take care of it for you.

And he did.

I'd never paid much attention to hockey before, but I made an effort to learn the rules, the positions, the penalties, the lingo. I Googled things. I lurked on forums, always looking for mentions of Joe's name. I'd go over to Austin's house or Xander's bar and watch Detroit games with them, asking questions and studying the plays. Pretty soon, I found myself cheering just as loud as anyone in the room, understanding why play stopped and started, and appreciating a beautiful breakaway or stellar pass.

But I liked watching Chicago best.

Joe's team was off to a fantastic start, and I kept track of their record on a piece of paper I stuck to the fridge with a Cherry Tree Harbor Historical Society magnet.

Often I texted Joe to congratulate him on a great game or tell him a penalty was bullshit or ask why something had gone down the way it had. He always explained things to me, and he was very patient, a good teacher. I told him I thought so.

> Have you ever coached little kids or anything?

No. I've helped out young teams here and there,
done things for charity, but never anything official.

> You'd be so great at it!

Thanks. Maybe someday.

How are you feeling?

> Pretty good. Eager to get past this first trimester,
> but I have a couple more weeks to go. Morning
> sickness is the pits.

Does anything help?

> Not so far.

The following evening when I got home from work, a brown paper bag was on my doorstep. Inside was ginger tea, some honey, a box of saltines, and a bag of peppermint candies. There was no note, but I didn't have to wonder long who it was from. By the time I'd brewed myself a cup of tea and eaten a few crackers, Joe had texted.

Did you get the stuff?

> Yes! Did you send it?

I had it delivered. After you mentioned your sickness was still bad last night, I reached out to my sister and asked her what had helped with hers. Those were the things she said.

My heart fluttered.

> That was very sweet. I'm already drinking the tea and eating the crackers, and I'm going to keep some of the candies in my bag and next to my bed. Thank you.

You're welcome. Let me know if there's anything else you need.

One night in mid-October, Chicago suffered a painful loss. After shouting expletives into a throw cushion on my couch, I messaged Joe.

> How come you weren't on that last power play? The puck was right there by the crease! You'd have scored.

Coach wanted me to rest my shoulder.

> Are you okay?

I'm okay.

Also yes. I'd have scored.

    I smiled at the screen. I could just hear him saying those words, and I knew the exact expression on his face.

How are you feeling?

> Great. Officially in the second trimester. Morning sickness gone.

Glad to hear it. It's 14 weeks now, right?

> Yes! I'm impressed you know that.

Good. I like impressing you.

What are you up to this weekend?

> I'm going to a birthday party for my niece Vivian. She's turning 3.

Who does she belong to again?

> She's Austin and Veronica's youngest. The party is at their house.

Do your brothers still want to murder me in my sleep?

> Austin has actually stopped growling when your name comes up. Progress!

I'll take it.

• • •

At Vivian's party that weekend, Austin came over and sat down next to me on the couch.

"How are you?" he asked. "Everything going well?"

"Yes. The dizziness has subsided. The morning sickness went away. And I have a little more energy."

"That's good." He folded his arms. "I wanted to ask you if you've bought a crib yet."

"A crib?"

"Yeah." He cocked a brow. "You know, where your baby will sleep?"

I laughed and slapped his arm. "I know what a crib is. But no, I haven't bought one. I'm going to turn the second bedroom at my house into the baby's room at some point, but I have to get my desk and bookshelves and office stuff out of there first, then get the walls painted. Why do you ask?"

"I thought I'd make you one."

My jaw dropped, and tears welled in my eyes. My oldest brother made gorgeous furniture out of reclaimed wood, mostly dining sets, but he could do anything. His work was featured in design magazines and showcased in high-end galleries throughout the Midwest. He had a waiting list a mile long. "Oh, Austin. Really?"

"Yes. We just need to talk about what kind of wood you'd like."

"I'd love that so much."

"When you're ready, I'll come over and help you clean out that room. Don't move any furniture on your own. And don't paint it by yourself either. You shouldn't be around the paint fumes."

"Okay." Slipping my arms through his, I tipped my head against his shoulder. "Thank you."

"You're welcome," he said gruffly. "I'm happy to do it. But

you know, it shouldn't *have* to be me."

"Austin, be fair—he doesn't live here."

He grumbled under his breath.

"And he's being so generous. Did I tell you he sends me enough every month to pay my mortgage plus my car payment plus utilities and my health care premium?"

"No."

"Well, he does."

"Is he going to move up here when the season is over? At least for the summer?" Austin wasn't giving Joe an inch.

"We haven't gotten that far," I admitted. "But I'm not asking him to."

"He should *want* to. You're going to need help. A baby is a lot of work, trust me. You shouldn't be alone."

"I'll be fine. Look, I know you're my big brother and you're protective of me, but ease up on him a little, okay? He's in the NHL. It's not like he's a mechanic or lawyer or something and could work anywhere. He has to live where he's contracted to play. But he's going to be here as much as he can. He promised he won't let me down."

Austin harrumphed, jerking his chin. "He better not. Or he'll have to answer to me."

I smiled. "Believe me, he would like to avoid that."

• • •

At the end of October, Kelly gave birth to a third daughter she and Xander named Dakota Mae. I went to visit them a few days after they got home from the hospital and found Xander in the kitchen, tiny Dakota nestled in the crook of one arm as he rooted around for something in the fridge.

"Here, let me take her," I said, quickly washing my hands at the sink before reaching for the sleeping baby.

"Thanks." Xander carefully transferred her to my arms. "I'm trying to make Kelly a sandwich and give her a little time with Jolene and Serena," he said, naming their two older daughters. "The three of them are all cuddled up in our bed watching a movie."

"How's everyone feeling?"

"Good," he said, taking out lettuce, cheese, tomato, mustard, and turkey. "The baby has been fussy and won't sleep unless someone is holding her, but that's how the other two were also. Nothing new."

I laughed and looked down at the adorable little thing, wrapped up like a burrito in a pink flannel blanket. The pudgy pink cheeks, miniature nose, perfect rosebud lips, and downy brown hair. "She's *so* cute."

"I know." Xander looked over at his daughter with tired but lovestruck eyes. "Doesn't she look just like Kelly?"

"A little. It's hard to tell when they're fresh out of the oven."

Xander finished putting together the sandwich and cut it in half. Then he added some carrot sticks to the plate, along with a little dish of hummus. My stomach growled loudly, and my brother looked over at me. "Hungry?"

"I guess I am," I said, laughing. "My appetite has been huge lately. And that sandwich looks tasty."

"Let me bring this up to Kelly, and then I'll come down and make you one."

"Xander, you don't have to do that. I didn't come here to make more work for you."

"I don't mind," he said. "And it's important that you get proper nutrition. By the time you're hungry, the baby's hungry, and what kind of uncle would I be if I let my niece or nephew starve?" He left the room before I could argue, and when he came back, he pulled two more slices of bread from the bag. "Turkey?"

"Perfect, thanks," I said. "I appreciate it."

"Well, who's gonna feed you if I don't?" He looked around. "I don't see anyone else around here making sure you eat right."

I rolled my eyes. "Can you guys all please stop picking on Joe? He'd make me a sandwich if he were here. He likes to cook. He made spaghetti for me when I went to see him in Chicago. With homemade meat sauce! Not from a jar!"

"Man of the year," Xander muttered, layering turkey on one slice of bread.

"He texts me just about every day asking how I'm feeling and telling me to take care of myself. When I told him about my morning sickness, he sent me ginger tea and crackers and peppermint candies."

Xander remained silent.

"Did I tell you he took me to Traverse City to meet his family? His dad is so cool—he's all tatted up like you. And his mom is so lovely and welcoming. She drove up here to have lunch with me and Dad and Julia already."

"I heard," he said grudgingly. "Dad and Julia said she was very nice."

Dakota started to fuss a little, and I rocked her in my arms. "Shhhh," I soothed. "Your dad is just acting tough. He's not really a big meanie."

Xander gave me the stink eye over his shoulder. "Austin said you need some help cleaning out the extra room at your house."

"Eventually, yes," I said. "I want to turn my office into the baby's room. But I'm waiting for the ultrasound next month to tell me if it's a girl or a boy, so I know how I want to decorate."

"Is Joe coming up for that appointment?"

"He can't," I said. "He's got a game that night."

My brother didn't say anything as he put some carrot sticks on my plate.

"Xander, if you were still in the navy and deployed somewhere and Kelly had an ultrasound appointment, you would not be able to fly home and go with her, but it wouldn't mean you're not a good dad," I pointed out.

He spun around and poked at the air between us with a carrot. "Don't even compare being a SEAL with being a fucking hockey player. It's *way* more badass."

I laughed. "You know what I mean. He's not choosing to miss it."

"I don't care," Xander said, taking a bite of the carrot stick. "I'm still mad at him, even if he did score a kickass goal last night against Boston."

"Were you watching?"

"I saw the replay." Xander set my plate on the island. "Dude can shoot, I'll say that for him."

Dakota began to fuss again, her little face wrinkling up in fury. "Guess I'm not the only one who's hungry."

"I'll take her." Xander reached for his daughter and carefully placed her over his shoulder. She looked so tiny against his massive chest, his wide hand spanning her flannel-wrapped bum. The look on his face was pure adoration as he kissed her head and patted her. "Let's change your diaper, huh? And then I'll take you to Mommy for a snack."

"Tell Kelly I'd love to see her if she's up for it," I said, taking a seat at the island. "I've got something for her and for the baby, and I brought gifts for Serena and Jolene too. I didn't want them to feel left out."

"I'm sure they'll all want to see you," he said. "But you need to eat first. Just come upstairs when you're done."

"Okay. Thanks for the sandwich."

"You're welcome." Then to the baby, he said, "Your Aunt Mabel needs her big brothers to look after her, Dakota Mae. And the lesson is, don't ever go out with any hockey players, okay?

Actually, don't ever go out with anyone. You'll break my heart."
He left the room, snuggling his little daughter tightly against his
chest.

I wondered if Joe would be like that. And what it would do
to me to see it.

• • •

In early November, my belly began to pop a little. My pants grew
tight. I started unbuttoning them at work and in the car, and once
I forgot to do them back up again, and I taught an entire class
with my pants undone.

Later that night, while I was online shopping for some
maternity clothes, I got a text from Joe.

How's my little avocado?

I laughed. Joe had found this website that kept him informed
of the baby's size by comparing it to different fruits or vegetables.
We'd been through cherry, fig, lemon, and peach.

Your little avocado is fine.

I read that at 16 weeks, they can make a fist.
Good practice for future hockey fights.

Stop.

What are you up to?

Shopping for maternity clothes. My pants don't
quite fit anymore.

Really?

Yes. I need some elastic waists and bigger
shirts.

A week later, I got a package from Joe in the mail. Excited, I ripped it open. Inside I found a Chicago jersey that said Lupo 19 on the back, size L. I squealed with excitement and put it on. After snapping fifteen selfies, I sent the best one to Joe.

> Thank you!!!! I love it!

Glad it arrived safely.

> My very first hockey jersey.

Call it a sweater. Then everyone will think you're old school.

> Lol okay! Are you excited for the game tonight?

Yes. But I might have to play a little rougher than usual so don't be surprised if you see me drop my gloves. And don't worry, I'm fine.

> Be careful! I'll be watching and wearing #19.
> Maybe I'll be your good luck charm.

> Well, charms. There are two of us in here.

I'll take all the luck I can get.

That night's game was rough, just like Joe had warned, the two teams intent on settling old scores. I watched from my couch, wearing my new shirt, as promised, shouting at the refs, cheering for the players, crossing my fingers and murmuring prayers when the action was down in front of the Chicago goalie. In the end, Joe scored in OT on a breakaway, and I jumped off the couch, clapping and shrieking with joy. Cleo took off running for the kitchen, spooked by the noise.

"Did you see that?" I asked my belly, both hands cradling the new bump there. "That was your daddy! He's a rock star!"

I sent Joe a quick text.

> FUCKING AMAZING!!! I screamed so loud, I scared Cleo. Congratulations!

> The avocado and I are very proud.

After I got ready for bed, I slipped between the sheets and grabbed my phone. Joe had replied to my text.

Thanks. I'm superstitious you know. Better wear that jersey all season long.

> It's a sweater.

He hearted the message, and I smiled.

Hey, would you like to come down here and go to a game sometime since you're such a big fan now?

> Are you serious? Of course!

Take a look at the schedule and see what home games you could make. Then I'll fly you down.

> I'll drive.

I don't like the idea of you making that drive alone.

> I'll be fine.

> And by the way, you sound like a dad already.

He laughed at that one, and I went to bed with a huge smile on my face, cradling my stomach with both hands.

This was good, right? We were friends. Buddies. Pals. We

were getting to know each other. Supporting each other. Learning what made the other one laugh.

And in just ten days, we'd learn whether our baby was a boy or a girl.

Chapter 14

JOE

The morning of the ultrasound appointment, I woke up in a panic. Tightness in my chest. Pulse like a jackhammer. Oxygen in short supply.

It used to happen to me all the time as a kid, especially on game days when I felt pressure to win or something big was riding on my performance. There was a scout in the audience. There was a new coach who thought I was overrated. There was a playoff victory at stake—if we didn't get it done, we'd be eliminated. An entire team depending on me.

It all comes down to this. Don't blow it.

The threat of failure was like a fucking predator in the room, prowling at the foot of my bed.

What if I wasn't good enough? What if I got out there and forgot how to shoot? What if there was some new guy on the ice who made me look like a clown? What if my NHL dreams were delusional, like so many people said they were?

After a particularly bad panic attack in college, my roommate convinced me to talk to someone. I saw a therapist on campus who taught me some coping strategies, which helped.

I hadn't had one in a long time—years, even—but I remembered what to do. Lying in bed, I forced myself to take deep, slow belly breaths. I concentrated on the sensations of things around me—the scent of fabric softener on my sheets, the sunlight just starting to peek around the shades, the warmth of my body heat beneath the comforter. As I grounded myself in the present, I felt the danger recede.

I hit a button to raise the shades, and for a few minutes, I just lay there while the morning sun warmed the room. Then I reached for my phone.

I'd gotten a text from Mabel about fifteen minutes ago.

Everything is all set. The tech was able to move the appointment back one hour so you could "be there," and Ari will be with me to FaceTime you on my phone. You won't miss a thing. How crazy is it that today we will know if this baby is a boy or a girl???

It was crazy there was a baby at all, but finding out whether it was a boy or a girl was going to make it very, very real. When I could think of the baby as an avocado or a peach or a fig growing in Mabel's belly, it was easier to keep the fear from swallowing me whole. But in a couple hours, it wouldn't just be an abstract idea sized like a piece of fruit.

It would be a boy or a girl.

A son or a daughter.

> Thanks for moving the appointment. I'll see you soon. Are you nervous?

JOE.

Immediately, I panicked.

> What's wrong? Are you okay?

I just felt the baby move.

I breathed a sigh of relief. Then I smiled.

> What did it feel like?

A tiny little thump. I wasn't even sure that's what it was so I just stayed completely still until I felt it again. It was the cutest thing ever.

> So was it a kick?

Probably. I think that's what you feel first are kicks. Later I'll be able to feel elbow jabs and rolling around. Things will get tight.

> That does not sound comfortable.

Lol not much about pregnancy is. I'm heading to work but I'll see you at 2:00 your time! I'm so excited!

I liked her message, set my phone aside, and rolled out of bed so I wouldn't be late for morning skate. As I made my way to the bathroom, I rubbed my shoulder, which had been bothering me this week. In fact, after practice, I had an appointment with the physical therapist.

After that, I'd have a few hours of rest before the pre-game meal, which was when I'd come home and jump on FaceTime so

I could see the ultrasound happening in real time.

I hadn't told anyone here about the baby yet—not my coaches or teammates or the media relations people. I knew I'd have to do it pretty soon, but I was putting it off because I didn't want to deal with the gossip that would follow. I was afraid Mabel would be hunted down and harassed, and there would be rumors and speculation about the two of us.

After Thanksgiving, I'd let the appropriate people know and explain the situation. I'd do whatever they advised in order to keep the chatter to a minimum and Mabel out of the public eye.

I didn't give a fuck what random people said about me, but I wanted to protect her.

• • •

"Okay, you guys ready?" the ultrasound tech asked. It was a different one this time, but the room looked the same.

"I'm ready," Mabel said from where she lay on the table. She looked at the phone in Ari's hand and smiled. "You ready in Chicago?"

"I'm ready," I said, wiping a sweaty palm on my pants.

The camera swung to the monitor, and at first all I saw was the same ghostly static I'd seen before.

Then I lost my breath.

Because right there on the screen was the shape of an actual baby's head and spine. I'd seen pictures of these scans before— my brothers and sister had sent them—but it was so different knowing it was actually my child in there. I could see its nose. Its chin. And then suddenly a hand, as if the baby had pressed its palm right up against the camera.

I got chills.

"Oh, look at that." The tech laughed. "Someone wants to say hello."

I heard Mabel laugh too. "Hi baby," she said. "I can't wait to meet you."

My throat tightened. I tried to swallow the tension away, but I couldn't. It slid and expanded, moving down into my chest and squeezing my heart. The tech continued talking, and I heard things about the arms and legs, the brain and heart, the kidneys and bladder and lungs. Everything was good, but I still couldn't breathe right.

"Okay, so as for other anatomy, do you want to know what you're having?" the tech asked.

"Yes," said Mabel.

"Do you want me to tell you now or are you planning any sort of reveal event where you and family all find out at once?"

"You can tell us now," Mabel replied, while I briefly wondered what the hell a reveal event was.

"Okay, let me just...ope!" The tech laughed. "There we are. It's a boy!"

A boy. That little hand belonged to my *son*. Those tiny arms and legs, that little nose, that flickering heart. The tech clicked something that made the graph pop up and turned on the sound, and I heard it again—the wondrous beating.

Would he look like me? Like my dad? Would he have the distinctive Lupo nose and chin? Would he have blue eyes like Mabel and I did? Brown hair? Would he get that dimple in her smile?

I was overcome with emotion, and my eyes began to sting. My chest ached.

"Joe? Are you still there?"

I realized Mabel had been talking to me. "Sorry." I cleared my throat. "I'm here."

She took the phone from Ari and flipped the view so I could see her face. Her smile lit up the screen, and her eyes glistened with tears. "It's a boy."

"I heard." My voice cracked. I laughed, and Mabel laughed too.

"Ari also got it on video with her phone—we had it set up—so I'll send it to you."

"Thanks. I'd like to show my parents."

"Of course. I'm going to hang up now and get dressed, but then I'll send."

"Perfect."

She smiled and waved. "Talk to you later. Good luck tonight! We'll be watching."

"Thanks." The call ended, and I set my phone aside. For several minutes, I remained on the couch, staring into space.

A boy. I was going to have a son.

Emotions swirled within me. Fear that I wouldn't know how to be a dad, gratitude for Mabel that she was taking such good care of him, happiness that he was developing perfectly, and a fiercely protective love I'd never known.

I wished Mabel were here. I wanted to put my arms around her. I wanted to place my hands on her belly and feel the little guy kick. I wanted to talk to him so he'd hear my voice and know it once he was born.

A boy. I was going to have a son.

We were about halfway there already—nineteen weeks down. He was the size of a mango now. And over the next four months or so, he'd grow to be the size of a watermelon. I tried not to think about how Mabel was going to get something that big through an opening I *knew* was considerably smaller. Was she scared? She hadn't talked much about the actual birth. I should ask her. I wondered if she'd want me in the room or out in the hall, and I couldn't decide which location I'd prefer.

My phone buzzed, and I checked it—Mabel had sent the

video. I watched it five times in a row.

A boy. I was going to have a son.

Should I start acting like it?

Filled with the sudden urge to do something mature and responsible, I jumped off the couch and went over to the kitchen, where I grabbed a broom from the pantry and began sweeping up crumbs from the floor. After that, I made my bed. Then I emptied the dishwasher. Put a load of laundry in the washer. Pretty soon, an hour had gone by.

It wasn't time to leave for the game yet, but I was too restless to sit still. I threw on a thick hoodie and left my apartment building. Pulling my hood over my head for privacy, I walked down the street and went into the drugstore. Some strange compulsion had me looking for the baby care aisle, where I stood there staring at things I'd never noticed before. Diapers and wipes. Bottles and nipples. Shampoo and powder and ointment. Things for their skin and hair and teeth and butts.

So many things for their butts.

I reached for a box of diapers and took it off the shelf. Holding it with both hands, I stared at the baby on the front, who was wrapped up in something that looked like a bag made out of a yellow blanket. Only his head poked out the top—even his arms were constrained. I turned the box over but didn't see any instructions on how to change a diaper. Maybe they were inside?

"Finding everything okay?"

I jumped like I'd been caught stealing and turned to see an employee smiling at me. "Um."

"Are you wondering if those are the right size?" she asked, indicating the box in my hands. Her smile was kind.

"Oh—no," I said, putting the box back on the shelf. "I was just looking."

Her face scrunched up and she shrank back a little. "Just

looking at diapers?"

"I'm going to be a dad soon," I blurted.

"Oh." Her expression relaxed with understanding. "Are you nervous?"

"Yeah. I don't know anything about babies. I'm an uncle, but I just play with my nieces and nephews. I've never had to actually feed them or change them or get them to sleep."

She smiled. "You'll figure it out."

"It's all just happening really fast. I feel a little out of control."

"When's the baby due?"

"April."

"You've got some time yet. Don't worry—a lot of it is instinct."

Instinct. I felt that way about hockey, too. A lot of what made me good was instinct—knowing where to be on the ice, who to pass to, when to shoot.

But what if those were the only instincts I'd been given?

I left the store and hurried home to get ready for tonight's game. The unsettled feeling in my stomach stayed with me throughout the pre-game meal, and a few teammates asked me if I was okay.

"I'm fine," I said. "Just a little tired."

But when I stepped out on the ice, I felt the tension dissipate as the usual rush filled me. Fueled by adrenaline, confidence in my ability, and the knowledge that Mabel was wearing my number and watching me play, I let my instincts take over.

I was in control again, and I liked it that way.

• • •

The day after the ultrasound, Mabel left me a voicemail message asking if it would be cool to come down and see the Friday night game the day after Thanksgiving. When I got home from a therapy session later that afternoon, I called her back.

"That sounds great," I told her.

"Are you sure? I wasn't sure if you'd have family in town for the holiday or anything."

"Nah, my parents do Thanksgiving at their place for everyone."

"Will you be there?"

"I can't. I've got a game Wednesday night in Columbus and Friday night here, and it's too far for a day trip. But I don't have a game Saturday. If you stayed, we could hang out or something."

"That would be fun. I'll book two nights at the hotel."

"Mabel, that's silly. Just stay here."

"I don't want to be a bother, I can just—"

"Hey, I owe you, remember? For letting me crash on your couch. I have a guest room, and no one ever uses it unless my mom comes to visit. She picked out the bedding and everything. It's very nice, lots of unnecessary pillows and shit."

She laughed. "I'm sure it's nice."

"And I promise I will stay at my end of the hallway. I can even put a lock on your door."

Another laugh, harder this time. "I'm sure that will not be necessary, I just..." She was silent a moment. "Actually, you know what? It's fine."

"It really is."

"I'll plan on leaving around eight in the morning, which should put me there around two or so. Does that work?"

"That's perfect. I don't have to leave for the game until about four. I'll get you a ticket to sit in the family section and introduce you to my buddy Dag's wife. She comes to all the home games."

"That sounds great."

"Then I'll see you a week from tomorrow. Just text me when you're leaving Cherry Tree Harbor. I'll let the parking guy here know you're coming and when to expect you."

"Okay."

"Drive carefully."

"I will."

"And don't forget the jersey."

She laughed. "It's a sweater. Get it right."

We hung up, and it hit me how excited I was to see her. But that was normal with a friend, right? To look forward to spending time together in person? Of course it was.

But I hoped the week passed quickly.

Chapter 15

Mabel arrived close to three the following Friday afternoon. When I opened the door, she wore an apologetic expression. "Sorry I'm late," she said. "I kept having to stop to go to the bathroom."

"Don't worry about it. I'm glad you're here." I scooped her into a hug, and right away I felt the bump in her belly. When I released her, I looked at her stomach, but she wore a sweater that was baggy enough to hide the pregnancy.

"Can you see it?" She smoothed the sweater over the small mound.

"Not unless you do that." I grinned. "You look great. It's really good to see you."

She smiled, her cheeks growing pink. Her skin was glowing, and her blue eyes were bright behind the lenses of her glasses.

"Thanks. It's good to see you too."

As I looked at her, I wondered if pregnancy made a woman even more attractive to the baby's dad. Had she always been so beautiful? Or was it some quirk of biology that had me wanting to pull Mabel against my chest and crush my mouth to hers?

Instead, I grabbed the handle of her roller bag and brought it inside. "How are you feeling?"

"Good."

"How's our little artichoke?"

"Kicked up a storm the whole way down," she said, following me into the guest room.

"We don't have to leave for a little bit, so if you'd like to take a nap or even just lie down and rest, you have time."

"I'm too excited to sleep!" She bounced up and down, clapping her hands. "I can't wait for the game."

I laughed, dragging her bag over to the window. "Should be a good one. Montreal is tough."

"Don't worry," she said, patting her stomach. "I brought your good luck charm. He's ready to cheer for his dad."

I smiled. "Have you thought about names yet?"

"Here and there. Have you?"

"Every time I try, it scares me. It seems like a lot of responsibility to name a human being. He'll have that name forever, you know?"

"We have time to think about it." Her fingers knotted at her midsection. "Have you told anyone here yet?"

"I haven't," I confessed. "But I will soon. I wanted to talk to you about it."

She held up both hands. "You can decide when. No pressure. The jersey is big enough to hide it for tonight. No one will guess."

"I just know there's going to be a lot of bullshit gossip, and I want to protect you from it."

"I understand."

"I spoke to Shea, one of the team's media relations people last week. She said probably the best thing will be to just tell the truth—or at least a version of it. It was a surprise, but we're friends, and we're going to co-parent. I'm going to be supportive and involved." It sounded so rote when I said it like that. Like a script, which I guess it was.

"That's cool with me." She tucked her hands into the back pockets of her jeans, making the bump more noticeable. "I'll confirm that, if anyone asks."

"I just don't really want it getting out there while you're here," I said, unable to take my eyes off her belly. "I don't want Chicago media to have any kind of access to you. Shea thought maybe it would be good around Christmas. A feel-good kind of post on social media or something."

"Okay. Ooh!" She placed a hand on her stomach. "He heard you talking about him."

Instinctively, I moved toward her with my hand out—then stopped. "Can I—is it okay if—"

"It's fine," she said, reaching for my hand. "Come here."

I placed my palm on the bump, over her sweater, and waited. After a long moment, she looked at me, her eyebrows raised.

"Did you feel that?"

"No," I said, disappointed.

"Hang on, sometimes he moves more when I'm sitting." She lowered herself onto the edge of the bed and leaned back on one hand. With the other, she lifted her sweater, revealing a stretchy navy blue panel where the zipper and button would normally be. Pushing the panel down, her rounded belly appeared. "Come sit," she said.

I dropped down next to her.

She reached for my hand and brought it to her skin, which

was warm and firm. "Okay, now just wait."

I waited, my breath trapped in my lungs, my pulse racing.

"Come on, little guy. Don't be shy," Mabel coaxed. "It's just your daddy. He wants to—"

And I felt it—beneath my hand, I felt the tiniest little bump you can imagine. But the reaction it provoked in me was huge. My heart blew up like a balloon, and my throat closed.

Mabel grinned. "Did you feel it?"

I nodded. I couldn't speak. I left my hand where it was, hoping to feel my son move again.

"Talk to him," Mabel urged.

"What do I say?"

"It doesn't matter. Just let him hear your voice."

I stared at my hand on her stomach, trying to wrap my brain around the fact that my child was in there—the kid I'd teach to skate and take to his grandpa's restaurant and run alongside as he learned to ride a two-wheeler. "Hey, buddy," I said. "Are you really in there?"

Thump.

Mabel laughed. "There's your answer."

"I can't wait to meet you," I said, feeling kind of stupid but also ridiculously happy. "And introduce you to your cousins and your grandparents. And teach you to skate and handle a stick and pass and shoot and how to be the kind of player coaches love."

"Maybe *you'll* be his coach someday."

I met Mabel's eyes and swallowed. "Maybe I will."

She smiled, and I had that urge again to pull her close. Bury my face in her hair and breathe her in. Lay my cheek on her stomach and listen. Put my lips on her skin.

Reimagine my future.

Removing my hand from her belly, I stood up. "I should

probably give you a minute. Bathroom is right across the hall, and it's all yours. I hung clean towels in there for you. Extra blankets are in the closet."

"Okay." She pulled the stretchy navy material up over the bump. "I just need to change out of my sweater and put my contacts in."

I nodded. "We'll head out in about twenty?"

"Perfect."

I left the guest room and headed down the hall. In my bedroom, I shut the door and dropped onto the foot of the bed, my hands curled over the mattress edge. My heart was beating hard, and I felt like a stranger in my own skin.

Get dressed, I told myself. *Put on your suit and tie. Go to the arena. Get the pads on. Lace up your skates. Get on the ice. That's where you'll feel like yourself again.*

I pushed myself up off the bed, certain it would happen.

• • •

"Are you sure you're up for this?" I paused in front of the Irish pub's door and looked at Mabel. I'd told my teammates we'd join them for post-game drinks, but it was so crowded and loud in there. Mabel couldn't even have alcohol—wouldn't she be miserable around a bunch of tipsy strangers?

"I'm positive, Joe." Wrapped in her winter coat, she tucked her hands in her pockets. "Let's go in."

"We don't have to, if you're tired."

"I'm fine." She smiled at me. "Plus, we said we'd be here. Your friends are expecting us. How can they celebrate the win without the MVP?"

With just a few seconds left on the clock, I'd scored the tie-breaking goal that clinched our victory. But I couldn't take all the credit. "I'm not the MVP. I got a great pass from Larsson."

"You're right, you're just a chump." Pulling a hand from her pocket, she gave me a light punch on the shoulder. "Well, let's go in so I can congratulate *him* then."

Laughing, I swung the door open. "Okay, but when you're done, let me know. We can leave whenever you want."

Inside, the pub was busy. A long wooden bar occupied the wall on the left, lined with people packed three deep. Bartenders moved quickly, pouring pints of beer or mixing drinks from rows of shiny glass bottles on shelves behind them. The rattle of ice in metal cocktail shakers could barely be heard over the loud Irish rock blaring from the speakers, and people shouted to be heard over the music.

Instinctively, I took Mabel's hand and pulled her through the room, where groups of people huddled over high-top tables or sat in booths over to the right. Many wore Chicago jerseys—Mabel was still wearing mine—and I could see people looking at me. Some even waved and called out.

"Great game, Lupo!"

"Nice goal!"

"Championship, here we come!"

I nodded or shouted thanks but kept moving, my grip on Mabel's hand secure. At the back of the pub, I opened a thick wooden door to reveal a private room with a pool table at its center and brown leather furniture grouped in cozy formations on either side. Several of my teammates and their wives or girlfriends had already arrived and were relaxing with drinks on the couches or involved in a game of pool.

Dag Larsson's wife, Anna, who'd sat with Mabel at the game, stood up from a couch. "Mabel!" she called, waving us over. "Come sit with us."

"Lupo!" Larsson shouted. "Grab a stick. I need a partner."

I hesitated, not sure if Mabel would rather I stay with her or leave her to hang out with the women.

She read my mind. "Go on," she said. "I'm fine. You don't have to babysit me."

"Okay. Do you want anything to drink?"

"Not right now."

"Let me know if you want anything. They do send servers back here, but when it gets busy, the wait can be long. We usually end up having to go to the bar."

"Where's the bathroom? That's probably what I'll need before anything else."

"It's just outside the door to this room."

"Okay." She smiled and patted my arm. "Go play. Have fun."

• • •

I drank a few beers and shot a few games of pool, and every time I looked over at Mabel, she seemed to be having a great time.

"So who's the girl?" My captain, a French-Canadian guy named Luc Tessier I respected for his leadership and admired for his deep understanding of the game, elbowed me, his eyes on Mabel. We stood off to the side, waiting our turn for the next game.

"A friend from back home," I said.

"She's visiting you?"

"Yes." I paused, taking a swallow from my beer, debating. I decided I trusted Tessier. He was a father of two. Maybe he'd have some advice. "Actually, Luc," I said quietly, "she's pregnant."

He looked at me, the question in his eyes.

"Yes. It's mine." For the first time, it actually felt good to say it out loud.

Tessier nodded, glancing over at Mabel again. "How far along?"

"Halfway. She just had the ultrasound where you can find out the sex last week."

"Oh yeah? And?"

"It's a boy." I couldn't help the grin that took over my face.

He smiled too, clinking his beer bottle against mine. "Congratulations."

"Thanks. Although it feels strange to accept congratulations. Not only because this was completely unexpected, but because she's doing all the work right now."

"There will be plenty of work for you to do, don't worry."

I turned to face him. "How do you manage it? The balance between hockey and your kids?"

He shrugged. "It's not always easy. I have to miss things, but I try really hard not to. My wife picks up a lot of the slack."

"She doesn't want to move here, because we're not together," I explained. "So I'll miss a lot."

"That's tough."

"But what's the alternative? I can't move away from Chicago."

He thought for a moment. "When is your contract up?"

"Next year."

"Will you sign a new one?"

"If they still want me."

"I think they'll still want you," he said confidently. "But do you still want to play?"

"Yes. Hockey is my entire life."

"Not anymore," he said, tipping up his beer.

"It's different for you." I felt the need to argue. "You already have a championship ring." Tessier had gone all the way with his previous team.

"Yeah, but after I'm gone, I don't want my headstone to say 'Here lies Luc Tessier, Stanley Cup champion.'"

"What do you want it to say?" I asked incredulously, since that's exactly how I wanted mine to read.

"'Here lies Luc Tessier, family man.'"

"That's it? Family man?" It was unfathomable to me. Anybody could be a family man. A Stanley Cup champion was rare. Special. Elite.

He chuckled, shaking his head. "You don't get it now. But you will. At least, I hope you will. The lucky ones do."

"Lupo! Tessier! You're up!" someone shouted.

I glanced over at the couch to make sure Mabel was still doing okay and saw that she wasn't there. Figuring she'd gone to the bathroom, I joined the guys at the pool table for another game.

But when she still wasn't back after ten minutes, I asked someone to shoot for me and went over to the couch. "Hey," I said, touching Anna on the shoulder. "Is Mabel okay?"

"Yes," Anna said with a smile. "She went to the bathroom and then she was going to grab something to drink. Service back here is slow tonight."

Frowning, I looked at the big wooden door.

"Want me to go check on her or something?" Anna asked.

"No, no. That's okay. I could use another beer anyway, so I'll head out to the bar."

I walked out of the back room and headed through the pub's main section, which had grown even more crowded. My eyes scanned the bar looking for the number 19 jersey, and when I spotted her at the far end, the first thing I felt was relief.

The next, blind fury.

Some guy next to her had put a hand on her lower back, which she swatted away. She also said something to him, but I was too far away to hear it. I doubled my stride, moving faster. When he moved his hand right back to where it had been, she pushed it away a second time. Now I was close enough to hear her say sharply, "I said no!"

Rage surged through me like TNT, a red haze hovering in my

peripheral vision. Reaching them, I wrapped my fist around the guy's forearm and wrenched him away from her.

"What the fuck?" he demanded.

I had at least four inches on him, and I got right in his face with a menacing stare. "You best keep your hands off the mother of my son."

"Or what?" The stocky frat boy jerked his chin at me.

"Or they'll be sweeping up your teeth from the floor when this bar closes tonight."

He yanked his arm from my grasp, and I let it go without blinking. After a roll of his shoulders, he stepped back. "I was just trying to buy her a drink, dude. Relax."

"Relax?" I moved for him again, but Mabel grabbed my arm.

"Joe, it's okay. Don't."

I gave him one last narrowing of my eyes and a crack of my knuckles before turning toward her. "You okay?"

"I'm totally fine." But she was white as a ghost. "I was just trying to get some water."

"I'll get it for you." I didn't often use my celebrity status to cut the line, but when the bartender saw me standing there, she came right over and asked what she could do for me. Less than a minute later, I handed Mabel a glass of water.

"Thanks," she said, taking a small sip. Her eyes still had that deer-in-the-headlights stupor.

"You sure you're all right?"

"I'm fine, I just…" She glanced right and left, then spoke low. "You said out loud that I was the mother of your son."

"Yeah, I guess I did."

"It might get out. A lot of people heard it, and some of them know who you are." She glanced down. "I mean, I'm wearing your name."

I realized something. "I don't care who heard it."

"You don't?"

"No."

Her lips tipped up, color returning to her cheeks. "Okay."

"I want everyone to know if they don't treat you with respect, they will fucking answer to me."

"Thanks," she said shyly.

"I told Tessier earlier tonight anyway. I'll tell the rest of the guys tomorrow."

"Okay." There was no denying she looked happy about it.

"You ready to get out of here?"

She nodded.

"Me too. Let's go." Placing my hand on the small of her back, I guided her toward the back room so I could settle my tab, get our coats, and say goodbye to the guys.

That's right, asshole, I thought as we passed the jerk-off who hit on her. *The only person allowed to touch her this way is me.*

But of course, that wasn't true.

Someone could come along at any time and touch her any way she invited him to. In fact, *I* was the one she didn't want touching her.

I was broody and silent in the car on the drive home, and Mabel was preoccupied trying to get rid of her hiccups. When we got inside my apartment, I hung up our coats in the hall closet and turned to find her standing there, looking nervous.

"Are you okay?" she asked. "I'm sorry if that guy ruined your night."

"Do not apologize for that asshole," I said, scowling. "He's lucky he walked out of there with two good legs. And I'm fine. I just got a little too worked up."

"Need a hug?" she offered, opening her arms.

I laughed a little, the hard edges of my mood softening. "Sure."

She rose up on tiptoe and wrapped her arms around my neck, and I embraced her with caution, careful not to let my hands stray out of bounds or my lower body make contact with hers.

After a few seconds, she released me and stepped back. "Thanks for bringing me to the game. I really loved it."

"You're welcome. I'm glad you were there." I stuck my hands in my back pockets so I wouldn't be tempted to touch her again. "Get some sleep."

"I will. Good night." She went into the bathroom and shut the door.

I stood there in the hallway for a moment before heading into my bedroom, where I dropped onto the edge of my bed in the dark.

After a few minutes, I heard her cross the hall and go into the guest room, the door shutting with a decisive thunk.

I exhaled.

It was what we'd agreed to.

But something about this didn't seem right.

Chapter 16

You best keep your hands off the mother of my son.

I shivered, cuddling deeper beneath the duvet in the dark. As long as I lived, I would never forget the tone of his voice as he spoke those words.

Dangerous. Threatening. Possessive.

It was *so hot.*

I couldn't stop hearing it. The deep, raw texture of his voice provoked memories of other things he'd said to me in the heat of passion.

What do you want? Tell me every filthy little thing.

My body warmed and tingled in sensitive spots, and I closed my eyes, letting the memory of his mouth and his hands and his body on mine crash over me like waves. God, what I wouldn't give to relive that night with him, to feel so swept away.

He was right down the hall.

No. Go to sleep.

But I lay there wide awake as the minutes ticked by, tormented by his nearness and the memory of our one night together, until I thought I'd go mad.

Was he feeling it too? Sometimes I thought he looked at me with something more than friendship in his eyes, but he hadn't said anything even remotely suggestive all night, and he'd kept his hands to himself. Even when he hugged me good night, it had felt sort of...careful.

What would he do if I tiptoed down the hall and knocked on his bedroom door? And what excuse would I give? If I was thirsty, I had a water bottle. If I was hungry, I could just go to the kitchen. If I was cold, extra blankets were in the closet.

I couldn't very well tell him the truth—that his possessiveness had turned me on so much, I couldn't sleep. What if he rejected me? What if he didn't find me attractive anymore now that I was pregnant? What if something happened and I started to catch feelings I couldn't control? A lot was riding on my ability to keep a level head and stay emotionally stable. I didn't want to end up brokenhearted and resentful. Joe and I would be in each other's lives forever. We had to preserve the peace between us.

Then I heard something—footsteps in the hallway? A creak of the wood floor?

I propped myself up on my elbows and listened carefully, holding my breath, praying for a soft knock on the door.

But the room remained silent.

Eventually, exhaustion caught up with me and I fell asleep.

. . .

I woke up disoriented.

This bed was comfortable, but it wasn't mine. The room

didn't smell the same. There was no light coming through the blinds. Slowly I came out of the haze and remembered.

I was in Chicago visiting Joe. This was his guest room, with the fluffy white bedding and the blackout shades. I'd gone to his game last night, and then we'd met his friends at the pub.

I reached for my phone, surprised to discover that it was already going on ten—I never slept so late. I also saw that Joe had texted me about five minutes ago.

Hey, I'm heading to practice, but it's a light day for us. I should be home by 2:00 and we can do whatever you'd like. There are decaf coffee pods and tea in the pantry since I wasn't sure you could have caffeine. Fruit in the fridge. Bagels on the counter. Help yourself to anything.

Thank you! Sorry I slept so long. This bed is too comfy!

I lay there for a few more minutes, hoping he'd find a moment to text back, but no new messages popped up. Setting my phone aside, I lay back and closed my eyes.

You best keep your hands off the mother of my son.

Then I reached for my phone again and called Ari.

"Hello?"

"Hey, it's me."

"Hi! You make it down to Chicago okay?"

"Yes."

"How was the game?"

"So much fun." I paused, running a hand over my belly. "But I have to tell you about something that happened last night *after* the game."

She gasped. "You slept with him."

"No," I said. "But I can't say I wouldn't have if the opportunity had presented itself."

"Tell me everything, right this second."

"So we were in, like, this private room at the back of a pub, and—"

"Wait, who's we?"

"A bunch of his teammates and some of their wives and girlfriends."

"Got it. Go on."

"Joe was shooting pool and I left the room to go to the bathroom, and when I came out I went to the bar to get some water. The bar was super crowded and there was this guy who offered to let me get closer, and I thought he was just being nice."

"Oh dear."

"He wanted to buy me a drink and put his hand on my back. I told him no, thank you, and pushed his arm away. He put it right back, and I got more forceful with him, and I was about to just walk away when Joe suddenly appeared, grabbed the guy's arm, and got right in his face."

"Really?"

"Yes. And he said, in like this deep, growly voice, 'You best keep your hands off the mother of my son.'"

She let out a shriek. "Ahhhh, I am *swooning* up here!"

"I know! And then the guy got belligerent—I cannot imagine what he was thinking, since Joe was way bigger—and I literally had to pull him back and tell him not to punch this asshole."

"Holy shit."

"I was in shock. I couldn't believe he said it out loud—he hadn't told anyone here yet about the baby and was planning to wait another month."

"Why?"

"Just to protect our privacy, especially mine. He knows people are going to be nosy and gossipy, if not downright rude."

"True. So did people hear what he said about his son?"

"It was loud in there, but that guy heard it for sure. I'm not positive he recognized Joe, but I *was* wearing his jersey."

"It will get out," Ari predicted.

"That's what I told him, and he said he didn't care."

"Really?"

"Yeah, he was like, 'I want everyone to know if they don't treat you with respect, they will fucking answer to me.'"

Silence. And then, "Damn. This guy is good."

"He *is* good." I squeezed my eyes shut. "And he's so hot. Like I was about to physically combust last night, he is so hot."

"I don't blame you. But nothing happened?"

"Nope. He was pretty quiet on the way home, and when we got back to his apartment, we just hugged good night and that was that."

"What kind of hug? Like a close, lingering embrace?"

"Not really. Just more of a friendly or brotherly thing."

"Boo."

"Then I spent the next several hours lying in bed, talking myself out of knocking on his bedroom door."

"Why didn't you do it?"

"Mostly because I'm afraid of rejection."

"Mabel, I highly doubt he would reject you."

"Okay, but that could be even worse! Because then I'd be afraid of opening the floodgates for feelings I won't be able to control. I could drown, Ari. Falling for him would be disastrous for me."

"Are you sure you'd fall in love with him?"

I thought about Joe's voice and his blue eyes and his laugh and his hand on my back—protective and strong. "Kind of."

She sighed. "Well then, be careful."

"I will. I'll see you when I get back." After ending the call, I lay there for another minute or two. When the baby gave me a little kick, I laughed. "Are you awake too? Are you hungry?" Sitting up, I swung my legs over the side and reached for my glasses on the nightstand. "Let's go find something to eat."

After pulling on some sweatpants and a Two Buckleys Home Improvement hoodie, I shuffled out toward the living room. I made a cup of decaf and popped a plain bagel in the toaster, then I took my coffee over to the living room window. Once again, the view took my breath away. The tree branches were bare now, their spindly fingers reaching up toward an overcast sky. Snow flurries danced outside the glass in a blustery wind. In the distance, the lake was gray and choppy. Sixteen stories below, people hurried up and down city streets, huddled in winter coats and scarves and hats.

I wondered what Joe and I would do today. If we were a couple, it was the kind of Saturday we might spend wrapped in blankets, cuddled up on the couch, watching nostalgic movies and stuffing our faces with bad-for-you snacks.

But we weren't a couple, he probably hated old movies, and judging by the condition of his body, he didn't eat things like potato chips and ice cream.

The toaster popped, and I headed back to the kitchen. I spread some butter on the bagel and ate it along with some strawberries. After breakfast, I took a shower and dressed in my maternity jeans, a ribbed white tank top, and a loose, fuzzy gray cardigan. I'd forgotten to pack my hair dryer and I didn't see one in the bathroom, so I just left my hair to dry on its own. Barefoot, I wandered back out toward the living room.

On my way, I peeked into his bedroom. Not because I wanted to invade his privacy, but just out of curiosity.

He'd left the door open and his bed unmade. His clothes from the bar last night were still on the floor. Glancing over my shoulder, I pressed my lips together and took a step inside.

The room smelled like him, and my body's reaction was swift and visceral. My nipples tingled. My core muscles clenched. Next thing I knew, I felt his bedroom rug under the soles of my feet. Knowing this was wrong and I was acting crazy, I hurried around to the side of the bed he slept on and stopped, listening for his key in the lock. Hearing nothing, I quickly slipped into his bed and pulled the blankets up to my shoulders. Closing my eyes, I inhaled the scent of his sheets.

Suddenly the heat clicked on, and the noise sent me bolting from the bed and scurrying out to the living room, my pulse pounding as hard as my heels on the wood floor. After catching my breath, I laughed at myself and vowed I would not do that again.

I had about an hour until Joe was due home, so I grabbed my phone and stretched out on the couch. But it wasn't long before I began to doze off. Figuring I'd just take a quick catnap, I closed my eyes.

• • •

When I woke up, I discovered someone had removed my glasses and covered me with a chunky, cream-colored knit blanket. I sat up slowly and saw Joe in the kitchen. My phone and glasses were on the coffee table.

"You're home already," I said. "Did you get back early?"

"No. It's two-thirty."

"It is?" I blinked in surprise. "Oh my God. I had no idea I'd sleep for that long. I just meant to close my eyes for a minute."

"That's okay. Your body must need the rest." He turned on the tap and filled a glass with water.

I slipped my glasses on. "Did you cover me up?"

"Yes. Your feet were bare and I was afraid they were cold."

"Thank you," I said, touched by the gesture.

He popped something into his mouth and took a few swallows of water. "Some ibuprofen for my shoulder," he explained. "It's bothering me a little today."

"Are you okay?"

"I'm fine." He came out from the kitchen and dropped into one of the chairs adjacent to the couch. "I told the guys about the baby."

Tucking my feet underneath me, I sat up taller. "What did they say?"

"Not much. Some said congratulations."

"Was it weird?"

He looked off into the distance. "You know, it wasn't as weird as I thought it would be. I think I'm finally getting used to it."

I laughed. "Good thing."

"So what would you like to do today? I mean, we don't have to do anything, if you're tired." He leaned over to tie one of his brown lace-up boots that had come undone. He was wearing faded brown pants and a navy quarter-zip sweater over a blue plaid button-down. His hair was tousled and his jaw was stubbled, and the whole rugged, up-north look of him was enough to put my hormones on high alert.

We want more of this man, please.

"I'm good," I said, fussing with my hair and hoping it wasn't too matted. "I've certainly slept enough in the last twelve hours."

He sat back. "Since we did hockey last night, I thought I'd let you choose today's activity. Want to drag me to a museum or something? Broaden my horizons?"

"Like a field trip?"

"Yeah." He grinned. "I bet you're a good tour guide."

"Maybe," I said, "but I don't want to *drag* you anywhere."

"I was kidding. I would willingly go to a museum with you."

"Well, the good thing is that most of them probably close at five, so the torture would last only a couple hours at most." I thought for a moment. "Paintings or dinosaurs?"

"Dinosaurs."

"Natural history museum," I said, getting excited. "Let's go."

• • •

We spent two hours at the Field Museum, and even though I'm sure I rambled on for way too long on topics like archaeological dig methods, artifact acquisition and conservation, and exhibition design, Joe was a good sport. He listened and asked questions, and when I'd get particularly excited about something, he'd laugh—but always with affection.

"Okay, the torture is over! What was your favorite part?" I asked as we perused items in the gift shop on our way out.

"It wasn't torture at all, it was very cool. I want to bring my nieces and nephews here next time they visit. And my favorite thing was Sue the T. rex, of course," Joe said. "I can't believe they found that thing in South Dakota."

"I know." I picked up a kids' book about the paleontologist who discovered the bones and thumbed through it. "Oh, look how cute this is." I showed Joe one of the illustrated pages. "The scientist who found the skeleton was a woman named Sue, so they named it after her. And this book talks about how when she was little, she was always hunting for treasures in her backyard."

He nudged me with his arm. "Sounds like someone else I know."

I laughed. "Exactly."

"We should get the book for the artichoke."

I looked up at him in surprise. "Really?"

"Yeah. And maybe one of these things." He picked up a pair of newborn footie pajamas with little dinosaurs all over them. Then he draped it on my stomach. "Will they fit?"

I couldn't speak right away. I almost felt like turning away from him so I could burst into tears. But at the same time, I wanted to throw my arms around him. "Not yet," I said with a smile. "But they will when he's born."

"Let's get them." He looked around for the cashier. "You can read him the story at bedtime and tell him about the day we were here."

I put a hand on his arm. "You can read it to him too, Joe."

"Right. Yeah." He looked down at the sleeper in his hands. "I just won't be there at bedtime as often as you will."

I had to swallow back sobs as I followed him to the cashier, where he purchased the book and the pajamas. I imagined reading the story to our son one day, and my heart filled with love and longing for a little dark-haired boy with pudgy cheeks and sweet-smelling skin and wide, curious eyes. And it ached for his father who'd miss out on everyday things like bedtime stories and babbling and those first wobbly steps.

"Maybe we should talk about names," I said to Joe as we made our way outside.

"Can we do it over dinner? I'm starved."

"Sure. I'm hungry too."

"Restaurant or takeout?"

"I'm good with either one," I said, buttoning up my coat against the wind. "But will you be recognized at a restaurant?"

He tipped his head this way and that. "Depends. But I know a little place where the manager will give me a table with some privacy if it's available. Do you like steak?"

"Yes."

He took my arm. "Okay, let's try it. Careful on the steps."

• • •

"Helmer?" I made a face at Joe from across the table. We were trying out different baby names by working our way through the alphabet, each of us suggesting one name per letter.

"Yeah, it's Swedish." He took a bite of his New York strip. "I've got a buddy named Helmer. A defenseman. He's badass."

"How about something classic like Henry?"

"Too boring. Our kid needs a cool name. Something different."

"Let's move on," I said, because I was not about to name my baby Helmer. "Letter I."

"Ivan. That's a good hockey name too."

Laughing, I reached for my water glass. "What if he's not a hockey player?"

"Of course he'll be a hockey player," Joe scoffed. "What else would he be?"

"Anything. He might be a chef like your dad. Or have his own home improvement business, like my dad. Or be an actor or a teacher or an astronaut."

Joe's eyes lit up. "An astronaut is badass too. Commander Ivan Lupo."

"Commander Jeremy Lupo?"

"Commander Jaxon Lupo." He pointed a potato wedge at me. "With an *X*."

"Maybe it should be an Italian name," I suggested. "Lupo is Italian, right?"

"Yeah. It means wolf. But that's the only Italian word I know, except for the names of foods." He paused with his beer halfway to his mouth. "Hey, we didn't even talk about this, but is Lupo the last name you want the baby to have?"

I nodded, pressing my napkin to my mouth. "I've thought about it, and I think he should have your last name."

"Are you sure?"

"Yes." I looked down at the napkin in my lap, twisting it around my fingers. "I mean, someday I hope to get married, and I'll take my husband's last name. Any kids I have then will have that last name too. So it doesn't make much sense to give our baby *Buckley* as a last name."

"You don't have to take his name," Joe said, an unmistakably defensive note in his voice, as if my future husband was being unreasonable about it.

"I know," I said gently. "But I hope I'll want to."

Joe was silent for a minute, his brow furrowed as he sliced his steak but didn't take another bite.

"What are some Italian names in your family?" I asked.

"There are a lot of Joes," he said. "My dad is Domenico, but he's always gone by Nick."

"Domenico is cool," I said.

"You think?"

"Yeah. It's kind of old world, but it has an edge too."

"It's a mouthful for a little kid."

"Right, we'd need a short version." I giggled. "And Dom is a little harsh for a baby. What about Nicky?"

Joe's eyes widened. "After my dad? You'd do that?"

"It's something to think about," I said. "I like the idea of respecting your family's history and traditions. This baby will grow up surrounded by Buckleys, you know? I want him to feel connected to his Lupo roots too. So yes, I would do that."

Joe swallowed and opened his mouth like he might say something, but he closed it without speaking. He took a drink from his beer.

"Do you think your dad would like it?" I asked.

Joe cleared his throat. "He'd love it," he said.

Chapter 17

JOE

*B*ack at my apartment, I asked Mabel if she wanted to watch a movie.

"Sure," she said, curling up in one corner of the couch with the blanket. "What should we watch? I picked the museum, so you can pick the movie."

"What kinds of movies do you like?" I picked up the remote and turned on the system.

"I like almost everything except horror. Nothing gory or scary. What kind do you like?"

"Slasher films," I joked.

She laughed. "What's your favorite movie of all time? Like from when you were a kid."

"You won't want to watch it."

"Is it *Texas Chainsaw Massacre* or something?"

I shook my head. "No. It's just a movie I used to watch with my family."

"I like classic films too."

"I'm not sure *The Sandlot* qualifies as a classic film."

She giggled, burrowing deeper under the blanket. "I've never seen it. Show me."

"Are you serious? You want to watch *The Sandlot*?"

"Sure. But I apologize in advance for the number of times I'll have to ask you to pause it so I can use the bathroom."

"You never have to apologize to me." I found the movie and put it on, then turned off all the lights before dropping onto the other end of the couch. "God, I haven't watched this in years."

"No?"

I shook my head, realizing that I'd never even wanted to watch it with Courtney because I knew she'd have been bored. And her disdain would have taken away from my happy childhood memory. But somehow, I knew Mabel was going to like it, or at least appreciate why I liked it.

I'd seen *The Sandlot* so many times in my life I could just about recite it, so my mind wandered as it played. Moments from last night and this afternoon ran through my head.

How furious I'd been seeing that jerk's hand on her—I'd have gladly mopped the floor with his face. How torn I'd been last night when I'd stood outside her bedroom door, wondering if I should knock, deciding against it in the end. How confused I was about these feelings I had for her.

Were they real? Would they last? Was it just the biological urge to protect my offspring that had me feeling so possessive of her? If she weren't pregnant, would I feel the same?

Maybe it was the name thing getting to me. The way she was willing to name our son after my dad. I hadn't even realized how much that would mean to me until she suggested it. And it was going to mean the world to my father, if that's what we decided.

I remembered how she'd said something about getting married in the future and taking her husband's name. It was reality, it would happen, but I fucking hated the thought. I fucking hated that guy. But what could I do?

She laughed at something happening on the screen, and my eyes drifted toward her. She was so fucking cute all cuddled up under that blanket. Her hair was kind of curly today, and several times at the museum I'd been close enough to smell her shampoo or her body lotion or whatever it was that made her smell like cupcakes.

And I knew.

It was more than just the baby.

I wanted to be close to her. I wanted to stretch out behind her and wrap my arm around her middle. I wanted to pull her into me. I wanted to share myself with her in a way I couldn't explain and didn't even fully understand.

At one point, she looked over at me—she'd probably felt my eyes on her—and smiled. Her dimple appeared. "You okay?"

"Yeah." Pausing the movie, I got off the couch before I did something drastic. "How about a snack? Popcorn? Pretzels? Chips?"

"You have all those things? You do *not look* like you eat that kind of junk food."

"I don't, normally. But I wasn't sure what you liked, so I added a few things to my grocery list this week." I grinned at her. "I remembered what you said about ice cream and potato chips."

She squealed. "My favorite!"

"So do I just scoop the ice cream into the bowl and put the chips on the side? Or do I crush them up like sprinkles?"

"Like sprinkles," she said, laughing. "But I can get it. I have to use the bathroom anyway." Setting the blanket aside, she stood and stretched. She'd taken her cardigan off earlier and wore just the tank top now, and it hugged the curves of her upper body. For the first time, I noticed that it wasn't just her belly that had grown. Her breasts were bigger too.

My mouth watered.

Turning away, I headed for the kitchen. "I'll get it. I like when there are things I can do for you."

"Thank you," she said, hurrying toward the bathroom. "I'll be right back."

While I scooped vanilla ice cream into a bowl, I thought of other things I could do for her. With my hands and my tongue and my cock.

Then I had to hope she wouldn't notice the bulge in my pants when she came back into the room.

• • •

When the movie was over and her ice cream bowl was empty— I'd watched her lick that spoon with envy burning in my gut—I switched off the television. "Well? What did you think?"

"Adorable. I love nostalgic movies like that."

I smiled. "Good."

She put her hands on her stomach. "You can watch it with Nicky someday."

I nodded, my eyes on her belly. "That would be cool."

"I think the sugar and salt woke him up," she said. "He was still during the movie and now he's moving around."

"Can I feel?"

"Sure," she said, scooting closer to me and taking the blanket off. "Here." She took my hand and placed it over to one side of her belly. "This is where I feel him kicking."

I molded my palm to her firm, warm skin but didn't feel anything. She pulled her shirt up and pushed the panel of her jeans down like she had yesterday afternoon, but I still didn't feel those little feet. We gave it a few minutes, Mabel moving my hand around in different spots. I started to grow warm beneath my clothes, the heat gathering between my legs.

"He's messing with me," I joked, trying to keep things light. "Or you are."

"I'm not! I swear to God, he was all kickety in there just before you put your..." She looked up at me. Her lips were so close to mine. I stared at them, and she tucked the bottom one between her teeth for a second. "Your hand on me," she whispered.

A few inches. That's all it would take.

She could lift her chin. I could lower my head. Our mouths would meet. She'd taste sweet and salty, and I'd stroke her tongue with mine. I'd put my hand in her hair. She'd touch the back of my neck. We'd lay down on the couch, and I'd—

I'd what? Violate the trust she had in me to be a good guy? To treat her with respect? To honor the boundaries she'd set?

I took my hand off her. "Maybe next time."

"I'm sorry," she said, her expression disappointed.

"It's okay." Rattled by how close I'd come to kissing her, I stood up and took her ice cream bowl to the kitchen sink and rinsed it.

Mabel rose from the couch and stretched, sending a current of desire surging through me. "I guess I'll go to bed."

"Okay."

"You have practice in the morning?" she asked, walking slowly toward the hallway leading to the bedrooms.

"We skate at ten. But it's a game day."

"Oh, that's right."

"What time will you leave tomorrow?" I picked up a dish towel and dried my hands just to have something to do with them that did not involve touching her.

"I'd like to get on the road by nine."

I nodded. "I'll see you in the morning."

"Okay." She stood there for a moment, then lifted a hand. "Good night."

I stayed right where I was, not trusting myself to get any closer to her, let alone hug her good night. "Night."

Her shoulders dropped a little as she disappeared into the hallway, and I exhaled, bracing my hands against the edge of the sink, head hanging down.

Turn off the lights, go to your room, and stay there, I warned myself. *You are not allowed to come out. You are not allowed to knock on her door. You are not allowed to touch her.*

You will ruin everything.

Summoning all my discipline, I did what I was supposed to do. And when my apartment was dark and silent, I didn't even glance at Mabel's bedroom door to see if it was closed or open, if the light was on or off, if she was still in the bathroom or already in bed.

Closing my own bedroom door behind me, I used the bathroom, brushed my teeth, and undressed. Naked, I got into bed and pulled the covers to my waist. Lay on my back and stared at the ceiling. Thought about her. Imagined what I'd be doing right now if the circumstances were different between us. I couldn't bring myself to wish she wasn't pregnant—I already loved my son—but I did wish that whatever this was I felt for her would mellow into something other than bone-crushing desire.

I wished I could forget the way she tasted. The sounds she made. The words she whispered. *I want you to make me come again.*

I slid my hand under the covers and wrapped it around my cock.

That's when I heard it. A soft knock on my door.

I froze. Had I imagined it?

No—there it was again. Three quiet little raps on the wood.

"Mabel?" I called out, quickly taking my hand off my dick.

"Yes," she said through the door. "Can I come in?"

"Sure." I sat up, my heart pounding. Hopefully, it was dark enough she wouldn't notice how I'd bunched the covers over my crotch to hide my erection.

The door opened, and she appeared. She wore a long white T-shirt, giving her a ghostly appearance in the dark. "Hi."

"Hi." I swallowed hard.

"He's moving again," she said tentatively. "I thought maybe you'd want to feel?"

"Okay. I mean yes."

She moved closer to the bed. "Is it okay if I..."

"Of course."

She climbed onto the bed and sat back on her heels, her knees brushing my hip. Her buttery vanilla scent filled my head. Taking my hand, she pressed it to her belly, molding it beneath hers over the thin cotton shirt. I didn't breathe or blink. Nothing happened.

"Shoot," she said, sliding my hand to a new spot. "Now he's not doing it. But a minute ago I was just lying there, and he was kicking away."

"Maybe if you lie down the way you were?"

"Maybe." She rearranged herself so she lay on her side, facing me, above the covers. "Okay, this is how I was."

Rolling onto my side, I propped my head in one hand and reached out again. She took me by the wrist, and this time she slipped my hand beneath the shirt. Heat struck me like lightning as my palm rested on her bare skin. Beneath my hand, nothing happened.

Beneath the covers, my cock grew harder.

After a moment, she sighed. "You're going to think I made it up," she said, "but I swear he was dancing around in there when I was down the hall."

"I believe you."

She slid my hand higher on her belly, so high my fingers brushed the bottom of her breast.

Immediately I pulled my arm back. "Sorry."

"It's okay."

We lay there facing each other, our eyes locked. The silence between us lengthened into something tight and tense, something that threatened to snap.

Finally she spoke. "Were you asleep when I knocked?"

"No. I was just lying here thinking."

"About what?"

What popped into my mind was not the kind of thing you said to a friend. "Stuff," I said lamely.

"What kind of stuff?"

"I'm not sure I should tell you."

"Why not?"

"Because my answer will cross the line."

She didn't say anything, and I thought I'd gone too far.

"Fuck. Sorry. Forget I said that."

"Which line?" she asked.

"The one drawn between us."

"So you're wishing you could be on my side of the line tonight?"

"Yes. But don't worry—I won't cross it. I know it's better this way." I paused. "I was just thinking about you is all."

"It's okay. I was thinking about you too."

We were at a standstill. It felt like a face-off where the ref had dropped the puck but neither player wanted to be the first to touch it, even though they both wanted to score.

"I should go back to my room," she whispered.

"Probably."

She began to roll away and my arm shot out, my fingers catching her forearm.

"But I don't want you to go," I said.

"You don't?"

"No. Stay."

She settled back onto her side, facing me like before, and I let go of her arm.

"We don't have to do anything," I told her. "I won't even touch you, if you don't want me to. I know what the rules are. I just want to be close to you."

"I *want* you to touch me, Joe," she said softly but urgently. "I know it's a bad idea. I know it's wrong. But I really want you to touch me."

I reached over and slid my hand from her thigh to her hip, slipping beneath the hem of the T-shirt. I kneaded her hip tenderly. "Is this okay?"

"Yes," she whispered.

My hand traveled over her rounded stomach and up to one breast, cupping it gently. She arched her back, pressing herself into my palm, and sucked in her breath as my thumb teased her nipple, making it hard. God, I wanted my mouth on her. Leaning forward, I closed my lips around the cotton-covered peak, sucking softly, wetting her shirt.

She groaned, cradling my head in her hands, threading her fingers into my hair, raking her nails across my scalp. "That feels so good."

Tipping her onto her back, I did the same thing to her other breast while my fingers played with the first, twisting its pebbled tip through the damp cotton. After a moment, she lifted my head from her chest.

"Let me take this off," she whispered before removing her shirt and tossing it to the floor.

Under the blankets, my cock was hard as granite and aching for her touch.

But I didn't want to push this farther than she wanted to take it.

"Do you want to get under the covers?" I asked.

"Yes." She started to climb beneath them.

"Just so you know, I'm naked under here."

That made her laugh a little. "Thanks for the warning."

"I didn't want you to be unpleasantly surprised."

"Joe, your naked body could never be an unpleasant surprise to me." She stretched out beside me, and I pulled her close, anxious to feel those voluptuous new curves against my skin. It wasn't anything I'd say out loud, but there was something so hot about the fact that *I'd caused* these changes.

And in fact, as my hands moved over her skin, I couldn't help feeling somewhat proprietary about her body—like it somehow belonged partly to me. I knew it was wrong to think that way. I knew it wasn't true. I knew I deserved a slap across the face from a thousand angry feminists for it, but not only did I *have* the thought, I *liked* it. It turned me on.

Bringing my lips to hers, I kissed her hard and deep, and she wound her arms around my neck, holding me tight. I slipped one knee between her legs and she squeezed my thigh with hers, rubbing against me. I ran a hand down her lower back, inside her underwear, curling my fingers around her ass. My hips flexed instinctively, pushing my cock into her hip.

She reached between us, and I gave her the space to close her fist around my shaft, groaning as she worked her hand up and down its hard length and teased the crown with playful fingers. When I felt myself nearing a breaking point, I rolled her onto her back and moved down her body until my head was between her legs. "Is this okay?" I asked.

"Yes."

I slipped my fingers over the edge of her underwear. "Can I take these off?"

"Yes."

I pulled the panties down her legs and tossed them to the floor. Then I hooked my hands beneath her thighs and buried my face between them. Inhaling her scent. Savoring her taste. Sucking her like candy.

She moaned and sighed, the sounds making me hungrier—especially when she said my name. I used my fingers and tongue in tandem until her hips lifted, her thighs clenched, and she cried out with abandon, her clit pulsing on my tongue. I didn't stop until I felt the tension in her body release completely, and her sighs grew softer.

"Oh God, Joe." Her fingers tightened in my hair. "The things you do to me."

"You want more?" I got to my knees, fisting my cock.

"*Yes*," she said, reaching for my hips, pulling me closer.

Bracing myself above her, I paused. "This is okay, right? We won't hurt you or the baby?"

"It's okay."

"Do you want me to wear a condom?"

"Well, I'm already pregnant." She hesitated. "Have you—are you—?"

"I hadn't been with anyone for months before we met. And there hasn't been anyone since. I haven't even thought about it."

"Me neither," she said softly. "So I think we're good."

"I can be gentle," I told her as I eased inside her body, hoping it was true.

"Don't be gentle. Be rough." She wrapped her arms and legs

around me, whispering in my ear. "I like it when you lose control. When you fuck me hard."

I groaned as I buried myself as deeply as I could. "Cupcake, you don't know what you're asking for."

"Then show me," she urged, digging her nails into my ass. "Teach me a lesson."

That was all I needed.

I remembered exactly what she'd liked from that night at the hotel—the pace and pressure and angle that brought her to the edge—and when I had her there, sweaty and grasping and begging and rocking her hips beneath me, I relinquished my gentleman's hold on the reins and allowed my most primal instincts to take charge. The crazy thing was, although my body had gone through these motions before and knew what it wanted and how to get it, my head was filled with new thoughts that made everything feel like the first time.

Bananas irrational possessive caveman thoughts.

She's mine. She belongs to me. I put a life in her body. No one else has ever done that before. I am powerful. I am more than a man. I am a god.

See what I mean?

I even thought about the future husband she'd mentioned, and the fury that coursed through my veins only made me more unhinged.

Fuck that guy. I was here first.

I couldn't pull back from it. It was stronger than the rush I got on a breakaway, bigger than the adrenaline spike after a goal, better than the euphoria from a critical win. When she came, my name dripping from her lips, her heels digging into the backs of my thighs, the feeling intensified. It drove me higher and faster and harder until I lost myself to it, my body throbbing inside hers in hot, explosive bursts.

I caught myself before I collapsed on top of her, rolling to my side and bringing her with me, one leg flung over my hip. Still connected, I held her close to my chest, both of us breathing hard.

For a few moments, my un-evolved inner caveman tried to stand his ground with my modern, rational self.

You can't let this woman leave tomorrow. You have to keep her here. You have to protect her. She's carrying your son, and that makes her your responsibility. Where's your honor?

It's her choice to go. She's not my prisoner. I can't keep her here against her will. And neither of us wants that. I'm taking responsibility the best way I can. But women don't need men telling them what to do. My honor is in respecting her decisions.

The caveman harrumphed and slunk away, but I had a feeling he'd be back.

. . .

Mabel used the bathroom off my bedroom, and when she came out, she scooped up her T-shirt from the floor and pulled it on. "Any idea where my underwear went?" she asked.

"I think they might still be on the bed."

She felt around. "Found them."

I watched her tug them on from where I lay on top of the twisted sheets, strangely reluctant to let her walk out of my room. "Are you okay?" I asked.

"Yes. I'm fine."

"Are *we* okay?"

"Yes." She played with the hem of her shirt. "Joe, I knew what was likely to happen if I knocked on your bedroom door tonight. And I still knocked."

"I'm glad you did."

"I am too. But I don't think we should do this again. Not that

I didn't love every second of it," she went on quickly, "but things are good with us, you know? And I just don't want to muddy that water."

"Does that mean you don't want to sleep in here tonight?"

She didn't answer right away. "Like, with you? In your bed?"

I laughed at how surprised she sounded, although I'd surprised myself by asking the question too. "Yes."

"But you hate sharing a bed."

"I never said I hated it. I said I wasn't good at it. But for you," I said dramatically, like I was doing her a big favor, "I will try."

"Joe, you don't have to. I can just go sleep in the guest room."

"I want you to. Is that better?" I put my hand on the mattress beside me. "I want you to sleep in here with me."

"Okay," she said, climbing onto the bed. She fluffed the pillow on the far side, her back to me. "I promise I will stay over here and not take up your space. I won't make you cuddle."

"What if I want to cuddle?" I hooked an arm around her hips and pulled her against me, curling my body around hers. "Is this okay?"

"Yes," she said, laughing a little. "I like cuddling. I just didn't think you did."

"Normally I don't. But this is a special occasion—our one and only sleepover. I'm a special-occasion cuddler." Somehow my hand found its way inside her T-shirt and rested on her belly.

"I like it."

I closed my eyes and breathed her in, the honeyed taste of her still on my tongue. Her breathing slowed, and she sighed softly. I sensed her body relaxing as she fell asleep in my arms.

But just as I was drifting off, I felt a tiny thump beneath my palm that kept me awake well into the night.

Chapter 18

MABEL

*W*hile Joe was in the living room calling down to the valet for my car, I snuck into his bedroom and left a gift on the bed— the book about becoming a first-time father I'd bought months ago. I'd tucked a little note for him inside the front cover.

He walked me down to the lobby, wheeling my roller bag, and waited with me by the building's front door. He hadn't said much this morning, and I wasn't sure if it was because he was tired or because he was upset about what we'd done. More than anything, I didn't want to hear him apologize. I didn't think I could stand it if he said he was sorry.

"Joe," I said quietly, "I hope you don't feel bad about what happened last night."

He looked confused for a second. "Why would I feel bad about it?"

"I don't know. You just seem so quiet, and I—I don't want you to be sorry, because I'm not."

"I'm not either. I think I'm just…tired," he finished, but I wasn't positive it was the whole truth.

"Did you sleep okay? Sorry if I woke you when I got up to use the bathroom all those times."

"Don't be. That's not what kept me up." He shoved his hands in his coat pockets. "I was just thinking about things."

I nodded, wondering what *things*. "Hockey things?"

"Some hockey things. Yes." He looked down at his feet. "My contract is up next year, and I'm starting to give some thought to what I'll do if it's not renewed."

"You think it won't be renewed? But you're the best player on the team!"

He laughed. "I'm not, although I appreciate the compliment. And it might very well be renewed. Or I could get an offer from another team."

"Another team?" For a moment, I wondered what would happen if he was offered a better contract somewhere else—somewhere far, like Seattle or Anaheim or Vancouver. He'd have to go, wouldn't he?

My face must have given me away because Joe reached out and touched my shoulder. "It's nothing you need to worry about, okay?"

"Okay." This was why, I reminded myself. This was why it was best not to get attached.

"So what's coming up for you?" he asked.

"Well, I have my big fundraising event in two weeks, and—"

"The one about the bootleggers?"

I laughed. "Yes. I'm excited because ticket sales have been very good. Now we just need donors to bring their checkbooks and channel their Christmas spirit a little early."

"Hey, speaking of Christmas, I have a couple days off then," he said. "I'll be up in Michigan. Can I see you?"

"Of course." My heart fluttered. "Just let me know when."

"I'm flying up on Christmas Eve, and I have to go back the twenty-sixth."

"Wow. They don't give you much time."

He shook his head. "Nope. If you're too busy, I understand."

"We usually do Christmas Eve at my dad's house."

"My siblings do Christmas Eve with their in-laws, so my parents always host everyone on Christmas Day."

"I could drive down," I offered. "As long as I wouldn't be intruding."

"Are you kidding? My mother would probably rather see you than me. You're all she asks me about."

I laughed. "She's been so sweet to me. She calls or texts me every week to see how I'm doing."

"See? They'd love to have you there."

"Okay." My car appeared in front of the building. "That's me," I said, wishing the valet had been a little slower.

Joe pulled me in close, wrapping his arms around me. "Drive carefully. And let me know when you get home."

"I will." I stayed right where I was, enjoying the warm, safe cocoon of his embrace. The solid bulk of his chest against my cheek.

"Thanks for coming down here," he said.

"Thanks for inviting me."

He released me slightly and pressed his lips to my forehead. I closed my eyes, willing the lump in my throat to go away. Crying would be pointless and embarrassing.

"I'll see you soon," he said.

Because what other promise could he make?

•••

I drove straight to Ari's house and let myself in the back door. I found her in the kitchen, stirring something in a big pot on the stove. The aroma made my mouth water.

"Hey," she said. "You're back."

"I'm back. Is Dash here?"

"No. He took Wren over to your dad's."

"Good." I shrugged out of my coat and hung it on the back of a chair. "Because I did something I probably shouldn't have. I'm not sorry, and I don't regret it, but I have to tell on myself."

"You slept with Joe."

"I slept with Joe."

"How was it?"

"Fucking magical. Fantastic. Even better than last time."

"Eeek! Sit down and tell me everything before he gets back or Truman wakes up." She set her spoon on the rest.

"What are you cooking?" I asked as I sat at the table. "Smells amazing."

"Pumpkin gnocchi soup. Want to stay for dinner?"

"Yes, please."

She came to the table and dropped breathlessly into the chair next to mine. "Okay, out with it. What happened to your rules?"

"They sort of went out the window after I knocked on his bedroom door last night."

"Oh my God!" She pounded the table. "It's me when I was sixteen sneaking into Dash's room! Except I got rejected, and you didn't."

I laughed. "No, I didn't."

"What made you do it? I mean, other than the fact that he's a hot professional hockey player and you're having his baby."

"Partly I did it because the baby was kicking and I knew he'd want to feel, but mostly because I just really wanted him. And I knew he wasn't going to make a move, because I'd told him in September I didn't think it was a good idea for us to mess around. He was respecting my wishes."

"Right up until you showed up at his bedroom door in your nightie."

"Exactly." I sighed, shaking my head. "God, it was so good. What if it's never like that with anyone else?"

Ari leaned forward, her elbows on the table. "Did you guys talk about anything?"

"Lots of things." I shrugged. "We talk so easily."

"Did you talk about the baby?"

"Constantly. Joe even bought him a book and a little sleeper with dinosaurs on it at the Field Museum gift shop."

"You went to a museum?" She laughed. "That's so you."

"It was his idea," I insisted. "He wants to learn about me."

"God." She sat back and dropped her hands into her lap. "He's making this so difficult. Not that I want your baby's dad to be a jerk, but when you're trying not to fall in love with someone while also carrying his son, it might be easier if he was at least mildly insensitive or annoying."

"I know. But he isn't. He's cute and sweet and generous and charming. And he's also fiercely protective. It's like he has two sides."

"Okay, so what's the problem? He obviously has some feelings for you. You have some for him. You're having a baby together. Why can't you guys give this a real chance?"

"He doesn't want that, Ari. And I'm not sure I do, either. This morning he was telling me that his contract is up next year. Chicago is one thing, but what if he's signed to another team and it's across the country?"

"I don't know. You move?"

"Move away from my family and friends? And be alone half the time because he's on the road?"

"Only during the season," she pointed out.

"That's a lot. And anyway, it hasn't come up." Too agitated to sit still, I abandoned my chair and started to pace. "No. I don't want to move. I want to be here where people love me and I love them. I want to raise my son around his grandparents and aunts and uncles and cousins. Even the Lupos are here!"

"That's true."

"This is the path I chose," I went on. "I knew it would not be easy. I was willing to go it alone, and I'm glad I don't have to. I'm happy he's supportive. But I have to keep my feelings in check."

"How will you manage that?"

"A little distance," I said. "No more staying with him. It's too tempting. And I clearly cannot be trusted to follow the rules."

She laughed. "Nope."

"But you know what? It's out of my system now." I brushed my hands together this way and that. "And his too. We're fine. We're good. We even cuddled."

Her eyebrows shot up. "You cuddled?"

"Yes." I squirmed a little. "I slept in his bed last night."

"I thought he didn't like sharing a bed."

"He made an exception for me." Feeling the heat in my face, I turned away from her and went over to the stove to smell the soup. "What time is dinner?"

"Six."

"Good. That gives me enough time to be back home by eight."

"What's at eight?"

"Hockey game. I promised Joe the baby and I would watch." I could feel her eyes on me.

"Mabel," she said gently. "Do you think it's wise to watch every single one of his games like this? I mean, it's really sweet of you to learn about his sport and root for his team, but is it good for you?"

I stared at the simmering contents of the pot. "It's all we have of him right now," I said. "And I'll be fine."

• • •

Late that night, I was reading in bed when I got a text from Joe.
Hey, thanks for the book.

> You're welcome. I bought it a while ago when you said you were nervous about being a dad.

I'm still nervous. I'll read it. Then you can quiz me.

> Haha, deal. You played a good game tonight.

Not good enough to win.

> How's the shoulder?

It's okay. I've got therapy tomorrow. That should help.

> Can you take some days off to rest it?

If it's necessary, but I hope it won't be. How's our artichoke?

> Fine. Almost a banana.

You're up late.

> I know. But I'm in bed already and I'm going to sleep now.

Good. Take care of yourself.

> You too.

I set my phone on the charger and turned off my lamp. Lying there in the dark, I thought about Joe in his bedroom, taking off his clothes and slipping between the sheets we'd shared last night. Or maybe he'd changed them already?

I rolled onto my side and hugged a pillow close to me, the way he'd held me last night as I'd fallen asleep, his body warm and strong behind me, his hand on my belly.

I missed him.

And I wondered for a moment if what I'd said to Ari about being fine was a lie.

• • •

On the morning of my fundraiser, two dozen red roses were delivered to me at the historical society.

"Oh my!" exclaimed my assistant, a retired nurse named Nell Howard who served on the board and volunteered her time to help me a few days a week. "Look how beautiful! Who sent them?"

"I don't know," I said, hunting in the box for a card. Finding it tucked among the stems, I slipped the card from the envelope.

Knock 'em dead, Montana Swift. Wish I could be there.
Love, Joe

I smiled as my heart boomed inside my chest. *Love, Joe!* Had he specified it should say love? Or had the florist just added it? "They're from a friend."

"A *friend* sent you two dozen roses?" She leaned over and sniffed the scarlet blooms. "That's a good friend."

"He is a good friend." I decided to be honest with Nell. Touching my stomach, I said, "He's the baby's father."

"Ah." Nell nodded and smiled, her expression free of judgment. "The hockey player?"

"Yes," I said, surprised she knew. When I'd told the board

about my pregnancy, I'd simply said I was having a baby and would need some time off next spring. They knew I wasn't married but hadn't asked me for any additional details, and after the next board meeting, they told me I could take up to three months maternity leave. "How did you know he was a hockey player?"

"Oh, my dear, this is a small town. Exciting news travels quickly." She looked worried for a moment. "Was it supposed to be a secret?"

"Not necessarily," I said. "I just haven't talked much about it. I guess I was a little worried what people might think."

She patted my arm. "It's your life. You get to choose how you live it."

"The baby was a surprise," I admitted. "But Joe has been really supportive. We won't look like a regular family, but we're going to make it work."

"Of course you are! And what does a 'regular family' look like anyway?" She waved a hand in the air. "Family is whatever you say it is, whether you share blood or a last name or even just love. What matters is that you're there for each other and that baby."

I teared up—I couldn't help it. "Thank you," I said, laughing as I wiped beneath my eyes. "Sorry about the tears. I'm so emotional lately."

"You should be emotional! You're having a *baby*." She smiled and gestured toward the roses. "With someone who cares deeply about you—enough to remember the important days in your life and send flowers."

"He's very thoughtful," I said.

And sending roses wasn't all he did for me that day. That night at the event, I was told that a nice donation had come in from an out-of-town donor who wanted to remain anonymous.

"Really?" I asked the board treasurer, who'd received the email that afternoon. "You have no idea who it is?"

"Well," she said, her eyes sparkling a little, "I do, but I'm ethically bound to keep the name concealed. All I was given permission to say was that it was someone who sat next to you on a recent flight and was very impressed with your passion for the historical society. The donation was made in your name."

For the second time that day, Joe caused my eyes to mist over from hundreds of miles away. "I believe I remember this person," I said, unable to keep from smiling.

She grinned. "You must have made quite an impression."

• • •

I got home around eleven and called him right away. It went straight to voicemail, which I was expecting, since I knew he'd still be at the game.

"Joe Lupo! What are you trying to do to me? I've been an emotional wreck all day—first the roses and then the donation! It's all too much. I don't know how to thank you, but please know how grateful I am." I sighed. "Anyway, I hope you won tonight. Talk to you soon."

I hit end and lowered myself onto the couch, slipping off my flats. I'd started the evening in heels but very quickly realized they were not comfortable or practical at twenty-two weeks pregnant. Cleo came and curled around my ankles, looking for attention. Absentmindedly, I reached down to pet her. The roses from Joe were in a vase on the coffee table, their petals vibrant and velvety, their scent soft and sweet. I leaned a little closer and inhaled.

Love, Joe.

He was so damn sweet. Rarely did a day pass without at least a text checking in with me, asking how I was feeling, wondering if there was anything I needed.

Yes, you, I'd think.

"Nope, I'm good," I'd say.

And it wasn't a lie. I *was* good. I had everything I needed—my health, a house, a job, my cat, my family and friends, financial security. What purpose would it serve to admit to Joe that sometimes at night I got lonely and scared and wished he were here to hold me?

No sense in going down a road that you knew came to a dead end.

Inside me, the baby kicked.

"Hey, Nicky. You're up late too, huh?" I'd taken to using that name, even though we hadn't settled the matter for sure. It just seemed to suit the little guy. "Should we have a snack?"

I'd been so busy at the event that I hadn't eaten much. Rising from the couch, I wandered into the kitchen and opened the fridge. As soon as I saw the jar of pickles, I wanted one desperately.

As I was unscrewing the top, my phone buzzed. Joe was FaceTiming me. Excited, I accepted and his face filled my screen. "Hey!"

"Hey, cupcake." He leaned back against his couch, a grin on his face. His hair appeared damp and messy. "You look nice."

"Thanks." I looked down at the navy maternity cocktail dress I wore. "There were lots of people dressed in 1920s costumes—fringed dresses and top hats and feather boas. I looked boring in comparison."

"You look beautiful. You got your surprise?"

"I got two of them!" Turning around, I rested my hips against the counter. "Thank you! You did not have to do either of those things. But you made my day—twice."

"How did everything go tonight?"

"It was a great success. The board was happy, the guests had fun, and we raised good money. Thank you again for the generous donation, by the way."

"No problem. It wasn't a big deal."

"It was to me. You know, for a guy who thinks he doesn't have a very good memory, you're very good at recalling things I say."

"Well, maybe that's the secret. If you say it, I'll remember it."

Smiling, I reached into the pickle jar and pulled out a spear. "Nicky wanted a midnight snack."

He laughed. "Yeah? How is the little papaya?"

"Twenty-two weeks strong and kicking." I took a bite.

"Is he moving around more?"

"Definitely. He's feisty." I took another bite. "You want to say hi?"

"Sure."

"Okay, I'm putting you down by him." I lowered the phone toward my belly. "Go ahead."

"Hey, buddy. I think about you all the time and can't wait to meet you. Be good for your mom and keep growing big and strong."

I brought the phone up again. "He definitely heard you. He's throwing some good punches."

Joe's smile lit up my screen and my heart. "How are you feeling?"

"Tired tonight, but I've had good energy this month. The second trimester has been great for me."

"Yeah, my book said that the second trimester is the best for a lot of women."

I smiled. "You're reading the book?"

"Yes. This afternoon I read that the baby is like one pound now and he can hear music and sirens and dogs barking. And I read that it's very important for you to be drinking enough water and getting enough rest."

"I am," I said. "I promise. Tonight's a late night, but I'm going to sleep in tomorrow."

"The book also said sleeping might be hard."

"So far, so good," I said, propping the phone against the coffeemaker so I could put the lid back on the pickle jar and put it away. "I'm still able to get comfortable at night. But I'm sure that will change."

"It said to make sure you're not doing anything too strenuous from here on out."

"I'm not. I still take my walks outside, since we don't have snow yet, but once that happens, I'll go to the rec center and use the treadmill." I picked up my phone and headed out of the kitchen. "My brothers are going to help me take the office furniture out of the spare room and get it painted after the holidays."

Joe grimaced. "I'm sorry I can't be there to do it."

"It's fine." I sat down on the couch. "You've got games to win so you can get to the playoffs. How was tonight?"

"Okay. We won, but my shoulder was giving me trouble so I was out for the third period."

"Oh no! It was that bad?"

"Yeah. I think I'm out for the next game too."

I frowned. "Will you get physical therapy or anything?"

"Yes. I'll know more after I talk to the orthopod tomorrow."

"Let me know what you hear."

"I'm looking forward to a few days off for the holiday. Are you still planning to come down on Christmas Day?"

"Yes!" I placed a hand on my stomach. "You'll hardly recognize me. I'm much bigger than I was at Thanksgiving."

He laughed. "It's only been a couple weeks."

"I know, but I feel like I really ballooned since then."

"I can't wait to see you."

My entire body tingled, right down to my toes. "I'm excited to see you too."

In the silence that followed, I wanted to tell him I missed him, but couldn't bring myself to say the words.

Instead I said, "Well, I should probably go to bed. It was a long day."

"Get some rest," he told me. "Good night."

"Night."

We hung up, and I went into my bedroom, sat at the foot of my bed, and flopped onto my back.

Love, Joe.

I sighed heavily. Dreamily.

Cleo, who'd followed me, hopped up onto the mattress and meowed.

"What?" I asked, as if she'd accused me of something.

Meow.

"I'm just emotional."

Meow.

"I don't really love him. Not like that."

Meow.

"I'm not allowed to love him like that, Cleo." I closed my eyes and swallowed hard. "Don't let me."

Chapter 19

JOE

I flew out of Chicago early on December twenty-fourth.

After takeoff, there was some turbulence due to a cold front, and I thought of Mabel and the day we met. The things she'd confessed as the plane shuddered and rolled. The look on her face when she realized she wasn't going to die. The surprise of seeing her again the following night. The fun we'd had in my hotel room.

The insane turn my life had taken because of it.

Reaching into my bag beneath the seat in front of me, I took out the book she'd left for me. It was called *From Dude to Dad: A Pregnancy Survival Guide*, and it was aimed at guys like me who were generally clueless but wanted to be good partners and fathers. Each week of pregnancy had its own chapter. I couldn't say I'd read every page, but I'd skimmed the beginning and I'd read the last three chapters word for word. It was insane, the things happening inside her.

How the hell did she even sleep with all the kicking and jabbing going on in her uterus?

One time I'd skipped ahead to the birth stuff, just out of curiosity, but I felt a panic attack coming on while I read, so I'd closed the book and didn't pick it up for a few days. It was probably better to work up to that day gradually.

The note she'd slipped inside the cover fell into my lap, and I unfolded the page and read it again.

> *Joe,*
>
> *Thank you very much for inviting me down for the weekend, and for being my friend through all this. It means a lot to have you by my side. I know you will be an amazing dad.*
>
> *Mabel xoxo*

It kind of blew my mind, the faith she had in me. From the very beginning, she'd been convinced I would be good at this. Sometimes I wondered if she was just saying that or if she honestly believed it. I wasn't sure what I'd ever done to earn that kind of trust from her, except deliver on the promise that I could put the puck in the net.

Either way, I wanted to live up to those words. For the baby, of course, but also for her.

For the first time in my life, I wanted to be great at something besides hockey.

I wanted to make her happy.

Every day, I tried to think of little things I could do for her to let her know I was thinking about her and how cool I thought she was. How beautiful and smart and kind and funny. How easy it was to be with her.

In my bags were Christmas gifts for her that were definitely over the top—not to mention the gift I was having delivered to her house. But I hadn't been able to help myself, and it wasn't like I couldn't afford them.

I wasn't sure what it all meant, this crazy need to please her, and frankly, it scared me. For so long, I'd wanted only *one thing*. It was so all-consuming, there hadn't been room in my head or my heart or my fucking schedule for anything else. And I'd been fine with that. I'd liked it. I'd liked the guy I was and the life I lived.

I didn't know this new guy all that well. He was foreign to me, with his meandering daydreams and possessive feelings and weird visions of the future that didn't involve the game. Sometimes I even felt angry with him and wished he would just leave me alone.

But he wouldn't give up.

• • •

My parents' home looked and smelled the same as it always did at the holidays, and the familiarity was comforting.

The huge tree in the living room was hung with colored lights and way too many ornaments because my mother was sentimental and never threw anything away. Boughs of greenery and strings of white lights decked the fireplace mantel, the banister going upstairs, and the exterior of the house. The scent of gingerbread lingered from yesterday, when my parents had all their grandkids over to bake and decorate cookies.

I spent the early part of the day catching up with my parents, wrapping the gifts I'd brought with me, and playing with my nephew Hudson, whom Paul brought over after his nap. He was walking really well now, loved to climb and explore, and he was even talking a little bit.

"What do you think? You ready for this?" my brother asked, preventing Hudson yet again from getting his hands on a string of lights around the tree. He'd almost pulled it over twice.

"If you can do it, I can do it." I was lying on my side on the floor, head propped in my hand.

He smirked. "How's the pregnancy going?"

"Good. Mabel saw the doctor a couple days ago, and everything is fine."

He nodded, moving a fragile ornament higher on the tree. "Baby kicking a lot?"

"Yeah. I got to feel it when she was in Chicago. So crazy." I recalled the firm, warm feel of her belly under my palm and experienced a tightening in my chest. "Can I ask you a question?"

"Sure. No, Hudson. That's not for you." Paul took a wrapped present and put it out of reach. "Here's one for you."

Hudson happily beat the wrapped gift box like a drum with his fists.

"Hope there's nothing breakable in there," my brother muttered. "Sorry, what was the question?"

"When did you know…about Alison? Or maybe *how* did you know?"

He glanced at me. "You mean, how did I know I wanted to marry her?"

"Yeah. Or just, like, how you felt about her."

He exhaled. "I feel like it happened gradually, but also like it hit me all at once. I'd always liked her, but one day I looked at her, and I wanted a backyard."

"A what?"

"A backyard—with a lawn and a deck and a grill where I'd stand flipping burgers while my kids hung off a playscape like monkeys. I wanted that life—and I wanted it with her."

Rolling onto my back on the rug, I stared at the ceiling.

"I take it your question means you have feelings for Mabel?"

I swallowed. "I do, I just...don't know what they are. Or what to do with them."

"Is dating her out of the question?"

"Kind of. From the beginning, we said we'd just be friends."

"Well, that's kind of what you do when you're a mature, single adult with feelings for another mature, single adult. You date."

"I know. But how are we supposed to date when she lives all the way up here and I'm in Chicago or on the road? And who knows where I'll be next year?"

"That's tough." He was silent for a moment. "I guess you just have to decide how serious your feelings are."

"I have no idea. For all I know, I could be inventing these feelings. We've only been together in person a handful of times. The rest of it has been long-distance. I mean, maybe I'm idealizing her because we're not together all the time."

"What's it like when you're together?"

"Easy," I said. "I don't know how else to describe it. It's just fucking easy."

Hudson waddled over to me and sat on my chest. Laughing, I grabbed him and lifted him high above me like an airplane. He laughed and kicked and squealed with delight.

"Do we ever get to meet her?" Paul asked.

"Yes." I set Hudson down and sat up. "She's actually driving down here in the morning. I invited her to come for Christmas dinner."

"Tell her to be careful. We're supposed to get a good amount of snow tomorrow."

I frowned. "I didn't know that. When?"

"I think it's going to start late tonight. Alison is all excited about a white Christmas. Hudson will be able to make a snowman this year. Right, buddy? No, no, don't touch that cord." Paul went racing across the room and swept his toddler away from a power strip. "Jesus. I better get him out of here. We'll see you tomorrow."

Jumping to my feet, I went into the kitchen to find my phone and check the weather. Sure enough, a winter storm was heading our way. After saying goodbye to my brother and nephew, I went up to my bedroom and made a quick phone call.

"Hello?"

"Hey, Bill, sorry to call you on Christmas Eve. But I wondered if I might make a last-minute change to the delivery schedule."

"So not tonight?"

"No. Would you mind delivering it on the twenty-sixth instead? Exact same plan, just two days later."

"No problem. In fact, that's even easier. What time?"

I thought for a moment. "Would morning work?"

"I can have it there by nine a.m."

"Perfect. Thanks, Bill. I appreciate this."

"No problem. Anything for an old teammate! Merry Christmas, Joe."

"Merry Christmas." Then I called Mabel.

"Hey! You made it home," she said when she picked up.

"I did. Flight was a little bumpy. I thought of you."

"Did the person next to you spew a bunch of hideously embarrassing things?"

"No. He slept the whole time."

"Lucky you."

"Listen, I heard it's supposed to snow tomorrow. I checked the weather and it looks like the storm is going to hit us after midnight, which might make driving shitty in the morning."

"Yeah, I saw that too. But it's okay. Austin checked my tires recently and said they were good enough for the winter. I'll go slow."

"I'm coming to get you."

"Joe, you don't have to do that."

"You heard what I said."

She clucked her tongue. "Okay, *Dad*."

That made me smile. "How's your Christmas Eve?"

"Good! Just about to leave to go over to my father's. How's yours?"

"Good. I wrapped presents, played with my nephew Hudson, and realized for the first time how hazardous a Christmas tree is for toddlers."

She laughed. "It is. Are you spending tonight at home?"

"No, my mom and dad and I are going to Abelard Vineyards."

"Oh, I've been there! It's beautiful. What's happening there?"

"It's owned by Gianni's in-laws, the Fourniers. My mom and Mia Fournier have been best friends for like a hundred years—she already went over there to help cook. But my dad must be making something to bring, too, because I hear him singing in the kitchen, and I smell onion and garlic."

"Mmmm. What's he making?"

"Probably something with fish, since that's traditional for Italians on Christmas Eve. What does your family do?"

"The usual American thing—ham and potatoes and green bean casserole. No one in my family is a particularly great cook, but it will be fun just being all together. The kids will open their gifts, which is always a riot to watch." She paused. "It's kind of crazy to think about next Christmas, isn't it? The baby will be here."

"I've been doing it all day," I confessed.

Another moment of silence passed. Was she wondering where we would be? What we would be to each other?

"I better get going," she said. "Have fun tonight."

"You too. Tell your family I said Merry Christmas."

"I will."

"I'll be in touch in the morning."

"Okay."

We hung up, and I wandered downstairs toward the aroma coming from the kitchen. My dad glanced up from his cutting board on the kitchen island, where he was slicing Roma tomatoes. "Hey."

"Hey." I slid onto a counter stool. "What are you making?"

"Baccalà." He poured the tomatoes into a large cast iron skillet on the stove, then added chunks of cod and a small dish of olives. Finally, he squeezed two lemon halves over the simmering skillet before adding the lemon halves too.

My mouth watered. "Smells good."

"Thanks. Hey, open the oven for me, will you?"

I did as he asked, watching as he slid the skillet inside and closed the door. After setting a timer, he looked at me. "So what's up?"

"Nothing."

He cocked one eyebrow. "Try again."

"Really, it's nothing." I rubbed my triceps.

"Shoulder bothering you?"

"A little."

"Any word on the contract?"

"Not yet. Probably February or March."

"Think Chicago will renew?" He began to clean up after himself.

"I hope so."

He turned the faucet on and began handwashing the cutting board and knives. "The guy who owns the gym I go to, Bayside Sports, told me he's thinking of buying the old Blue Lake Arena, where you used to skate."

"Oh yeah?" I smiled, a thousand happy childhood memories

on the ice running through my mind. "That old place is still standing?"

"Barcly. It needs renovation. For a while, the rumor was that a minor league team was going to play out of there, but that deal fell through. They ended up in Ohio." He reached for a clean towel and carefully dried a knife. "Now there's talk of tearing it down. But Tyler Shaw—the guy who owns Bayside—thought maybe it would make a good training complex."

"For kids? Like camps and stuff?"

"Yeah. Teams, groups, one-on-one. Whatever. He doesn't know a ton about hockey training because he was a baseball player, but he knows I have a son who plays professionally and grew up playing around here, so he asked what I thought." He shrugged, setting the knife aside. "But I don't really know what that kind of program should look like, either."

"I know exactly what it should look like. I can talk to him," I said.

"I didn't want to volunteer you without asking."

"It's fine. You can give him my number."

"He'll probably try to hire you to run it," my dad said with a grin.

I shook my head. "I'm not ready to retire yet."

My dad picked up another knife and began to dry it. "How are things with Mabel?"

"Fine. I decided I'm gonna go pick her up tomorrow. Weather is supposed to be bad, and I don't want her driving in the snow."

He nodded. "Mom said she went down to visit you in Chicago."

"She did. We had a good time."

I could tell he had questions, but he kept his mouth shut.

"It's complicated, okay?" I blurted.

"I didn't say anything," he said, focusing on his task.

"Well, I can feel you over there judging me."

"Judging you for what?"

I frowned, rubbing my temples with a thumb and forefinger. "I don't know. Never mind."

"I'm here if you need to talk about anything."

"There's nothing to talk about." I got off the stool. "What time are we leaving?"

"Mom says to be there by five-thirty."

"Okay," I said, heading out of the kitchen. "I'm going to get dressed."

But when I got back up to my room, instead of pulling out my dress clothes, I lay down on the twin bed closest to the window. It was the same bed I'd slept in as a kid, the bed where I'd dreamed of playing professional hockey, where the only thing that mattered was being the best. Maybe I thought being back in that place would bring back those feelings.

But it didn't. Instead I lay there thinking about Mabel, counting the hours until I'd see her tomorrow and imagining her face when she got her presents. She'd probably say she couldn't accept them, but I'd convince her.

Maybe after I drove her back to Cherry Tree Harbor, I could stay the night with her. I wouldn't really have a reason, since my flight back to Chicago on the twenty-sixth wasn't until the afternoon. I just wanted more time with her. I'd sleep on the couch. The floor. A nearby hotel. Whatever she wanted.

I didn't even know what the fuck to call these feelings for her that churned and billowed and bruised me on the inside, but they refused to let up.

I just wanted to be with her.

Chapter 20

MABEL

*W*hen I woke up Christmas morning, my room was suffused with a soft light that I knew meant one thing—the world outside was white.

Tossing the covers aside, I went over to the window, shivering a little at the cold. When I peeked between the blinds, I gasped at the breathtaking winter wonderland on the other side of the glass—everything was covered with a blanket of snow, and it was still falling.

Climbing back into bed, I snuggled under the blankets again and reached for my phone. It was barely nine, and already there was a text message from Joe.

You awake? I'm coming to get you.

He'd sent it about five minutes earlier, so I quickly called him. "Don't try to argue with me," he said instead of hello.

I laughed. "Merry Christmas to you too."

"Sorry. Merry Christmas. But don't you dare get behind the wheel. Have you looked outside?"

"I have. But now I'm back in bed."

"Good. Stay there. I'm leaving soon."

"Joe, if it's too much to drive all the way up here, you don't have to."

"It's not too much."

"I don't want to take you away from your family on Christmas."

"You're part of this family now too. And besides, I want to see you. I have presents for you."

I smiled, sinking deeper into my pillow—and my feelings. "Fine."

He laughed. "Was it the presents that did it?"

"Maybe." I giggled. "What time will you get here?"

"I'm not sure how bad the roads will be, but I'm hoping by noon at the latest."

"I'll be ready."

After we hung up, I stayed in bed for a little while longer. The baby was moving around a little, and I rubbed my belly under the covers. "Are you excited to see your daddy? I am too."

Ari had asked me yesterday how I was feeling about seeing him.

"Fine," I'd said, my heart quickening. "Good. It will be great to see him."

"Things are still platonic?"

"Yes. Totally."

She gave me a look that said she obviously didn't believe me.

"What, you think I'm going to tear his clothes off and jump his bones under the mistletoe with his parents in the room?"

"No," she said, "I just think it might not be as easy as you think to keep your hands to yourself."

"Please. I'm five months pregnant, Ari. He's going to look at me and see someone's mother."

She snorted. "I doubt it. Your body looks amazing with all those new curves."

I did like the new curves. My breasts had never been so round and full, and the knit dress I was planning to wear definitely clung to my new shape. "Thank you, but we both agreed Chicago was a one-time thing."

"That might be true," she said, "but you've got a weak spot for this man. He gets to you. And you get to him."

I narrowed my eyes, recognizing a certain look on her face. "What do you know?"

"Nothing." She took a sip of her wine. "It's just a hunch. Same as it was the night of the wedding, and we know what happened then."

I shook my head. "We are not the same people we were that night. Nothing is going to happen."

But when I saw him pull up in front of my house and get out of a black pickup, my resolve faltered. God, he was hot. And the way he hurried up the snow-covered walk like he couldn't wait to see me was adorable. By the time he knocked on the front door, my heart was about to burst out of my chest.

I yanked the door open, and he swept in on a cold breeze, snow flurries dusting his dark hair. "Hi!"

He stomped the snow from his leather dress boots and shut the door behind him. His eyes popped when he saw me. "Hi. Wow, you weren't kidding when you said you've grown since Thanksgiving."

"I know." Laughing, I patted my rounded belly.

"You look great." He opened his arms and I went into them, my eyes closing as I rested my cheek on the scratchy, damp wool of his coat. He didn't let go right away, and neither did I.

Finally, Cleo meowed from behind me, and we both laughed. "Hi to you too, Cleo." Joe crouched down and gave her some attention.

"I'm ready," I said. "Just let me grab my bag."

"Hang on, I want to shovel the front walk first."

"Joe, don't worry about it. It's still coming down, isn't it?"

"Not really. Just some light stuff. The heavy snow is done. I brought a shovel from home."

"But what about your shoulder?"

"It's fine."

I looked at his feet. "And you're wearing leather boots."

"Stop being difficult. Just stay inside a few minutes, okay? Think of it as a Christmas present for me."

Sighing, I gave in. "Okay."

Warmth coated my insides like melted chocolate as I watched Joe shovel the walk from the front window. After he replaced the shovel in the truck bed, he came back up to the house to collect me. I let him in, tugged on my boots, and opened the hall closet door to grab my new maternity coat.

"Let me," he said, taking it from my hands and holding it open for me. "Is this new?"

"Yes." I slipped my arms in and buttoned it up. "It was a gift from Julia and my dad. I opened it last night."

He frowned. "I have something for you too, but I was so concerned about the drive, I left home without it."

"It's okay. We can open gifts later." I smiled. "I have something for you too."

He held my arm as we walked through the lightly falling snow. When he opened the passenger door for me, I laughed. "Remember the night of the wedding when you gave me a piggyback ride out to the car?"

After helping me into the passenger seat, he said, "I remember everything about that night." He closed the door and went around to the driver's side while I clenched my thighs together and tried not to recall his body moving over mine.

And I realized Ari was right. This man *got* to me.

• • •

"I was thinking, we should probably talk about the birth day," I said on the drive down to the Lupos' house.

Joe winced a little. "Yeah, I haven't exactly gotten to that section of the book yet. I've been scared."

"Scared of what?"

"*Knowing* things. Right now I only suspect them."

I laughed. "It's up to you what you want to know, but you definitely don't have to *see* anything you don't want to see. I don't expect you to be in the room."

He glanced at me. "You don't want me there when you have him?"

"Well, I wasn't sure it would even be possible. I mean, I don't know exactly when it will be. What if you're in the middle of a game when I go into labor?"

"I'm going to give you the number of someone who can get word to me right away—one of the manager's assistants. And I'll get there as quickly as I can."

"Okay. First labors take a long time, so unless you're super far away, you'll probably make it." I hesitated. "But I don't expect you to abandon a game to get there. What if it's a must-win for the playoffs or something?"

"Let's not jinx anything, okay? Right now we're playing well, and that's what we need to keep doing. And I want to be there when the baby is born."

"Like, in the room?" I asked tentatively. "Or out in the hall?"

"In the room. If it's okay with you."

"It's okay with me," I said, growing nervous about it. I honestly hadn't thought he'd want to watch the delivery. "But I have to warn you—it's not going to be pretty."

"I understand."

I twisted my hands together above my belly. "Like I almost wish you didn't want to be in there so your memories of my body would be more aesthetically pleasing."

"Hey." He reached over and took my left hand, giving it a squeeze. "Nothing can touch those memories. And for the rest of my life, I will be grateful for what your body is doing. I want to be there for you."

With my free hand, I unbuttoned my coat. Despite the winter weather, I was starting to overheat.

He kept my other hand in his the whole ride.

• • •

When we entered the Lupos' house, my mouth watered immediately. "God, it smells good in here!"

"My parents have been cooking and baking for days," Joe said, closing the door behind us. "Let me take your coat, and I'll hang it up."

I shrugged out of my coat and brushed snow off my knee-high boots. As I straightened up again, Coco came into the front hall.

"Mabel! You look gorgeous!" She enveloped me in a tight hug. "That burgundy color is stunning on you. And look at that little belly!" She reached out her hands and then pulled them back, her expression frightened. "Sorry! I should ask first."

I laughed. "It's okay. Go ahead."

She placed her palms on my stomach. "Is he moving?"

"Not right now, but I'll let you know when he does. He's been quiet on the car ride."

Nick entered the front hallway. "Mabel, it's great to see you." He took both hands and kissed my cheek. "You look wonderful."

"Thank you." Reaching for my bag, I pulled out a gift-wrapped package and handed it to Coco. Inside was a scented candle and soft throw blanket from one of my favorite Cherry Tree Harbor boutiques. "Merry Christmas. And thank you very much for having me today."

"Of course!" Her smile was bright. "We're so happy you were able to come. The food is in the dining room and it's all-day buffet. There are all kinds of things, but if your appetite is funny and there's nothing there that looks good to you, let me know and we'll make you something else."

"I'm sure everything will look good to me. My stomach is growling just from the smell!"

She squeezed my hand. "I'm just so happy you're here. Joey, why are you just standing there? Get her something to drink."

"I will, Mom." He looked at me, and now that he had his coat off, I saw how the cornflower blue dress shirt he wore matched his eyes. "What would you like?"

"Water is good," I said, desperately thirsty all of a sudden. "Thank you."

We moved into the dining room, where a feast was laid out on the long rectangular table, which was covered with a snowy white tablecloth. I'd never seen such a gorgeous display. There were platters and bowls and tiered stands, all overflowing with things that made my mouth water. A wooden board laden with cured meats and cheeses and olives. A basket of crusty white bread. Bowls heaped with pasta. A tureen full of soup. A roasted chicken and a beef tenderloin. Vegetables like brussels sprouts, roasted fingerling potatoes, and sautéed spinach.

"My goodness," I said, my eyes wide. "I don't even know where to start."

"Just make sure you leave room for dessert," Joe said. "The sweet stuff is in the kitchen. You'll definitely want to try the cannoli."

"I always have room for dessert. You're going to need a bulldozer to get me home." I began piling a plate with as many things as I could fit.

Joe returned with a bottle of water and laughed. "You can have seconds, you know. You get more than one trip."

"Hush." I took the water from him. "Make a plate and show me where to sit."

After piling his plate even higher than mine, he led me into a high-ceilinged family room, where his siblings and their families were spread out on couches or at a round table and chairs. In the large stone fireplace, flames jumped and crackled. Holiday music played softly, and a tall Christmas tree dominated one end of the room, hung with all kinds of ornaments and strung with lights that gave the room a festive glow. Three older kids sat on the floor near the tree organizing gifts into piles by names, while a toddler did his best to "help."

One couple sat at the table—it had to be Joe's older brother, Gianni, and his wife, Ellie—and I realized I'd seen them before, probably at Dash and Ari's wedding. Two more sat on the couches. I recognized Joe's twin, Paul, from the wedding, and the blonde next to him must be his wife, Alison. The toddler, I knew, belonged to them. On the other end of the L-shaped sectional was a woman with Coco's coloring holding a baby just a few months old, and seated next to her was a blond guy with a beard. Francesca and Grant, I assumed, and their new baby girl, Isla.

"Everybody, this is Mabel," Joe announced.

Joe's family all smiled and nodded or said hello, and Ellie gestured toward the two empty chairs at the table. "Nice to meet you," she said. "Would you like to sit here?"

"Sure, thank you." I walked over and set down my plate, and Joe followed.

As I ate—the food was incredible, and I not only went back for seconds but thirds, plus dessert—I chatted with Ellie about the pregnancy, her kids, the snowstorm, and being a working mom. Later we moved over to the couches and watched all the kids tear the bows and wrapping paper off their presents, shouting gleefully about what they'd gotten, holding the longed-for gifts over their heads, or jumping up and down with excitement.

Then Gianni and Ellie's two older kids played elves and brought the adults any gifts with their names on the tags. "This big one says, 'To Mabel, from Nick and Coco,'" read Joe's niece Claudia. Smiling, she carried the giant gift bag over to me with both arms and set it at my feet.

Inside the bag was a beautiful, soft white fleece robe, a pair of matching slippers, and a gift card for a manicure and pedicure at a Cherry Tree Harbor salon. "Oh my goodness, this is so sweet of you." I touched my heart and looked at Joe's parents, who were seated together at the hearth. "Thank you for thinking of me."

"Of course," said Coco. "Every expectant mama needs a little pampering."

When all the gifts had been opened, Joe and Gianni got down on the floor to help free Barbies and action figures from their plastic packaging and assemble toys. Ellie came to sit by me, a glass of red wine in her hand. "Can I get you anything?" she asked.

"No, thank you."

"So it's not really my business," Ellie said quietly, "and you don't have to answer this, but is there anything happening with you and Joe?"

I watched him putting together some kind of Barbie Dream House for his little niece Gabrielle and smiled wistfully. "You know what? I don't even know how to answer that question."

She laughed softly and sipped her red wine. "No?"

"No. I mean, originally, there wasn't—not after the initial night that got us into this situation." I patted my stomach. "We sort of agreed that was best. I didn't want to complicate things."

"Totally get it," Ellie said.

"We were never together," I went on. "And in fact, before we even fooled around, he told me he'd just gotten out of a relationship and didn't want to get into another one. He said he just wanted to focus on his career and wasn't a good boyfriend."

Ellie exhaled and took another sip from her glass. "I don't know if that's true or not. In my opinion—and of course, I wasn't there or anything, but I did meet the ex-girlfriend a couple times—he just didn't care about the relationship all that much. He always made it seem like it was casual, but I think she wanted more."

"That could be." I watched as Joe said something that made the little girl laugh. My heart thumped hard, and I swallowed. "I'm trying not to want more."

She looked at me. "But you do?"

"I mean, it's hard not to. Joe took the news of this pregnancy really well, all things considered. He's been nothing but supportive, and he's so generous. He checks in with me all the time. He sends me thoughtful gifts. He wants to know everything about the baby and how I'm feeling. Not to mention…" I sighed as my eyes traveled over his wide shoulders and muscular legs. "He's really hot."

She laughed. "Seriously, it is criminal how hot the Lupo brothers grew up. They were such devils as boys. If you'd have told me I'd end up with one, I'd have screamed and wondered what I possibly did to deserve such a hideous fate."

I laughed too, because I could imagine it perfectly. "That bad, huh?"

"Awful." She shook her head. "But they were raised right. Nick and Coco are the best."

"They have been nothing but wonderful to me."

"And Joe is really great with our kids. He'll be a good dad."

"I think so too." I smiled as he let Gabrielle brush his hair with a tiny Barbie brush.

"So is there really nothing between you two?" Ellie sounded surprised as she looked back and forth between Joe and me.

"I wouldn't say *nothing*," I allowed. "Despite our best intentions, we broke the rules when I visited him after Thanksgiving. But I keep telling myself that was a one-time thing, and it can't happen again."

"Why not?"

"Because I'm scared," I admitted, cradling my belly with both hands. "I don't want to end up pining for him, living for the days he passes through town to see his son. I know what his career means to him, and I'd never ask him to give it up."

"Can't he have both?" she wondered. "Plenty of pro athletes have families."

"He hasn't led me to believe he's interested in that. He'll be a good father, I know he will, but I think he always saw having a family as something in the hazy distance, something he'd get around to after he was done playing. Right now, hockey is still the love of his life." I took a breath. "And I want to be with someone who sees *me* that way."

At that moment, Joe looked up and smiled at me. *You okay?*

he mouthed. I nodded and smiled back, yearning for him with my whole heart.

Next to me, Ellie sighed. "Hockey might be the love of his life, but I'll tell you something. I've known Joey Lupo since the day he was born, and I have never seen him look at anyone the way he looks at you."

I could feel the heat creeping into my cheeks as Coco approached and sat on the other side of me.

She smiled warmly and patted my leg. "How are you doing, Mabel? Did you get enough to eat? Can I get you something warm to drink? Some tea?"

Laughing gently, I shook my head. "I'm fine. I ate so much I could burst. Everything was delicious." Then I noticed the ring she wore on her left hand—an emerald-cut diamond in an art deco setting on a platinum band. "What a beautiful ring!"

"Oh, thank you. My wedding ring."

"The design is such a lovely combination of modern and vintage."

She smiled happily. "You have a good eye. It's actually a replica of a ring from Nick's family history. His great-grandfather gave it to his great-grandmother back in the twenties."

"Oh! I think Joe has mentioned them before. The bootleggers?"

Coco laughed in surprise. "As a matter of fact, yes."

"I love that story—I love family history."

"I do too," she said. "I was a history major in college."

I warmed even more toward her. "Coco, thank you so much for having me here tonight. Your family is so wonderful, and your house is so warm and inviting. I appreciate being included."

"Of course! You're family now too, so it wouldn't have been complete without you."

For a second, I wondered what would happen in the future

if Joe and I each went on to be with other people—we'd have to trade holidays with our son. I wouldn't be family here anymore. The thought was so horrible it turned my stomach.

She took my hand and squeezed it, glancing at her son, who was now playing Barbies with his niece. "Is Joey treating you right?"

Pushing the unpleasant thought aside, I smiled at the way everyone in his family still called him Joey, like he was a little boy. "Yes. He is." Suddenly, the baby kicked. "Ooh! He's moving!"

Coco gasped. "Can I?" she asked, a hand hovering over my belly.

I nodded. "Of course. It's right…" I placed her hand where I'd felt it. In just a few seconds, he kicked again.

"I felt it!" She laughed. "He's strong!"

Joe popped to his feet and came over. "He's moving?"

"Yes."

"Sit here, Joey." Ellie rose to her feet. "I'm going to get another glass of wine." She smiled at me before heading for the kitchen. "Nice chatting with you, Mabel."

"You too," I said as Joe dropped down next to me.

"Mom, you're taking up all the room," he complained, trying to find space for his wide palms on my stomach.

Coco sighed. "Fine, I'll let you. It was over here," she said, removing her hands. "On the side."

Joe slid his palms over to where hers had been, and a moment later, the baby gave them a thump. He grinned. "I felt it!"

I laughed. "He's all hopped up on sugar. I ate so much dessert, he'll probably be awake all night."

At that moment, Nick moved to the front of the fireplace and stood with a glass of wine in his hand. "Since we're all here, I'd like to make a toast."

The adults in the room quieted, and someone turned down the music. The younger kids continued to make noise, but Gianni shushed them.

Joe sat back, placing his arm along the back of the couch above my shoulders.

"Days like today make me feel so grateful for all that I have," Nick said, "especially this house, the love that makes it a home, and this family. Four incredible children, the amazing partners they've chosen, the five gorgeous grandkids they've given us, and those yet to come." He looked over at me and smiled before his eyes moved to his wife. "And every day, I am thankful to wake up next to the most beautiful woman in the world. I don't know how I convinced her to choose me, but she did, and I'll never take it for granted."

"It was the tattoo," Coco said, and everyone laughed.

I wondered which tattoo, since he had so many.

Chuckling, Nick raised his glass. "To family!"

"To family!" The voices in the room echoed his sentiment, and those with drinks lifted them up.

I smiled but didn't move, enjoying the way my left side was nestled beneath Joe's arm.

$$\cdots$$

Around five o'clock, Joe asked me if I was ready to go home.

"Sure," I said. "I just need to use the bathroom first."

"No rush. I'm going to warm up the car."

He helped me up from the couch and went to find his keys while I made my way to the first floor bathroom. The door was open, but I heard girls' voices coming from inside. As I got closer I realized it was Claudia and Gabrielle.

"Today I want to go for a natural look," Claudia was saying. "Not like too bronzed, but more like sun-kissed, you know?"

"I'm gonna use this pink blush," said Gabrielle.

When I reached the doorway, I discovered them standing in front of the mirror applying the makeup they'd gotten for Christmas and narrating the process, as if they were giving a tutorial. I hid a smile at the garish amount of blush on their cheeks, their thick black eyebrows, and the extreme highlighter usage.

"Oh hi," said Claudia, catching my eye in the mirror. "We're just making a 'get ready with me' video. Except we don't actually have a phone, so we're just pretending it's a video."

"That's a good idea," I said.

"Are you having a baby?" Gabrielle asked out of the blue.

I laughed and touched my belly. "Yes."

"With Uncle Joey?"

"Um, yes."

"But you're not married," she said, her expression perplexed.

Claudia slapped her sister's shoulder. "Gabby, Mom said not to talk about that."

"But I don't understand," the little girl said. "I thought you had to be married to have a baby."

"You don't." Claudia applied more bronzer. "You just have to *do it*."

"Do what?"

Claudia sighed heavily. "Never mind."

"But how did Uncle Joey get the baby *in there*?" Gabrielle demanded, pointing at my stomach. "I want to know."

"Um, is there another bathroom I could use?" I asked, eager to escape this conversation.

"There's one upstairs," Claudia said.

"Okay." Turning around, I headed for the stairs and ran into Joe coming in the front door, stomping snow from his boots.

"Ready?" he asked.

"No," I said, flustered. "Your nieces are in the downstairs bathroom putting on makeup and talking about how babies are made, so I ran away."

Joe laughed. "How babies are made?"

"Yes! Gabrielle doesn't understand how you got the baby *in there*." I pointed at my stomach. "And I didn't want to be the one to explain it to her."

"I don't blame you." He took my elbow and guided me toward the steps. "Second floor. First door on your right."

"Thanks," I said, heading up the steps. "I'll just be a minute. Then I want to say goodbye to your parents."

"Okay." He waited at the bottom of the stairs a moment. "Hey, Mabel?"

"Yes?"

"I was wondering. Would it be okay if I stayed with you tonight?"

Reaching the top of the steps, I paused. Closed my eyes. Swallowed. "If you want to."

"I just feel like we didn't get much of a chance to talk with everyone around. And you still have to open your presents."

I turned around and looked down at him. He stood with his feet slightly apart, hands in the pockets of his gray dress pants. The cuffs of his blue dress shirt were rolled up, exposing his thick forearms. His dark hair was slightly tousled, probably from the wind outside, and his cheeks were flushed from the cold. *I could warm you right up*, I thought. *In fact, my body is an inferno just looking at you.*

"I'll just crash on the couch again," he said.

I didn't want him to crash on the couch. I wanted him to want me like I wanted him. I wanted to spend tonight with his naked body pressed against mine. I wanted to feel him moving inside me, deep and hard.

But I forced myself to smile. "Sure. That's fine."

"I'll get my bags," he said, starting up the stairs.

I hurried into the bathroom and shut the door, hiccups coming on with a vengeance.

Chapter 21

JOE

It was after six by the time Mabel and I got on the road. "Sorry about that," I grumbled. "Goodbyes in my family are endless. By the time you hug the last person, it's been so long, the first person wants another hug."

"I think it's sweet. Everyone really loves one another. And your parents are so adorable." She was quiet for a second, then she turned to me. "Hey, what's the thing about the tattoo?"

"My dad has my mom's name tattooed on his chest. They have this crazy history, which they didn't tell us about until we were a lot older, but evidently they eloped to Vegas when they were like twenty-one or something, and they got tattoos of each other's names and their wedding date."

"That's so romantic!"

"Well, it *was*, but then for some reason, my dad decided

they'd made a mistake. He wanted my mom to take a year to study abroad like all the women in her family had done, and she wasn't going to do it because she didn't want to leave him. Her family was really mad about it, and he didn't want to be the reason she didn't go. So he broke it off."

She gasped. "No way."

"Yeah, with a real dick move—a note by the side of the bed." I shook my head.

"No!"

"Of course, now he says he never meant that marrying her was a mistake, just that they'd rushed it. But my mom was devastated. She covered up her tattoo, took the trip abroad, and didn't speak to him for seven years."

"Wow. How'd he win her back?"

I thought for a moment about what I'd been told. "I'm not entirely sure about the details, but somehow he got her to give him another chance, and she saw that he still had that tattoo. She said she was toast after that. She knew he'd always loved her."

Mabel sighed. "That's so romantic. He knew she was the one all that time."

"I guess."

"What, you don't believe in soul mates?"

"I've never really thought about it. It just seems kind of unlikely that there's only *one* perfect person for somebody."

"Even so, there's something wonderful about someone believing you're the only one for them, isn't there?"

"Seems like a lot of pressure."

She made a noise. "Unlike your dad, you are *not* romantic."

I laughed. "My dad is a hard man to live up to, but I'm trying. What about your parents?"

"The story goes that it was love at first sight. On their first date, he told her he was going to marry her. And six months later, he did."

"Seriously?"

"Yes. And then they had five kids."

"Funny how we both come from big families." I glanced at her. "Do you want a big family?"

"I don't know. Four or five kids seems like a lot. I'm still trying to wrap my head around one."

"Me too."

"But I would like at least one more. It's fun to grow up with siblings. I'd like for you to meet mine."

When I remained silent, she laughed.

"They're not going to come at you with an axe, Joe."

"No?"

"No. They can see that I am being taken care of. That I'm happy."

I rubbed a finger beneath my lower lip. "Are you happy?"

"Yes. I mean, I wouldn't have *chosen* this way to go about starting my family. But I'm ready to be a mom. I can't wait to just love him with everything I have, you know? To hold him and hear him cry and feed him and kiss him and rock him and watch him sleeping and just know that he's mine—I mean, ours," she said with a laugh.

I wanted to laugh too, but I couldn't. I was picturing her standing over a crib and watching him sleep—alone. I was imagining her hearing him cry in the middle of the night and going to soothe him—alone. I was envisioning her rocking him, singing to him softly, holding him close—alone.

It was all wrong.

But I didn't know how to make it right.

Should I ask her to move to Chicago? Live with me? That's probably what my dad would do. But that was crazy! It *felt* like we knew each other really well, but we'd literally spent like three nights under the same roof, ever. And two of those were in separate beds! A lot of our closeness had developed over texts and phone conversations, which wasn't the same as living together.

Like I'd said to my brother yesterday, maybe I was idealizing her. I'd thought Courtney was easygoing too, but as soon as we got more serious, she got clingy and demanding. She constantly accused me of being unfaithful. Mabel was nothing like Courtney, but the experience had put me on edge.

Maybe I should ask Mabel to move to Chicago, and I'd rent a separate place for her so she'd have her own space? That way we could get to know each other better with less pressure. Like Paul said, we could date.

But she'd still be alone a lot of the time, especially when I was on the road, and she'd already told me she didn't want to move—she wanted to be up here surrounded by family and friends. She liked her job. She loved her small town. Cherry Tree Harbor was home to her.

And what if Chicago didn't renew my contract? I was having a decent season, yes, but it was still early. And I wasn't getting any younger. They might sacrifice an aging stalwart with a torn rotator cuff for a healthy, hotshot rookie who had the potential to be a superstar for years to come. I'd seen it happen. And my agent had said I wouldn't hear anything until at least February.

Maybe I should just wait. Maybe the holidays were messing with me, making me think about things like future Christmases and watching kids open their gifts and making a toast to family like my dad had done. Maybe my priorities were fine the way they always had been, and once I got back to Chicago tomorrow, I'd realize it.

Tonight, I'd sleep on her couch and keep my hands to myself. Probably.

. . .

When we arrived at her house, I told Mabel to wait in the passenger seat and I'd come around to get her. "It's snowing again, and I don't want you to slip. I'll bring the bags in once you're inside."

She sighed heavily but indulged me, and I took her arm, guiding her to the front door. After she unlocked the door, I went back for my luggage, and then for the gift bag my parents had given her.

"Where do you want this?" I asked, stomping the snow off my feet.

"You can just set it down. I'll take it into my bedroom."

I left the bag on the hallway floor and removed my shoes while Mabel went into the living room and switched on the Christmas tree lights. "Want to open your present?" she called.

"Sure. You can open yours too."

I shrugged out of my coat, hung it in the closet, and opened the large suitcase I'd brought to bring gifts home. Mabel's presents were the only two packages left in there. I pulled out the boxes, then joined her in the living room.

She was sitting on the couch with a gift-wrapped box on her lap, and her jaw fell open when she saw the two presents stacked in my arms. "Joe! What did you do?"

"It's Christmas." I sat down next to her, placing the gifts on the coffee table in front of us. "And only one of them is for you. One is for the baby."

Shaking her head, she handed me the box on her lap. "You start. I have no idea if you'll like this or not. Now I'm scared you won't."

"Stop. I'm sure I'll like it." I slipped the ribbon and bow from the gift and tore off the paper. Beneath it was a shirt box, and when I lifted the lid I discovered a gray shirt with some kind of giant pocket on the chest. I held it up by the shoulders in front of me.

"It's a kangaroo shirt for dads," she said. "The pouch is for the baby."

"It is?" I'd never seen anything like this.

"Yes. It's so you can carry him close to you without a sling or anything. My brothers said this brand is the best. But you don't have to use it if you—"

"No, I love it," I told her. "I just had no idea this was a thing, wearing your baby in a shirt."

She laughed. "It's supposed to help babies bond with dads. He'll be calmed by the contact with your body and your heartbeat and your smell."

I tried to imagine feeling comfortable walking around with the little guy tucked inside this pouch on my chest and couldn't, but I would try. "Thank you," I said, laying it back in the box. "I love it."

"You're welcome."

"Okay, your turn. Let's start with the one for the baby." I reached for the package on top and handed it to her.

She unwrapped it, and when she opened the box, she gasped. "Oh my God!" One by one, she lifted out the tiny crocheted helmet, jersey, hockey pants, and black and white bootie skates. The jersey had the Chicago logo on the front and the helmet had my number on it. "I'm going to cry! This is so adorable!"

"I saw the idea online," I said, smiling because she looked so happy. "I couldn't resist."

"I love it. I can't wait to show these to Ari." She carefully placed all the pieces back in the box and replaced the lid.

"Speaking of Ari…" I handed her the last box. It was a light brown shoe box, tied with a red satin ribbon. "I had a little help from her with this next one."

She untied the bow and gasped when she saw the label on the box: Christian Louboutin. Her hands flew to her cheeks. "You didn't. Tell me you didn't."

"Open it," I said eagerly.

Gingerly, she lifted the top off the box, like she was scared a snake might jump out. When she saw the black patent leather heels with the bright red sole, she squealed. "Joey Lupo! You did!"

She'd covered her entire face with her hands, so she couldn't see how I smiled at the use of my family's childhood name for me. "You said on the plane the day we met you were so practical, you'd never even bought a pair of designer shoes. I asked around and was told these are the ones to have."

She shook her head in disbelief. "I can't believe you remembered that." Lifting one shoe from the box, she admired its spiky heel, shiny leather and candy-apple bottom. "They're so beautiful. How did you even know my size?"

"I had to do a little research. I asked Gianni if he knew how I could get Ari's number, and he came through."

"Ari knew about this?" Her voice rose to a high-pitched squeak. "I can't believe her! She didn't say a word to me!"

"Don't be mad at her. She was sworn to secrecy."

"I knew she was up to something when I saw her yesterday. She had this smug look on her face like she knew something I didn't." She sighed, rubbing the side of one shoe against her cheek. "I love them. But they're too nice for me."

"They were made for you. You deserve them."

"I went the opposite way and got you something overly practical."

"That just means we're a good team."

She laughed, replacing the shoe in the box and setting it on the table. "Stiletto heels are definitely impractical for a pregnant woman. But I'm going to wear the hell out of them after this baby is born."

"Good."

Our eyes met, and her smile faded. Seconds ticked by as we sat there in the glow of the tree lights. "I appreciate all the things you're doing for me."

"I wish I could do more."

Her eyes dropped to her belly. "Because you feel bad?"

"No," I said, taken aback. I put a hand on her knee. "Because I care about you."

She was silent a moment, like maybe she didn't believe me. "It's not just about the baby?"

"No." Slipping my hands into her hair, I took her head in my hands and forced her to look at me. "It's not just about the baby, cupcake."

She licked her lips. "I care about you too. I think I'm just getting...confused. Or maybe I'm just emotional because it's Christmas and I'm pregnant and no one has ever been as good to me as you are and I'm all—worked up. I have these feelings and nowhere to put them. I have..." She hesitated before blurting out, "I'm having urges."

Closing my eyes, I rested my forehead against hers. "Believe me, I'm having urges too."

"You are?"

"Yes."

"I wasn't sure if the pregnant belly would be a turn-off."

"Are you kidding me?" I pulled back slightly and allowed my eyes to travel over her curves. "Your body is driving me crazy."

She laughed breathlessly. "In a good way?"

"Yes. But I don't want to do the wrong thing, Mabel. I

remember what we said in Chicago."

"Right. Chicago." She was breathing faster now. Her hand was on my thigh.

"And if you want me to take my hands off you, I will. If you want me to sleep on the couch, I will. If you want me to leave right now, I will."

"Joe," she panted. "I want you to kiss me."

In an instant my mouth was on hers, our lips open, our tongues meeting with hot, desperate need. I fisted my hands in her hair as her palm slid over the bulge in my pants. My cock surged to life, a growl tearing from somewhere in my chest.

Reaching around her back, I hauled her across my lap, slipping a hand up her dress. She threw her arms around my neck and clung to me as the kiss deepened. My palm moved up her inner thigh, and she moaned as I stroked her. Nudging the edge of her panties aside, I teased her clit with my fingers.

I put my mouth at her ear and spoke low. "I want to bury my face between your legs."

"Oh God," she murmured, clinging harder, opening her thighs.

"I dream about the way you taste," I told her, sliding a finger inside her and rubbing the silky wetness over her clit. "About the way you move. About the sounds you make when you come on my tongue."

My mouth moved down her throat, my tongue caressing the delicate skin. When she moaned, I felt the vibration on my lips. "Can I?"

"Yes," she whispered.

Moving her off my lap, I dropped to my knees in front of her and pushed her dress up to her hips. Hooking my fingers in her panties, I pulled them down and tossed them aside. Then I slung her legs over my shoulders and yanked her closer to me.

At my first long stroke, she sighed. When I drew circles with my tongue, she put her hands in my hair. When I sucked her swollen clit, she tightened her fists. In mere minutes, her heels dug into my back, her cries grew more frantic, and her body released all its tension in a thumping pulse against my tongue. My cock ached with envy.

As soon as her grip in my hair loosened, I jumped to my feet. My plan was to carry her off to her bedroom and explore all her new curves, but before I could scoop her into my arms, she sat up and unbuckled my belt. Unbuttoned my pants. Dragged down the zipper. Untucked my shirt. Her hands moved so fast I barely had time to register what she was doing. Then she yanked the sides of my pants down, my cock springing free like a jack-in-the-box.

Gripping it with both hands, she lowered her head and teased me with her tongue and fingers—slow, circular strokes over the crown that made my abs flex and my thighs tense. I slid my hands into her hair, lifting it off her face. Then I groaned as she dipped her head and licked her way from the base of my cock all the way to the tip. Like it was a popsicle in August and she wanted every melting drop in her mouth. Once. Twice. On the third long sweep of her tongue, my knees trembled. My cock thickened and twitched.

She looked up at me, her face lit by the lights on the tree, her eyes catching their gleam. Smiling mischievously, she took only the tip into her mouth and sucked gently, eyes still on mine.

I growled in frustration, battling the urge to thrust in deeper, to fuck that perfect strawberry mouth until I came, to watch her swallow me down.

Lowering her eyes, she slid her lips down to her fingers, sheathing my cock completely. Moaning softly, she worked her mouth and her hands together in tandem, sucking and stroking me with tight, wet pulls that shot electrical pulses down my legs and up my spine. Heat swirled and gathered at the center of my body, and my muscles hummed like live wires. I was close, and if she kept going like that—

"Mmmmm." She took me from her mouth and licked the crown again. "I can taste you."

My jaw tensed. "Fuck."

She slipped me between her lips, dropping one hand and taking me all the way to the back of her throat. I cursed through gritted teeth again. My hands clenched in her hair, and she gasped.

I loosened my grip. "Sorry."

"Don't be," she panted, tilting her face up to me, that wicked little spark in her eye. "You know I like when you lose control. When you come hard for me."

My dick throbbed in her hand, and I tightened my fist again in her hair. "It's going to happen in your mouth if you don't stop."

She smiled seductively, and that fucking dimple nearly put me over the edge. "That's right where I want it." Lowering her head, she moved her lips and tongue up and down my cock, and I fought off the climax that hovered like a storm on the horizon, wanting to prolong the sweet agony of her mouth on me.

But before long, the furious, fiery tension building up in my body demanded release. With my hands grasping her head, my hips began to flex—quick, hard jabs that forced her to take me in deeper. She gasped and moaned, her breaths coming in choked little pants, but she didn't ease up or push back. Grabbing my ass, she dug her fingers into my flesh as I fucked her perfect wet mouth faster and faster, my body growing tighter and tighter, until suddenly the orgasm erupted within me and I groaned loud and long, coming down her throat in hot, streaming bursts without even giving a warning.

Falling backward, she gasped for air and wiped her mouth.

Hitching my pants up, I dropped to my knees again in front of her. My heart was still pounding. "Jesus. I'm sorry."

She paused with the back of her hand against her lips. "You are?"

"Well, no. That was fucking amazing." I slid my hands up her thighs. "I just hope I wasn't too rough."

"You were rough. But I liked it. I wanted it."

"Was it the shoes?"

She laughed, tousling my hair. "No. It was not the shoes. It was just you."

"Good."

"So do you really want to sleep out here on the couch?"

"No. I was just trying to respect the rules."

Her eyes widened. "We are so bad at that."

"I feel like we should get a pass on Christmas, you know?"

"Definitely. So in the spirit of Christmas, would you like to sleep in my bed?"

I rose to my feet and offered her a hand. "Yes, I would. After all, I'm a special-occasion cuddler, and Jesus's birthday is a very special occasion."

Placing her hand in mine, she laughed as she stood up and adjusted her dress. All day long, I'd been admiring the way it coated her curves like a second skin, exaggerating the changes to her body. Changes I liked. Changes that were beautiful. Changes that meant my son was growing bigger and stronger because she was taking such good care of him.

As she walked away from the couch, I caught her from behind and buried my face in her neck, my arms cradling her belly.

She giggled. "Joe, we didn't even make it to the bedroom yet."

"I know. I just really love the way you feel."

Falling silent, she let me hold her.

It hit me how hard it was going to be to leave her tomorrow.

Chapter 22

MABEL

"Want to hear something funny?" I lay facing Joe, my hands tucked beneath my cheek on the pillow. I couldn't believe we were actually naked in my bed, where I'd spent the last five months dreaming about him.

"Yes." He had one arm bunched beneath a pillow, the other hand on my stomach, waiting to see if the baby would move. The bedside lamp was on its lowest setting, and the room was cozy.

"Before you came and sat next to me on the plane, I was planning to ask whoever was in that seat to switch with me, because I like the aisle seat better. But when you got there and sat down, you were so hot, I couldn't do it."

He laughed. "You should have asked. I would have given you the aisle seat."

"I couldn't! All I could do was stare at your face." I reached out and pushed the hair off his forehead, then touched his temple. "I noticed a scar right here. And another one here." I traced his lips.

"I remember you asked about that one." He smiled and kissed my fingertip. "Want to hear something I noticed right away about you?"

"Yes."

He cupped my jaw, rubbing the side of my mouth with his thumb. "The dimple."

I laughed. "Really?"

"Yes. It was adorable and sexy at the same time, which sums up what I thought about you."

"You thought I was sexy?"

"Fuck yes. Maybe not on the plane—although I did think you were cute—but when I saw you at the wedding in those heels and that dress? Forget it. I knew what I wanted."

I laughed. "To knock me up?"

"No, smart-ass." He grabbed me beneath the arms and rolled onto his back, taking me with him so I straddled his hips. "To give you what nobody else could."

"Well, you did both. Congratulations." I was slightly self-conscious sitting up there like that, but Joe's eyes drank me in thirstily.

He reached for my breasts, covering them with both hands, teasing me with his fingers. "This fucking body. You have no idea what it does to me."

I exhaled slowly, my nipples growing hard beneath his touch. I closed my eyes, savoring the sensations—his solid hips between my thighs, the ridges of his stomach muscles under my palms, the warmth of his skin. "God, I love your hands."

Between us, his cock thickened, and I began to rock my hips along its hard length, need building in me.

"Mabel," he said urgently. "Will we hurt the baby?"

"No."

"Will we hurt you?"

"No." Reaching low, I rose up on my knees and positioned his cock between my thighs. As I sank down on him, we both moaned.

"Oh fuck." Joe gripped my hips. "Go slow. You have to go slow. I beg you to go slow."

Laughing breathlessly, I did what he asked, the unhurried pace its own delicious torture. I swiveled and circled my hips over his, leaning forward to get the angle just right, gasping at the way he filled me, and the sharp twinge that blurred the line between pleasure and pain. "You're so deep," I whispered. "It feels so good."

Somewhere in the back of my mind was the fear that this was it, this was the last time with him. I had no idea when we'd see each other again or what the situation would be or even how big I'd have grown. I wanted to savor every single second.

But even a slow climb will take you to the top, and we found ourselves there together, reluctant to jump but craving the rush of the fall. Joe's breathing was quick and hard, his skin hot and sweaty. He kept closing his eyes, his expression pained, like the sight of me was too much to bear. I'd never felt so beautiful, or so alive.

"Cupcake." It was a warning.

"I know," I breathed, my hands braced on his chest, riding him harder and faster. "I know."

My hair swung around my shoulders. A sweat broke out on my skin.

"I can't—I'm gonna—fuck!"

I felt it then, the rhythmic beat of his climax, and I went with him, moving through it, my muscles contracting, my body determined to take every last drop. When I finally slowed to a stop, I could feel the quick hard thump of his heart under my palms.

His eyes opened. He swallowed. "My God."

I laughed, still a little breathless. "Did I wear you out with my second trimester energy?"

"In the best possible way." He glanced at my belly. "Are you okay?"

"I feel great. Just give me a minute." Carefully sliding off him, I went into the bathroom.

After cleaning up, I washed my hands and splashed some cool water on my face. In the mirror, I turned my face this way and that, taking in my disheveled hair and flushed cheeks and swollen lips. I was a mess. But I was happy.

Hurrying back to my bedroom, I switched off the lamp before crawling into bed. Immediately, Joe pulled me close and curled his body around mine like a question mark. He rested his hand on my stomach. "Is he awake?"

"I don't know." I giggled. "Maybe we rocked him to sleep." I lay very still, and a few minutes went by before the baby jabbed me. "There. Did you catch it?"

"Yes." Then he slid down and rolled me onto my back, putting his lips on my belly. "Good night, Nicky. Be good in there. Let your mommy get some sleep."

In response, the baby punched me again.

"Our son is a smart-ass," Joe said. "I'm afraid he's gonna take after me like that."

"I'll keep him in line, don't worry."

Joe moved back up and resumed his position, tucking his knees under mine, his chest warm against my back. "Thanks for letting me stay."

"You'll always be welcome here."

Of course, my anxiety chose that moment to raise her hand and remind me that this cozy little arrangement was not in my best interest long-term. *Remember what you said to Ellie? How you didn't want to end up pining for him, living for the days he passes through town? Hoping he hasn't met someone in the meantime? Stop pretending this is all fine and you're okay. You're not okay. You're in love with him.*

It was true. I was so in love with him, I didn't care how much tomorrow would hurt.

Tonight, it was Christmas.

And this felt like a gift.

• • •

When I opened my eyes the next morning, Joe wasn't beside me. I sat up and blinked, reaching for my glasses. Had he left without telling me?

"Joe?" I called out.

"I'm here." He entered the room, appearing freshly showered and wearing just a pair of sweatpants, carrying a tray with two steaming mugs on it, along with a plate. "I made you some tea and myself some coffee. And my stomach was growling, so I made some toast for us to share. Hope that's okay."

"Of course it is."

He set the tray on the foot of the bed and handed me the mug of tea. "Careful, it's hot."

"Thank you." I reached for a piece of toast and took a bite, trying not to think how lovely this would be every morning.

"I didn't want to wake you, so I just grabbed a quick shower."

"Did you find a clean towel?"

"Yes. I remembered where they were from the last time I stayed overnight."

"Good." I took a sip of hot tea. "What time do you have to

leave for the airport?"

"My flight is at two, so I should probably clean up and get out of here by ten, just to give myself enough time to return the rental car and all that."

"Is it still snowing?" With any luck, there would be a blizzard to strand him here.

"Just a little. The roads look fine."

Dammit. I hated the thought of watching him drive away from me. I didn't want to think about it. "What time is it now?"

"It's just after nine."

Less than an hour left with him. "Okay."

He set his coffee down and squeezed my foot beneath the blanket. "There's one more gift I have to give you before I go."

"What is it?"

"It's a surprise." His blue eyes glittering, he finished off a piece of toast.

"Joe, you've already given me enough for Christmas."

"This is about more than just Christmas."

And despite everything I knew to be true, to be real, to be sound and logical, my heart began to pound. "What's it about?"

"Just get dressed. And then I'll show you."

Trying to remain calm, I got out of bed and threw on some jeans and a sweatshirt. While I was pulling a sock on, I asked, "Do I need shoes?"

"Yes. We have to go outside."

Straightening up, I looked at him over my shoulder. "Outside?"

"Yes." He grinned, bringing his coffee to his lips.

"Okay." I tugged on my second sock and stood up. "My boots are by the front door."

In the hallway, Joe took my puffy coat from the closet and helped me into it. I stepped into my snow boots while he put on his coat and shoes. The whole time, my insides were knotting themselves up until I felt so tightly wound I might snap.

Joe laughed when he saw my face. "You look nervous."

"I'm just trying to figure out what you're about to show me."

He put his hand on the door handle. "Are you ready?"

"Yes. The suspense is killing me."

His grin grew even wider as he opened the door. "Take a look."

I stepped onto the front porch, my eyes scanning the front yard.

Then I froze. I gasped. I covered my mouth with both hands.

Parked at the curb in front of my house, topped by a giant red bow, was a shiny black SUV.

"Joe Lupo, tell me I'm seeing things."

He laughed. "You're seeing your new ride. Look, the keys are right here in the mailbox. Santa left them for you."

"No." I closed my eyes and shook my head. "No. When I open my eyes, there will not be a new car in front of my house."

"Try it out."

I peeked with one eye. "It's still there."

"Then maybe you should go touch it. Make sure it's real." Pulling a key fob from the mailbox, he took me by the hand. "Come on, cupcake."

In a complete daze, I let him lead me down the snowy walk to the street. He unlocked the driver's side door and opened it for me. When I stood there in a stupor just staring at the gorgeous black leather interior, he laughed and took my arm again. "Come on. I'll help you in."

Once I was seated behind the wheel, he went around to the passenger side and got in. "Well? What do you think?"

"I can't think. I'm in shock." My breath made little puffs of white in the freezing air.

"Start the car, so we can have some heat. Look, you even have seat and steering wheel warmers."

I did what he said, but as the vehicle warmed up, I shook my head. "Joe. I can't accept this."

"Sure, you can."

"I won't."

"You have to. Listen, this is a brand new Honda CR-V. It has a five-star safety rating from the National Highway Traffic Safety Administration. I have been assured of its *robust safety features,* including front-crash prevention, backup camera, rear child safety locks, and more. It's got four doors, which will make dealing with a car seat easier. And it's got plenty of room in the back for Nicky's hockey equipment."

I stared at him in disbelief. "Who *are* you?"

"I'm just a dad in the making who wants to make sure the mother of his son—and his son, once he arrives—is safe on the road. So I did some research." He shrugged. "Plus, turns out I used to play hockey with the guy who owns your local Honda dealership. He got the car in and delivered it for me."

My eyes filled. I slipped my glasses off and placed them in my lap. Pinched the bridge of my nose. "I'm…I'm overwhelmed."

"Listen to me, Mabel." He reached over and took my hand. "On that plane you thought was going down, you said you regretted being so practical and careful. You said you'd never splurged on a new car, and you didn't even know what a new car smelled like."

Tears were leaking from the corners of my eyes, and I tipped my head back, staring at the car's pristine ceiling. "Why do you remember everything I said on that stupid flight?"

He stroked my hand with his thumb. "I don't know. I just do. And clearly I have made it my mission to make sure you have all the things you thought you'd missed out on—designer shoes, a new car, a good puck."

I sob-laughed. "Right."

"So now…are you ready to inhale?"

Wiping my cheeks with my free hand, I nodded.

"Count of three. One, two, three!" At the same time, we both breathed in deeply. "Well? Do you love it?"

The smell was divine—new leather and crisp winter air and a trace of gasoline.

But what I loved was the man who had given it to me. What I wanted was his heart.

"It's even better than I imagined," I said. Then I met his eyes, and my insides unraveled. My voice trembled. "Everything with you is. That's the problem, Joe."

Joe swallowed. "Why is that a problem?"

"You're too good to me."

"All I want is to make sure you're taken care of, cupcake."

"I know." I smiled through my tears. "But this isn't good for me."

He frowned. "What do you mean? What's not good for you?"

"These feelings for you. The sense of belonging with you." Taking my hand from his, I balled it up against my chest. "This *hope* in my *heart* that just keeps *growing* every time we're together."

"Oh." His eyes dropped. "I didn't think of it like that."

"Don't say anything, okay? This isn't your fault." I took a breath. "When I came down to Chicago to tell you about the baby, I told you I didn't expect you to change, and I meant it. I knew hockey was your priority. And I didn't suddenly expect you to have feelings for me just because the condom broke—I didn't have them for you either. After all, we were practically strangers." I paused, thinking of that day. "I remember turning down your offer to stay the night because I didn't trust us not to have sex, and I knew sex would complicate things. I just wanted us to get to know each other better. Become friends."

"I wanted that too."

"The problem was, the better we got to know each other, the more I wanted you in all ways."

"And now you regret it?"

"No! I love being with you that way, Joe, I really do, but my heart did not get the memo it was all in fun, no matter how many times I sent it. And I'm scared. I don't want to get hurt."

"I never want to hurt you," he said quietly.

"I know you don't. And you wouldn't intend to. It's just that your dreams and my dreams don't overlap. We've always known this. And I couldn't live with myself if I thought for one second that I'd stepped between you and your dreams."

His blue eyes were shining. "And I couldn't live with myself if I made you a promise I couldn't keep."

"Don't," I said, my lower lip trembling. "I don't want that promise, Joe."

Exhaling, he slipped one hand around to the back of my neck and tipped my head toward his, our foreheads touching. "So now what?"

"I think we should cool off for a bit," I said, even though it was the last thing I wanted. "Take some time to think about what's going to be best for the baby long-term."

"Can I still call you?" He sounded aggrieved. "I need to know you and the baby are doing okay."

"Of course. We can still talk. And I promise I'll keep you up to date on all the baby things." I spoke more gently. "I just need a little space to give my heart some time to accept reality."

"Okay." He kept his hand on the back of my neck, kneading it gently. "I wish things were different for us."

"I do too. But I wouldn't change who you are, Joe."

"I wouldn't change you either. Not a single thing." He released me, his expression pained. "But you're keeping this car, Mabel Jane Buckley. No backsies, no givesies."

As I wiped my eyes, I laughed. "Okay. Deal."

• • •

We said goodbye thirty minutes later at my front door with a long hug. "Let me know when you get home," I said, determined not to break down in front of him. "And I hope you have a safe flight."

"I will." He let me go and planted a quick kiss on my forehead. "You take good care of yourself," he said gruffly. His eyes were uncharacteristically dark.

"I will." I tried to keep things light when I really wanted to sob into his chest. "And you rest that shoulder. I need my favorite team to make the playoffs."

He smiled, but it didn't reach his eyes. "I'll give it my best shot."

After closing the door behind him, I went to the front window and watched him walk away, holding back the tears. And then halfway to the sidewalk, he stopped.

My breath caught.

He bounced his right leg at the knee a few times. Agitated, like he was torn.

My lips moved in a silent prayer. *Come back inside. Love me. Stay.*

But a moment later, he continued the walk toward his car, which was parked in my driveway. After tossing his bags in the back, he got behind the wheel, started the engine, and looked at my house. I held my breath once more.

Again, I was disappointed. Ten seconds later, he backed out of the driveway, and then his rental car disappeared down the block. I closed the door, walked into my bedroom, and curled up into a ball on my bed, inhaling the scent of him clinging to the sheets.

Cradling my belly, I wept.

• • •

"Whose car is that?" Ari stared past me out to the street where I'd parked in front of her house. She'd invited me to come for dinner, and since I'd done nothing but mope around my house for the day and a half since Joe left, I jumped at the chance to be around family.

"It's mine." I held up the fob. "Christmas gift."

"From *who*?"

"Joe." In the cold winter air, I felt the heat in my cheeks.

Ari's jaw fell open. "He bought you a *car*? Are you kidding me? I was aghast about the Louboutins, but this is next level!"

"Well, it's more about the baby," I said, entering her house. "He knew my car was old and wanted me to have something newer and safer, something easy to get a car seat in and out of."

"Jesus, Mabel." Ari shifted Truman in her arms and shut the door. "What is going on with you guys?"

"Nothing," I said, hanging my jacket in the hall closet. "Well, now it's nothing. Christmas Day, it was something. Actually, it was everything." Sighing, I followed her into the kitchen and plunked down at the kitchen table. Her house smelled delicious, as usual. Like roasted chicken.

"Ha! I knew something would happen Christmas Day!" She set Truman in the baby swing and peeked in the oven. "Did you sneak into his childhood bedroom?"

"No, he stayed the night at my house after driving me back. He wouldn't let me drive myself that day because it was snowing."

"You know, he is suspiciously protective of you," Ari said,

pulling a huge cast iron skillet from the oven. "It's almost like he's in love or something."

I shook my head. "He is not in love with me. If he was, he wouldn't have let me push him away yesterday morning."

"What do you mean?" Setting the skillet on the stove top, Ari turned around and faced me. "Why'd you do that?"

"I felt like I had to." I played with the edge of a place mat. "I was getting too invested in him. In *us*." I swallowed hard against the lump trying to form. "I think I'm in love with him. Actually, I know I am."

"Oh Mabel."

I dropped my head into my hands. "God, I feel like I've done nothing but cry for twenty-four hours. In bed. In the shower. Facedown on the couch. Have you ever cried on the toilet? I assure you, there is nothing that makes you feel more pathetic."

"Poor baby." She came and sat down next to me, rubbing my arm. "Tell me what happened."

"I just basically told him I caught feelings I didn't intend to catch, and I was scared of getting hurt. But I assured him that I wasn't going back on my word."

"What word?"

"Not to make any demands on him. Not to ask him to change or prioritize me over hockey."

"But it's not like he'd have to give up hockey," Ari argued. "Why can't you give the relationship a chance inside the existing parameters of his life? You could move to Chicago."

"He didn't ask me to. He's never asked me to."

"Well, he's dumb."

I almost smiled. "He's not dumb. He's careful. He doesn't want to say something he doesn't mean."

She sat back, folding her arms. "I can't help it if I think he's dumb for not realizing he'll be sorry if he lets you get away. I'm not saying you have to get married tomorrow, but he obviously loves you. Why not say it?"

"I don't know, Ari." I jumped up from the chair and went over to the sink to look out at the snow-covered yard. "It's not like I can ask him."

"Why not?"

"Because I'm too afraid. What if the answer isn't what I want it to be? Maybe that makes me a coward, but I can't help it if I feel it's better to be safe than sorry." I took a deep breath. "At least this way, I'm safe."

Ari said nothing, but she got off her chair and came over to the window. Standing next to me, she tipped her head onto my shoulder. "I get it," she said softly. "And I'm sorry if I upset you. I want you to feel safe."

"I know you do."

"But I want you to be happy too, and sometimes you have to risk a little safety to get there."

"If it were only about me, maybe I would have. Maybe I'd have put my feelings out there and asked him to give us a fighting chance. And if he'd turned me down, I'd forget him and move on. I'd never have to see him again and be reminded of the hurt. But I have the baby to think about, Ari. I can't just forget Joe exists. He'll be in my life forever."

"True," she said with a sigh. "So how are the shoes?"

"Stunning. Wait till you see them. And the new car is beautiful too."

"Of course it is." She shook her head. "You know, I'm not one to wish anyone ill, but when you finally find the one who loves you the way you deserve, I hope Joe Lupo pines away for you for the rest of his cold, lonely days."

I laughed. "Thanks."

Chapter 23

JOE

*O*n a Saturday night in mid-January, after a shitty defeat to a team we *hated* losing to, a bunch of the guys went out for a few beers.

"You were off tonight, Lupo." Next to me at the bar, Tessier's voice held a trace of irritation, and I didn't blame him. We'd lost seven games out of the last ten since Christmas, and our division standings had slipped. I was blowing passes and shots I should have been able to make in my sleep. My skates felt like they were made of lead. I'd started playing too carefully, too tentatively. It wasn't my game. And my fucking shoulder hurt like a bitch.

Worse, there was some hotshot player that management was talking about bringing up from the minor league affiliate—and they were calling him *the next Joe Lupo*, which pissed me the fuck off.

If I didn't get my shit together, the only hockey I was going to be playing next year was on the Dad Bod Squad.

I was trying to do what I'd always done before—tune out everything else in my life and just play hockey—but even that wasn't working. I couldn't compartmentalize the way I had in the past. I didn't feel in control.

"Sorry," I said with a grimace. "I'll do better."

"Something wrong?"

I wasn't even sure how to answer that question. Since I'd driven away from Mabel's house three and a half weeks ago, *everything* had felt wrong. We weren't talking as much, and when we did, there was a formality to our conversations, a stiffness that wasn't there before. We didn't tease each other. We didn't make jokes. I didn't flirt with her or tell her she looked beautiful or call her cupcake.

I fucking hated it. I missed the way things had been before, and at night I lay awake thinking about where we'd gone wrong. What I'd done wrong. Or hadn't done right.

But that was nothing I could offer up to my captain as an excuse for my poor performance, so I only shrugged. "My shoulder is bothering me."

"You sure that's it?"

"Yeah." I lifted my beer.

"How's the pregnancy?"

"Good." Mabel had texted me yesterday that her doctor's appointment had gone well. Baby was growing right on track.

"When's he due again?"

"April."

"How's the girl? Sorry, I forgot her name."

"Mabel." I took another pull from the bottle. "She says she's fine." Actually she'd mentioned that her blood pressure was a little high, and I'd panicked and called her.

"Hi Joe," she'd said when she picked up.

"Hey. Are you okay? I saw your text about the blood pressure."

"I'm fine," she assured me. "The doctor told me it's common at this time during a pregnancy."

The sound of her voice hit my bloodstream like a drug. I wanted more. "What else did she say?"

"That the baby is probably just under two pounds. And guess what?"

"What?"

"He got the hiccups while we were there!"

I laughed. "He's got some of his mom in him."

"Right?" She laughed too, and it made my chest hurt.

"Are you sure you're okay?"

"Positive. How are you?"

"Fine," I said.

"How's the shoulder?"

"Not great, but I'm icing it and resting it when I can. Doing PT a few days a week."

"Be careful. I know you must be down about the last few losses, but I worry about you playing too hard."

"You don't have to worry about me. Just take care of yourself."

"I am." She paused. "I should go. Austin and Xander are here to help me move the furniture out of the office so we can get it painted."

"Okay." My gut wrenched—*I* wanted to be the one helping her move furniture and paint the baby's room. "Let me know how it goes."

"I will. Good luck tomorrow night." She hadn't said anything about watching the game or wearing my number or cheering me on, and it dragged me down even deeper into the funk.

"Hey, Tessier, can I ask you something?" I turned to my captain, and he nodded.

"Shoot."

"Do you ever think about what you'll do after this?"

"Sure. All the time. I'm fucking thirty-five years old. And some days my body tells me I'm twice that."

"I get it. So what will you do?"

"My contract is up next year. At that point, I'll probably just move back to Canada and buy some land. Watch my kids grow up in the country. That's what my wife wants." He shrugged. "We've been down here for eight years, in Boston before that, and she misses her family. She wants the kids to have some good years with their grandparents."

It surprised me. I thought for sure he'd look for a job in management or coaching. "Aren't you worried you'll miss it?"

"I'll miss parts of it, sure. But not all of it. And it's not just about me."

"Maybe that's my problem," I muttered before tipping the bottle up again. My entire life, everything had been about me. My family took vacations around my hockey schedule. My parents spent countless hours driving me to tournaments in places like Saskatchewan and Manitoba. My professors gave me extended time on assignments and tests because a winning team was good for the school. I'd never had to put anyone else's needs before my own.

"What's that?" Tessier leaned a little closer to me. "Didn't hear you."

"Nothing," I said. "I guess I'm just having some doubt that I'm as good a man as my dad and brothers are."

"Why?"

"Because I'm kind of a selfish prick off the ice. I've always known it, and I used to just laugh it off. But I can't do that anymore."

"Nope. You can't."

"I don't even want to." I spun the beer bottle around in my hand, its bottom leaving wet rings on the wooden bar. "But I don't know any other way to be. I've never wanted to be anyone but the old me. And suddenly I've got these fucking complicated feelings that are tearing me apart."

"Feelings about the baby?"

"No. Those feelings are simple. These are about the girl." I closed my eyes, and she was in my head—her laugh, her dimple, her yellow cupcake scent. "Mabel."

"Why not try to make it work?"

"That doesn't seem to be a risk she's willing to take."

"Are you?"

I took a sip of my beer without tasting it. "Yes. But even saying that just now, I get this panicked feeling, like I need to slow down and think some more. Until I'm absolutely one hundred percent sure it's right. I feel like there's no room for uncertainty."

"Let me ask you something. When you're lining up a shot, are you always one hundred percent certain you're going to score?"

"No."

"But you take the shot. Because it's worth a chance."

I rubbed the back of my neck. "But that's hockey. I'm *good* at hockey. And this isn't a puck I'm playing with. It's someone's feelings. It's someone's life."

"Still. The Joe Lupo I know would take the shot."

His words stuck with me.

• • •

Our next game was Monday night in Montreal.

We'd gotten off to a good start with a 1-0 lead, but then took six straight penalties in a row. When it was finally five on five again, I passed the puck to Larsson on a breakaway and went to skate around the defenseman, but he tripped me—and the ref either didn't see it or didn't call it. As he skated past, fury surged through my veins. I wanted to retaliate, but forced myself to keep the urge in check. That was how the game was played. Things got rough sometimes.

I got up and continued to play, but the anger didn't dissipate. It grew and festered and boiled. They were up by two goals going into the third period, coaches were pissed, tempers were hot, and my shoulder was fucking killing me. But when I saw that same defenseman take a cheap shot at Larsson, I made up my mind I was going to do something about it.

I tripped him the same way he'd tripped me, only when he got up, he pitchforked me and I went down hard on my bad shoulder. We both came up swinging. We were separated fast and handed penalties, although someone else had to serve mine for me— because of the injury, I was out of the game, which we lost.

Later, I'd get even worse news… I was out for at least two weeks, which meant missing the All Star game. Adding insult to my injury was the doctor's opinion that most of the damage to my shoulder was due to "overuse and aging."

My agent was mad. "What the fuck, Joe?" he demanded when he called me on Tuesday. "Why would you do something so stupid? That's not the kind of hockey you play."

"He came at me first!" I shouted, sounding like an eight-year-old. Lying on my couch with ice on my shoulder, I winced at the pain that lanced through my arm.

"Listen, if you expect Chicago to renew your contract, you need to be in top form. Rehab the shoulder, get back on the ice, and do what you're paid to do—fucking score goals, not get in fights!"

I hung up on him, too angry to reply, knowing I didn't really have a good argument anyway. I hadn't expected my agent to be warm and fuzzy about it. His job was to get me the best deal possible, and I'd just made that harder.

Mabel called Tuesday afternoon, too. She'd also texted *and* called late Monday night, leaving panicked messages asking if I was okay, begging me to call her back when I could, saying how sorry she was and that she was worried about me. I'd been too mad at myself to call her right back—it was almost like a punishment, denying myself any of the sweet things I knew she'd say, her care and concern.

But I answered her call now.

"Hello?"

"Joe! Are you okay?"

"I'm fine." But I wasn't.

"What happened? I've been so worried!"

"Sorry I didn't call you back. I was traveling today, and I'm on some strong pain meds, so I slept a lot."

"That's okay, I just didn't know what happened. I was so scared."

I felt even worse for frightening her. "Sorry," I said again. The word felt inadequate, but what else could I offer her besides an apology?

Mabel was silent for a moment. "What's wrong, Joe?"

Everything, I wanted to say. "I'm mad at myself. I should have just played my game."

"That guy deserved it."

Her comment, delivered with a venomous tone I rarely heard from her, made me smile a little. "Yeah. He did."

"What's the news on your shoulder?"

"I'm out for at least two weeks. I have to miss the All Star game."

She gasped. "Oh no! I'm so sorry."

"The biggest problem right now is my contract. Being old is

hard enough. Being old and injured is two strikes against me."

"Come on, this is just an unlucky streak. Your season got off to such a great start—you'll find that groove again."

"I don't know. Maybe I'm past my prime."

"I don't believe that."

"Maybe I'm just fucking tired." I kept thinking about what Tessier had said about moving to Canada and buying land, watching his kids grow up in the country. Something about that sounded so fucking good. I imagined sitting on a back porch, Mabel on my lap, Nicky running around with a dog or a buddy or a little sibling.

Was I crazy?

"You sound so sad," Mabel said. "I wish I was there to watch *The Sandlot* with you and cheer you up."

"That would definitely cheer me up." I recalled sharing this couch with her the night she'd ended up in my bed, how closely I'd held her, how I'd felt my son moving beneath my palm. God, I wanted that again, and I'd never have it. She was never going to be mine again, not like that.

The pain in my shoulder moved into my chest.

"So the baby's room is coming along," she said with a new energy to her voice, probably because I was depressing her and she wanted to change the subject. "We painted, and the carpet is in. I'll have to send you pictures."

"I'd like that. How are you feeling?"

"Great. Officially in the third trimester."

I glanced at the pregnancy book on the coffee table. I hadn't looked at it much lately, because it just made me feel worse about everything I was missing. "Twenty-eight weeks, right?"

"Right. What's the fruit this week?"

"I'm not sure. Sorry." I closed my eyes.

"Oh. That's okay. I know you've got a lot going on." The

disappointment in her voice was obvious.

Don't excuse me, Mabel. Stop being so sweet. "I'll look as soon as we hang up," I promised.

"Don't worry about it. I just want you to get better, okay?"

"Okay."

"I'll talk to you soon. Bye, Joe."

"Bye."

After ending the call, I checked the website with the fruit chart. At twenty-eight weeks, the baby was the size of an eggplant. Setting my phone aside, I picked up *From Dude to Dad* and caught up on the last couple weeks.

The baby was fifteen to sixteen inches long and weighed between two and three pounds. I tried to imagine carrying around a three pound eggplant in my belly and quickly shoved the thought from my brain. The book said Mabel's stomach was getting cramped, and the baby's movements probably felt less like sharp kicks and jabs and more like softer pokes and rolls.

The author talked about not letting his wife lift anything heavy or climb any ladders to change lightbulbs—he insisted on taking over any and all projects. He mentioned that his wife experienced sciatica at this time, and how he'd help her stretch and give her massages. He described painting the nursery and shopping for a rocking chair together, so that when she was exhausted, he could help get the baby back to sleep at three a.m.

My pulse quickened with concern. Who was making sure Mabel didn't lift anything heavy? Who would rub her back when it hurt? Was she shopping for furniture alone? Why hadn't I asked any of these questions before? I hadn't even inquired about the high blood pressure just now.

I scowled. No wonder she didn't want to trust me with that hope in her heart. I could do better. I had to do better.

Grabbing my phone, I searched for rocking chairs online.

But there were so many options, I was totally overwhelmed. Swivel gliders, rockers, electronic recliners, ergonomic designs, ottomans...and they came every style and color under the sun. How was I supposed to choose? I didn't even know what color the walls were in the baby's room, which made me feel even worse.

Friday afternoon, I sent Mabel a text.

Hey. How are you?

Good! Just standing in the baby's empty room
mentally arranging the furniture lol.

Can you show me the room?

Sure. Want to FaceTime?

My pulse kicked up at the idea of seeing her, hearing her.

Yes.

I called her, and her smiling face appeared on my screen. "Hi."

My entire body warmed. "Hey."

"How's the shoulder?"

"Getting better."

"Good." She nodded in satisfaction. "So you want to see the room so far?"

"Yes, please."

She switched the view of the phone, and I saw that the walls were painted a soft sage green. "Okay, I'm standing right at the doorway. The crib will go over to my left against the wall." She turned and aimed the phone along a bare wall, and I imagined the crib there.

"The one your brother Austin is making?"

"Yes. It's almost done."

"Cool." I was unreasonably jealous, not only that he had the incredible skill to make something like that with his hands, but that he could do these things for her in person.

"On this wall will be the changing table." She pivoted and showed me another bare wall. "And this is his view." She went over to the window and aimed the phone at the glass. "It will be the backyard, which is currently covered in snow."

"You're not shoveling it, are you?"

"No, *Dad*," she teased. "I'm not. Austin or Xander have been doing the driveway and front walk for me."

Again, I felt the unreasonable sting of envy that I wasn't there doing those simple, everyday chores for her. I was sending money, yes, but that wasn't the same. It wasn't good enough.

She aimed the phone at an empty corner. "Right here is where the rocker will go. Veronica is going to give me the one she used for Luke and Vivian."

"Nice," I said, trying to gauge the size of the space so I could send her a new chair.

She opened the closet door. "And look!"

I was not prepared for the way my gut wrenched when I saw the little dinosaur pajamas we'd gotten at the museum hanging there. I couldn't even speak.

"Remember the day we bought them?"

I cleared my throat. "Yes."

"And the carpet is amazing. So soft and plush." She aimed the camera toward her feet, which were bare. Laughing, she wiggled her toes, which were painted bright red. "My feet are swollen, so I didn't even bother with shoes today. Although now they're cold."

I wanted to take her chilly feet in my hands and rub them for her while she ate potato chips and ice cream on the couch. We could watch *her* favorite movie this time. Then I'd carry her off to bed and massage her back, and if she'd let me, I'd give her an orgasm with my tongue or my hand or however she wanted. As many *times* as she wanted. As long as I got to hear my name on her lips while it happened.

Then she turned the camera back on her face, pushing her glasses up on her nose. "So what do you think?"

I think I should be there and not here. Or you should be here and not there. I don't want to be apart from you anymore. Or ever again. "It looks great. He'll love it."

She laughed. "He knows we're talking about him. He's moving around."

I smiled, but I felt like my heart was splitting in two. "I really wish I was there right now. I'm sorry I can't help with the baby's room."

"That's okay. Just get that shoulder back in shape so we can watch you play again. We miss it."

"I will."

Silence fell between us, and I could have filled it with so many things. *I miss you. I want you. Give me a chance.*

Instead what came out was, "I should go. I have a PT appointment at three-thirty."

"Okay," she said.

"I miss you," I blurted.

"I miss you too, Joe." She waited for me to say something else, but when I didn't, she said goodbye.

I felt worse than ever.

• • •

I spent a good chunk of Saturday looking at rocking chairs again, but even though I knew what color the walls were, I felt just as lost as I had yesterday. Finally, I gave up and made a phone call right before I had to leave for the arena.

"Hello?"

"Hey, Ari. It's Joe Lupo."

"Oh. Hi." Her tone wasn't unfriendly, but it wasn't warm.

"I wondered if I could get your opinion on something."

"You can get my opinion on a lot of things."

I grimaced. "Specifically, I'm calling about a rocking chair."

"A rocking chair?"

"Yes. I'd like to get one for the baby's room at Mabel's house, but I don't know what style or color or anything. I saw the room on FaceTime yesterday—"

"I heard."

"Oh." I cleared my throat. "Anyway, I'm still not sure what to get. Can you help me?"

She sighed heavily. "I suppose I could. Do you want me to send you some links?"

"Yes," I said with relief. "That would be perfect."

"Do you have a budget in mind?"

"No. I don't care what it costs. Pick something she'll love."

She was silent. "Joe, this might be none of my business—in fact, it is absolutely none of my business—but I'm going to ask this question anyway."

I braced myself. "Okay."

"What do you want from Mabel?"

The question surprised me. "I don't want anything *from* her. I just want her to be happy."

"And that's what all the gifts are about? Making her happy? The shoes, the car, the rocking chair?"

"Yes. What else would they be about?"

"Keeping her in love with you while you decide what to do with your life."

The words pierced my heart like an arrow. "That's not what I'm doing."

"You know she is, though. She's so in love with you, it breaks my heart."

"I—" I swallowed hard. A sweat broke out on my back. "She's never said that to me."

"Because she's scared! And she'd rather be safe than sorry. Look, I shouldn't even be saying this stuff to you, and I wouldn't, except that something tells me that you love her too. But if you're not going to love her the way she deserves—with your whole heart—then stop with all the gifts and the attention."

"She's carrying my son," I argued. "I'm allowed to support her."

"That's not what you're doing, and you know it."

Damn. This girl was ferocious. But even though she was baring her teeth and growling at me like a guard dog right now, I was glad Mabel had a friend like Ari in her corner.

"Look, I'm trying to figure things out," I said. "But if what you're saying is true, Mabel hasn't been honest with me about what she wants."

"She wants a love story, Joe! It's what she's always wanted—to meet the one and be swept off her feet. To feel chosen. To get married and have a family. But she didn't meet the one. She met you."

"I could be the one," I said, more offended than I'd ever been in my life.

"Then prove it." And she hung up on me.

. . .

Her accusation made it impossible to sleep that night.

Keeping her in love with you while you decide what to do with your life.

It rankled. It stung. It gnawed at my insides.

I lay on my back in the bed we'd once shared and scowled into the dark.

It wasn't fucking true!

I wasn't doing all these things just to string Mabel along. I was doing them because I genuinely wanted to. Because it felt right. Because she deserved them. Because she was the mother of my son.

Because I loved her too.

I had nothing to compare it to, because I'd never felt this way before, but that's what this all-consuming, under-my-skin, gut-raveling feeling had to be.

I loved her.

"That's right. I love her," I said, as if someone had dared me to admit it out loud.

And maybe someone had.

"You're goddamn right about that, Ari. I fucking love her too. But you're wrong about the other thing. *I* am the fucking *one*."

Saying it out loud felt good. It felt true. It made me feel whole.

I kept talking as I jumped out of bed and threw on some clothes, even though it was four o'clock in the morning. "I am the fucking one, and it's time everybody knows it. It's time for Mabel to hear it. It's time for me to say it right to her face."

It was time to take the shot.

Chapter 24

*a*fter my alarm went off, I stayed snuggled under the covers for a few extra minutes, Cleo curled up at my side.

I thought of Joe on Sunday mornings like this. I would imagine what it would be like to scoot over and press up against the warm, hard length of his body. To feel the shelter of his arm come around me. To lay my cheek against his chest and inhale the woodsy, masculine scent of him.

But maybe it wouldn't be like that. Maybe the two nights I'd spent with him were not indicative of how things would be. Maybe, like he said, he was only a special-occasion cuddler, and if I tried to tuck myself along his side, he'd push me away or roll in the other direction.

In my fantasies, though, he always pulled me closer. He was the protective guy who held my hand on the airplane. The romantic guy who kissed me in the rain. The possessive guy who got in someone's face and said, *You best keep your hands off the mother of my son.*

I missed that guy.

Since I'd asked him for space, I sensed a reserve between us, neither of us quite sure how to act. For so many months, the intimacy between us had been allowed to grow and flourish. It had felt like a dance as we'd circled around each other, then joined hands, and finally held each other close as we spun around the floor.

Now it was like we were walking on broken glass, each of us unsure where to put a foot.

The distance was what I'd asked for, but I missed the easy way it used to be. I missed feeling free to text him whenever I felt like it. I missed chatting with him nightly about what the baby was doing and how I was feeling. I missed that flutter in my heart when he'd say something a little suggestive or pay me a compliment or call me his cupcake.

Had I let my anxiety have too much sway? Was safe really better than sorry? Would I regret not throwing caution to the wind and taking a chance on this man I loved? Maybe he wasn't perfect, but damn, he tried hard. And he was good to me.

I could spend hours second-guessing myself this way.

I miss you, he'd said the other day. I'd seen the expression on his face as he said it, and it was tortured. That was how I'd described it to Ari when I told her about the FaceTime call, which might have been a mistake because she said, "Good. He deserves torture."

But I didn't want him to hurt. I loved him.

Not just because he was the father of the child I carried, but for the man he was. The good in his soul. The gold in his heart.

And I couldn't stop hoping he'd wake up one morning and choose me to share it with.

"Am I a fool, Nicky?" I asked, running my hands over my belly. "To keep on hoping this way?"

The baby was silent on the matter.

"Okay, fine. Be that way. It's time to get up anyway." Sighing, I swung my legs over the side of the bed and got up to head for the bathroom. "Your uncle Austin is bringing the crib over this morning, and—" Suddenly my vision went blurry. I backed up immediately and sat on the bed again. Something was not right. There was a ringing sound in my ears. As I groped for my phone, I broke out in a cold sweat.

I dialed Austin.

"Hello?"

"Hey, can you come a little early?"

"What's wrong?"

"I'm not sure. I feel strange."

"I'm calling 9-1-1."

"No, don't!" I blinked a few times. "I think I just got light-headed getting out of bed. I'll be okay. Maybe I just need to eat."

"Stay where you are. I'll be there in ten minutes. Don't move, Mabel. I have a key."

"Okay."

But as soon as we hung up, I realized I had to go to the bathroom. My bladder was not going to last ten minutes. I looked at my bedroom doorway. It was just a few feet from there to the bathroom. I could make it.

Moving more slowly, I lowered my feet to the floor and took a few tentative steps. But my legs were unsteady. Or maybe it was the room. Instead of moving toward the door, I'd veered toward my dresser. I reached out, grabbing for the edge, but lost my balance, my upper body falling forward.

Something hit my temple, and I sank to the bottom of a deep, dark pool.

Chapter 25

JOE

Exactly six hours after I'd left Chicago, I pulled into Mabel's driveway and parked right behind her new SUV. The front lawn was covered with snow, but I was too impatient to go back to the sidewalk and use the shoveled front walk, so I stomped through six inches of snow in my shoes like a madman.

On the front porch, I stamped my feet and knocked on the door at the same time. Impatient, I shoved my hands in my coat pockets and shifted my weight from side to side. When she didn't answer after thirty seconds, I knocked again. When she didn't answer thirty seconds after that, I put my hands to the small window pane within her front door. The front hallway looked exactly how I remembered it, but there was no sign of Mabel or even Cleo. The hall light was on, though, and at the back of the house, I could see the kitchen lights were on. That was a little strange. Maybe she was in the shower?

I knocked again and waited a couple more minutes, but she didn't answer. Hustling back to my car, I got back behind the wheel and turned on the engine for some heat. Then I called her. It went to voicemail. Without leaving a message, I hung up and texted.

> Hey, cupcake. I have a surprise for you. Are you home?

Five minutes went by. Then ten.

A bad feeling had worked its way beneath my excitement. Something prickled at the back of my neck. I wasn't usually someone who overreacted or assumed the worst, but I couldn't shake the feeling that something was off. What if she was in the house but she couldn't get to her phone or the door?

Blood pumping, I jumped out of the car and strode back onto her porch. I banged on the door with both fists. I called her name. I went around to the back door and pounded there too.

Nothing.

"Fuck!" I tugged on my hair, which I hadn't even combed before leaving my apartment.

I was heading for my car again, trying to decide what to do, when another car pulled up in front of Mabel's house. Hidden behind my SUV, I watched as the driver got out and hurried up the front walk.

It was Ari.

"Ari!" Again, I waded through half a foot of snow to get to the porch. "Where's Mabel?"

Ari squealed and jumped, placing a hand over her heart. "Oh my God, you scared me!"

"Where is she? Is everything okay?"

"Jesus." Ari took a couple deep breaths. "She's okay. They're just keeping her for observation for twenty-four hours."

My blood pressure spiked as I pictured my girl in a hospital bed hooked up to machines. "Who's they? Where is she? Observation for what?"

"She passed out in her bedroom this morning and hit her head on the dresser. She's at Northern Medical Center."

"Oh my God." My heart. My heart. "Tell me she's okay."

"She's fine. A bump on the head. Austin arrived within minutes and called 9-1-1. She was confused when he found her but was awake and talking by the time paramedics got here."

"And the baby?"

"Baby is fine too." She pulled a key from her pocket and stuck it in Mabel's front door. "Let's go inside. It's freezing out here."

"I want to go see her!"

"I'm here getting together a bag of things she wants. You can take them to her."

I fidgeted, glancing at my car, but reluctantly followed her into the house. If there was something Mabel needed, I wanted to bring it to her. Following Ari inside, I caught sight of Cleo in the front hall. I crouched down to pet her while Ari removed her shoes.

"I'm sorry about the outburst yesterday," she said. "I'm just protective of Mabel."

"It's okay." I straightened up. "I needed to hear those words. After you said all that stuff to me, I couldn't think about anything else. I couldn't even focus on hockey—thank God I'm not back on the ice yet, because I watched an entire game without seeing a fucking thing. I went home and couldn't sleep. Because I realized you were right about one thing—I love her—but wrong about the other."

"The other?"

"You said Mabel wanted a love story. You said she wanted to meet the one and be swept off her feet. But then you said she didn't meet the one—she met me."

Ari tilted her head. "And?"

"And you're wrong. I *am* the one. And I drove here at four in the morning to tell her that."

Her eyes widened. "You did?"

"Yes! I love her, and I'm so mad at myself for waiting until now to tell her. She should not have been alone this morning. She shouldn't be *living* alone. She should be living with me."

"She needs to hear all this, Joe."

"She will. As soon as I can get to her."

"Right. Okay, come on." She disappeared into Mabel's bedroom, and I followed.

Moving quickly, she gathered things from Mabel's dresser and then from the bathroom, tossing them all into a cloth bag she took from a hook on the back of Mabel's door. I stood by the foot of the bed with guilt pummeling my chest as I imagined her losing her footing and falling to the floor, her precious head hitting the dresser.

I should have been there.

When the bag was full, Ari handed it over to me. "Here," she said. "Northern Medical Center. You'll have to sign in when you get there, and they'll give you the room number."

I grabbed the bag and was halfway to the front door before I turned around again. Poking my head back into the bedroom, I looked at Ari and touched my chest. "Thank you."

"You're welcome, Joe." She smiled at me. "Go get her."

. . .

After parking in the hospital structure, I ran as fast as I could for the stairwell, taking them down three at a time. I bolted into the lobby, skidded to the reception desk, scribbled my name on the sign-in, slapped a visitor tag on my chest, and raced for the elevator. It was about to close when I yelled, "Hold the door!" A hand shot out, and I slipped inside the car.

"Thanks," I said breathlessly to the tall, dark-haired guy holding a cardboard cup of coffee. "Four, please."

"No problem." He studied me as the doors shut.

I kept my eyes straight ahead—I didn't want to talk hockey with any fans right now. My leg bounced as the elevator rose. It seemed to take forever to go up four floors. When the doors began to open, I shot through them sideways and took off down the hall.

When I arrived at her room, I didn't even stop to catch my breath. Throwing open the door, I rushed in, tossed the bag from Ari on a chair in the corner, and threw myself down on my knees next to Mabel's hospital bed. My chest ached at the big purple welt near her temple.

"Joe?" She stared at me like I might be a ghost, her face registering shock. "What are you doing here?"

"Ari told me what happened," I said, out of breath.

"When? Did you fly here?" She shook her head. "I don't understand how you heard in time to get here so fast. I just called Ari an hour ago."

"I left Chicago at four o'clock this morning," I told her.

"I don't understand," she said again. "My head is so fuzzy."

"It's not your head. Your head is perfect." I looked at her, worry and relief and affection radiating throughout my whole body. Her dark hair was a mess, her face was pale, and she wore a ratty blue hospital gown. But no one had ever looked so beautiful to me. "Are you okay?"

"I'm fine. I just got dizzy and lost my balance. Low blood sugar or something."

"I'm so sorry I wasn't there."

"It's okay, you weren't supposed to be." She half smiled at

me, like she was afraid something was too good to be true. "Joe, what's going on?"

"God, Mabel. I've been so miserable. And so stubborn. So afraid to make the wrong move that I made no move at all, and that's not who I am."

Her lips parted, but she didn't say anything.

"When I want something, I go after it," I said with conviction. "When I dream something, I make it happen. And when I love something, I will dedicate my life to it. For as long as I can remember, that something was hockey. I devoted practically every waking hour to being the best player I could be—for the people who believed in me, for my team, for the adrenaline rush I got from it. I thought hockey was the answer to every question. I thought winning was my purpose in life. I thought nothing would ever make me feel as good as the game. But I was wrong."

"You were?"

"Yes. None of it matters to me nearly as much as you do. It doesn't make me feel as good as being with you does. And I don't love it the way I love you."

"Joe Lupo," she whispered, her eyes filling. "What's happening right now? Am I dreaming this?"

"No. I'm *the one*, Mabel. I don't care that we haven't been dating forever or that we're doing all the things out of order or that people might say we're crazy. I'm the one." I thumped my chest, getting worked up. "I'm the one you were destined to sit next to on that plane. I'm the one who couldn't stay away from you at that wedding. I'm the one who couldn't stop thinking about you afterward. I'm the one who fell in love with you. And I'm the one who drove all the way here to ask you to live with him."

"Live with you?" Her blue eyes widened. "But—but we barely—"

"Don't say it." I took her hand again, rising to my feet and sitting at her side. "Don't say I don't know you, because I do. I know how much you hate to fly because some dipshit fifth grader told you a lie about your future. I know you like the aisle seat more than the window, and I'll always give it to you. I know you had an alter ego named Montana Swift when you were young. I know you ran cross country in high school. I know you make a little sniffle noise in your sleep. I know you got the dimple in your smile from your mom. I know you're scared to lose people you love, but Mabel—cupcake—" I brought her hand to my lips and kissed her fingers. "You will never lose me. I will fight harder to win you than I have ever fought to win anything in my life. *You* are the prize—you and our baby."

She smiled through her tears. "We are?"

"Yes. I forgot to mention it, but I'm also the one who put that baby in you." I leaned closer, lowered my voice. "And when you let me, I'm gonna put another one there. I know how to put the puck in deep."

She burst out laughing, but it turned into a sob.

"That's you too," I told her. "Laughing and crying at the same time. I love how your emotions show up on top of each other like that. I love everything about you, Mabel Jane Buckley."

When she held her arms up, I pulled her closer, gently pressing my lips to hers before holding her to my chest, careful not to jostle her too roughly. "I feel like maybe I didn't wake up yet," she said, her voice muffled in my coat, which I hadn't even bothered to remove. "I'm scared to open my eyes."

"You don't have to be scared." Releasing her, I put two fingers beneath her chin and lifted it. "There's nothing to be scared of. I'm here, and I'm not going to let anything happen to you."

She smiled, and her dimple about broke me. "When do you have to go back? How did you even get today off?"

"I took a personal day," I said. "Don't worry, I didn't miss a game. Just a practice. But I did promise to be in Philly by tomorrow morning."

Her eyes glistened. "You really took a day off and drove all the way up here just to tell me you love me?"

"Yes." I grinned at her. "But I'm getting a little anxious to know how *you* feel."

Color rose in her cheeks. "Joe, you know how I feel."

"I want to hear it."

"I love you too," she said.

"You'd better," I told her. "Because I am not easy to live with. I hog the remote, I leave kitchen cupboard doors open, I take my shoes off anywhere I feel like it, and I take up all the space in bed."

"You really want me to live with you?" she asked.

"Yes! I'd carry you out of here right now and force you to come back with me today if I could. I don't want you living alone anymore. And I don't want to be without you." I took her hands again and held them in my lap. "We'll figure this out, cupcake. It's you and me from now on. But I know your family and friends are up here. And if you say you don't want to move to Chicago, I'll understand. I'll finish out the season and move up here to be with you this summer."

Her eyes widened. "You would?"

"Yes. Would you move to Chicago in the fall when I have to go back for the season, assuming Chicago renews my contract?"

"Yes," she said without hesitation. "I would. And as long as I can find a doctor I like and trust down there, I'll move before the baby is born."

My heart bucked wildly. "You will?"

"Yes."

"We will find you the best doctor in the city, cupcake." I

pulled her close again, kissing the top of her head. "I promise."

A nurse knocked on the open door. "Hi there," she said, smiling as she entered the room wheeling a cart with some machinery on it. "Just coming to check on you. How are you feeling?"

"Like a million bucks." Mabel laughed as the nurse looked at the bruise on her temple. "Like I hit my head and woke up in dreamland."

"Well, good." The nurse smiled as she took her temperature and blood pressure and oxygen level. "Your vitals are all good. Let's check that baby's heartbeat."

Mabel smiled at me as the sound of our son's beating heart filled the room. "It sounds good, doesn't it?"

"It sounds perfect," the nurse said. "The doctor still wants you to stay overnight to keep an eye on that bump, but you should be good to go in the morning."

I stayed out of the way, but as soon as the nurse was gone, I moved right back to her side and sat down. Took her hands in mine. "I wish I could stay all night with you."

"I know," she said. "It's okay."

Someone knocked on the door behind us. I looked over my shoulder expecting another nurse or maybe the doctor, surprised to see the dark-haired guy who'd held the elevator for me standing there. "Okay to come in?"

"Yes," Mabel said, sitting up a little taller. "Austin, this is Joe. Joe, this is my brother Austin."

I stood up immediately and held out my hand. "Nice to officially meet you, Austin. Mabel talks about you all the time."

"Likewise," her brother said. His grip was firm and friendly. Then he looked at Mabel. "How are you?"

"Doing great. Hey, can we get that crib you made to Chicago? I'm going to be moving soon."

Her brother looked surprised. "Oh. Okay. Uh, yeah, sure. We can do that."

Mabel smiled. "Thank you."

Behind Austin, another wide-shouldered, dark-haired guy appeared. This one was even taller and held a little girl on his arm. "I heard," he said, his brow furrowed in concern. "You okay, Mabel?"

"Yes." She laughed and waved at the child. "Hey, Serena! Did you come to visit me?"

"You fell down," the little girl said.

"I did, but I'm better now." She glanced at me. "Joe, this is my brother Xander and my niece Serena."

I stood up and moved toward them, holding out my hand. Xander shook it but eyed me a little more suspiciously than Austin had. All in all, her two big brothers were slightly menacing, but I kept my smile friendly. "Nice to meet you, Xander. I was in your bar last summer. Great place."

"Thanks." He looked back and forth from Mabel to me. "Everything okay with the baby?"

"Everything is fine," Mabel assured him. "Actually," she went on with a laugh, "other than this bump on my noggin, everything is the best it's ever been."

• • •

I stayed as long as I could, long enough to meet Mabel's dad and his wife, Julia, who could not have been kinder or more welcoming. Long enough to see Ari again, who came later that afternoon with a chubby baby in one of those car seat carriers I'd have to learn about. Long enough to meet the doctor and hear for myself that Mabel was going to be perfectly fine, and there was nothing to worry about.

Finally, I couldn't delay leaving any longer.

Leaning over, I gently kissed her forehead. Mabel's eyes filled as I straightened up and pulled the blankets higher. "I'm sorry to get sad," she said. "I know you have to go."

"I hate leaving you." My chest felt like it was ripping down the center.

"Soon we won't have to say goodbye so much."

"I hope not." I squeezed her hand. "I love you. Everything is going to be okay."

She smiled. "I remember you said that to me once before, when I thought my life was ending."

I chuckled. "And I was right, wasn't I?"

"You were right."

"This is only the beginning, cupcake." Leaning down once more, I kissed her lips. "It just gets better from here."

Chapter 26

MABEL

EARLY MARCH

"What time is he going to call?" I asked for the tenth time.

"He said by eight tonight." Joe indulged me by answering again anyway. He stopped rubbing my feet long enough to check his watch. "And it's just before eight."

We were on the couch, me stretched out with a book in my lap, Joe sitting with my feet in his. ESPN was on the television, but he wasn't really watching. And truthfully, I wasn't really reading.

His agent was calling tonight to let us know whether or not Chicago wanted to offer an extension on his contract. If they didn't, Joe would become a free agent in July. Another team—anywhere—could make him an offer. And if he wanted to keep playing hockey, he'd have to take it. If I wanted to be with him, I'd have to go too.

And I did. I would.

I'd moved down here a few weeks ago, right after my baby shower, and I knew immediately it had been the right decision. Everyday life with Joe was amazing. He was sweet and generous—he'd cleared space for me in his walk-in closet, in his dresser, in his bathroom. He had the guest room painted and carpeted just the way I had done the baby's room at my house (Ari with the assist there...she was suddenly Joe Lupo's second biggest fan). He bought a rocking chair for the room so he could help get the baby to sleep and let me get some rest. And he bought a litter box, cat bed, cat food bowl, and even a cat carrier for Cleo. "I want to make sure she feels at home too," he said.

I laughed and burst into tears all in one breath, of course.

Austin was bringing the crib down this weekend. I hadn't sold my house yet—we figured it would be good to have a place to stay when we visited Cherry Tree Harbor with the baby, until we had our own permanent home.

The historical society was sad to lose me, but they understood my family mattered most. I said I would always be happy to help with anything they needed and to please let the new curator know she could reach out at any time. They threw me a little going-away party/baby shower on my last day.

My due date was just six weeks away now.

Every time Joe left for an away game, he was more nervous. But I'd found a doctor I really liked, and she had assured me everything was looking great with the pregnancy and there were no troubling signs. I'd had no more fainting spells, my blood pressure was normal, and the baby was now the size of a pineapple. I got tired early these days, so I was often in bed by the time Joe got home from a game. But he'd crawl in behind me and wrap his arms around my stomach, warm and protective. And every single night, without fail, he whispered that he loved me.

One morning I woke up to a text from Ari that said just one thing.

Better than pining.

Then a screenshot arrived—Joe had posted a photo of us on Instagram in which he was standing behind me, arms wrapped around my middle, his face buried in my neck. I'm laughing with my mouth open and my eyes closed, and the shot is kind of blurry. But the caption made my heartbeat quicken.

Never letting her go.

I felt chosen and cherished. Just like I'd always wanted.

Joe had told me not to worry about the contract and just get settled in, so we hadn't discussed it yet. But over the last few weeks, I'd made up my mind.

"Joe," I said, setting aside my book. "I want you to know something."

"What, cupcake?"

"No matter where the offer is, I'll go with you."

His fingers stilled on my foot. His eyes met mine. "Really?"

"Really. We're a family." I put my hands on my stomach. "Where you go, we go."

He didn't say anything for a moment. Then he reached for me. "Come here," he said, his voice thick with emotion. I gave him my hands and let him pull me toward him so I lay across his lap, my arms around his neck. "You mean it?"

"Of course I do. If you still want to play, and you feel good enough to do it, you should do it." Ever since he'd gotten back on the ice after rehabbing his shoulder, he'd been playing well.

The team had turned their bad luck around, and they were on a winning streak again. If they stayed consistent, they were assured a playoff spot and had a good chance to win it all.

"It's funny you say that. Because I've been thinking, if Chicago doesn't extend, I'll retire."

"Retire?" I raised my eyebrows. "And do what?"

"Move up north. Buy some land. Watch our kids grow up."

I laughed. "Are you serious right now?"

"Yes." He pulled me close, nuzzling my neck. "It sounds so good to me."

"It sounds good to me too." My heart was beating so fast.

"My dad told me about this guy he knows up in Michigan who's thinking of building a hockey training facility. He's looking for someone to design and run the youth program."

"And you'd do that?"

"Sure. I think I'd be good at it."

"I know you would be. But what about a championship win?"

He shrugged. "I mean, that would be cool if it happened. But if it doesn't, I had a good ride."

"I can't believe I'm hearing this."

"Believe it." He pulled back and looked me in the eye. "I can imagine my life without professional hockey. But I can't imagine my life without you."

"You have me, Joe. Body, heart, and soul." I pressed my lips to his. "I just want you to have that championship ring too."

"There's another ring I've been thinking about that will mean more to me."

My breath caught.

His phone buzzed, and we looked at it. His agent's name was on the screen.

Trembling, I moved off his lap and stood up. "I'll let you take this."

He nodded and took the call, while I went into the bathroom. My legs were wobbly. My hands shook. What ring was Joe referring to? Although we spoke about the future a lot, we hadn't really talked about getting married. I hoped we'd get there eventually, but living together was such a huge step, I felt like we should breathe for a minute before making that leap.

But what other ring could he mean?

Trying to remain calm, I looked at myself in the mirror, marveling at my reflection. Even now, nearly eight months later, sometimes it still caught me off guard that I was having a baby with the hot hockey player next to me on the plane. That we'd fallen in love. That somewhere along the way, he'd begun to imagine a life with me in which we watched our kids grow up on a piece of land we called our own. It was better than a dream.

When I opened the door, I didn't hear anything. Not wanting to interrupt, I wandered down the hall toward the baby's room. Inside, I looked at the rocking chair, at the wall where the crib would go, at the changing table we'd picked out together. The carpet was thick and soft beneath my bare feet. I walked over to the closet and looked at all the little clothes hanging there, a rush of excitement moving through me.

I turned and saw Joe leaning in the bedroom doorway, a familiar grin on his handsome face.

"They offered," I said breathlessly.

"They offered," he confirmed.

Letting out a squeal of excitement, I ran for him and threw my arms around his neck, feeling him sweep me off my feet. "Oh my God, this is great news! Congratulations!"

He set me down, but kept his arms around my back. "I haven't said I'll accept yet. They want a two-year extension, and I'm not positive I want to commit to two years. I told him I had to talk it over with my wife."

My jaw dropped. "Your *what*?"

"My wife. It just slipped out. And it sounded so fucking good."

My eyes filled with tears as I began to laugh. "Joe Lupo! What does this mean?"

"It means I know what I want. It means you're it for me, cupcake. It means I finally understand how my dad felt when he got that tattoo on his chest—you know forever when you feel it." He cocked his head. "So what do you say? Will you marry me?"

"Yes!" Pulling his head down, I rose up on my toes and kissed his lips. "Yes, yes, yes! God, I'm so happy right now!"

Laughing, he kissed me back. "I'm sorry I don't have a ring."

"I don't care about a ring. And we don't have to rush anything."

"You don't want to get married before the baby is born?"

I shook my head. "No. Let's wait. Let's just enjoy this time together, get Nicky into the world, celebrate your Stanley Cup win, and then we can think about what's next."

He grinned. "Mabel Jane Buckley, I love you beyond words."

"I love you too. And as far as the contract, whatever you want to do is good with me."

"I'm going to think about it. My body has some wear and tear on it already, and I'd rather go out by choice and not by necessity."

"Your body is my favorite thing on earth, so you definitely need to take care of it," I told him. Between us, Nicky kicked in agreement. "I think someone wants to be heard." Turning within Joe's embrace, I put my hands over his and placed them on my stomach. Inside me, our son moved again.

"You're the best thing that has ever happened to me," Joe

whispered in my ear. "And I want to spend the rest of my life making sure you know it."

Melting back against his chest, I closed my eyes and wiggled my toes in the softness of the carpet, just to be sure I hadn't floated away.

Chapter 27

MID-APRIL

"Cupcake, I'm not sure this is a good idea." Joe looked worried—and absolutely gorgeous—standing in the bedroom dressed in his suit and tie.

"Joe, it's the conference semi-finals. I'm going." Sitting on the bed, I leaned back on my hands and stuck my bare feet out. "But I need you to put my socks on. And maybe my shoes."

Lines appeared in his forehead as he knelt to deal with my socks and sneakers. "But today is the due date."

"Do you know what percentage of babies are actually born on their due date?"

"No," he said, tying my shoelaces.

"Five. Five percent."

"Remember how effective condoms are? Ninety-seven percent. If we were in the three, we could be in the five."

"We won't." I held out a hand. "Now help me up, please."

He gripped my hand and helped me to my feet. "I feel like maybe you should just stay home and rest."

"I've been doing that all week! I want to go out!" I pointed at the shirt stretched over my massive belly that said MY DADDY PUTS THE PUCK IN DEEP, a gift from the team wives and girlfriends, who'd thrown me a little baby shower. "Plus, I have this awesome new outfit. Don't ground me, Dad."

He laughed. "You're not grounded. I just worry about you."

"I know." Rising on tiptoe, I kissed his scruffy cheek. He hadn't shaved since the quarter-finals began. "But you don't have to worry tonight. I haven't even had any Braxton Hicks today. I feel great, lots of energy. I want to cheer my team on for the win!"

Joe didn't look convinced, but he relented. "Okay, but you and Anna sit in those seats I bought you so I can see you." Instead of sitting in the usual family section, Joe had gotten us seats on the glass right next to the bench.

I saluted him. "Yes sir."

He rolled his eyes and bent down to kiss my belly. "You stay in there until I'm off the ice, Nicky. Do we have a deal?"

"He says yes. Now go to work."

Joe scooped me into his arms. "You know I only worry because I love you guys."

"I know." I nestled my body against his, the best I could with my belly in the way. "We love you too. But tonight is not about me or the baby, it is about you winning this game. Pucks in deep!"

He laughed. "Pucks in deep."

• • •

The game was a nail-biter, fast-paced, physical and ferocious, both teams fighting to stay alive. Anna and I clutched each other in fear, screamed with excitement, and jumped up and down when our team scored. Joe was having a great game—he'd scored in the first period on a gorgeous breakaway, in which he skated so fast and so beautifully, I couldn't breathe. During the second period, he had an assist, but a few reckless penalties resulted in power plays that allowed Denver to score two goals, tying it up. Tension was mounting. The crowd was wild.

My back was killing me, so occasionally I had to sit down. "Are you okay?" Anna kept asking me.

"I'm good. Just need a rest."

But it wasn't long before I was back on my feet. By the third period, the game was tied at three. The goalies were making phenomenal saves. Players were killing penalties with incredible defensive skill. Both teams were out for blood. My brothers were texting me frantic messages about what Chicago needed to do, like I could just bang on the glass and give the coaches the Buckley brothers' advice.

Xander
They need to shoot more! You can't score if you don't shoot!

Austin
They're taking too many penalties! They need to stay disciplined!

Dash
They should keep the shifts shorter so their legs are fresh!

Devlin
They're not picking up the loose pucks! They need to focus!

While it was a little scary being close enough to hear the players cursing and shouting, I did like being able to see the focus on Joe's expression, see the sweat on his face, feel the incredible drive and dedication he had to his sport. He was so fucking good—no matter what happened on the scoreboard tonight, I was so damn proud of him for giving so much of himself to this game. Occasionally, I'd catch him looking over at me, and I always smiled. He didn't smile back, but I could tell he was reassured I was okay.

Which was why I didn't let on that I thought I might be having some contractions. I wasn't positive, and they weren't horrible, so I didn't even say anything to Anna as the game went into overtime.

But a few minutes in, she noticed me breathing hard, kind of hunched over. "Mabel!"

"I'm fine," I said, fighting through the ache. "It will go away in a minute."

"What the hell! Are you having labor pains?"

"I don't know," I panted. "Maybe."

"Well, let's go! We have to tell Joe!" And she would have banged on the glass if I hadn't stopped her.

"No!" I said, grabbing her arm. "No. I'm okay. Let's just give it the first overtime at least. Maybe someone will score."

Her eyes widened. "Are you nuts?"

"No, I'm just a really big fan." I laughed, feeling relief as the pain eased. "But first labors take forever anyway. And it's not like my water broke."

"Oh my God. Okay, but you have to tell me if you get another contraction. You do not want to have the baby here."

"I'll tell you," I said, watching the teams head onto the ice again.

As soon as the puck dropped, I forgot all about labor pains, riveted by the action on the other side of the glass. But five minutes later, my body was gripped again by pain. Determined to hide it, I took quick, short breaths and pretended I was fine. Anna was preoccupied because Dag was on a breakaway, and she grabbed my arm, digging her fingers into my skin. The pressure was a good distraction.

We watched with rising hopes as he skated closer to the net and took the shot, letting out our breath when their goalie caught the puck in his glove. The entire arena moaned with disappointment. My insides twisted and raveled as play moved back down toward the Chicago goal. I was about to tell Anna I thought maybe I should call the doctor when she grabbed my arm again. "Oh my God," she said. "Look."

I watched in disbelief as a pass from one of our defensemen was intercepted by a Denver forward. But it hopped over his stick before he could control it, and suddenly Joe was there to scoop it up, easily corralling the loose puck. I couldn't even breathe as he breezed past center-ice and skated fast up the wing, no one able to catch him. And then at the blue line, he raised his stick and unleashed a slap shot that no one saw coming—especially not the Denver goalie. It flew right past him and hit the back of the net, the crowd roaring as the sirens and air horns went off.

Anna and I screamed as loud as the rest of the fans, and tears blurred my vision as the players all poured onto the ice and piled on top of Joe. But the pain across my lower back and the tightness in my belly refused to be ignored any longer. "Anna," I said, "I think I need to go to the hospital."

"Let's go," she said, taking my arm to help me walk.

"Wait! I have to get word to Joe." With difficulty, I moved over to the glass and banged on it. Joe was still on the ice, but I caught an assistant coach's eye and pointed to my belly.

His jaw dropped and he yelled, "Now?"

I nodded. "Now!"

He tapped a player on the shoulder, and the player glanced at me before taking off from the bench and skating across the ice toward the celebratory pile-up. Immediately, Joe extricated himself from his teammates and flew to the glass where Anna and I stood. The crowd was banging on it, trying to get his attention, but he only had eyes for me.

"Now?" he shouted.

"Now!" I shouted back, pointing to my belly.

The people surrounding us laughed as Joe spun around and skated faster than he ever had toward the locker room, ditching his helmet and gloves and shirt along the way. A guy wearing a Lupo jersey offered to help Anna herd me up the steps, and people were kind enough to move out of the way.

Joe and I were reunited in the family lounge, and I could tell he'd taken the fastest shower of his life. His hair was wet and there were damp spots on his shirt and jeans, like he hadn't even bothered to use a towel, he'd just jumped right into his clothes. Even his shoes were untied. He swept me into his arms and held me close, and I burst into tears, overwhelmed by it all.

"You did it," I wept, clinging tight. "You won!"

"I don't even care. I can't think about hockey right now," he said. "I *knew* I was right to be worried!"

I laughed through my tears as we moved toward the exit. "You were," I admitted. "So now just get me to the hospital before our son is born next to a locker room. He'll spend enough time in one later."

"Or not," Joe said. "He doesn't have to play hockey. He can do anything he wants."

I leaned against him in gratitude, in relief, in awe that he was mine.

• • •

By early the next morning, Domenico Buckley Lupo had made his entrance into the world. Joe held my hand the entire time, just as calm, steady, and reassuring as he had been when I'd thought that plane was going down. His voice was a constant source of strength when I was scared or exhausted or in pain. He told me over and over again how much he loved me, how amazing I was, how proud he was.

Only when we heard our baby cry for the first time, and they placed him on my belly did Joe break down, tears leaking silently from his blue eyes.

"Oh. God. He's perfect. He's beautiful." He wiped his eyes on the hospital gown he wore. "Do you think he looks like a Nicky?"

"I do," I said, even though he had the pinched, wrinkly old-man look of all newborns. But once he had his first bath, Joe brought him over to me, all wrapped up in a soft flannel blanket. Then we could see the big blue eyes, the dark hair, the precious little dimple on his chin.

Seeing Joe hold our son in the crook of his arm, the look of pure love on his face, made my heart ache in the best way. I took a video while he changed his first diaper, his huge hockey player hands struggling with the tiny tabs. It was almost as adorable as watching him rock the baby in the chair by the window. I dozed off, and when I woke up, I heard Joe talking to the baby.

"And then," he said softly, "I picked up the puck mid-ice and skated it down. I knew it was kind of a crazy shot to take, but I didn't even hesitate. And you know what? It went in. I'll teach you how to do it someday."

Later that afternoon, Joe's parents arrived. When they heard the name we'd chosen, they both cried. Nick embraced me carefully and kissed my cheek, saying he was honored beyond belief. Coco held me close and whispered how much this meant to them both. As I watched Joe hug his dad, my throat grew unbearably tight.

"You'll be a great father," Nick said. "I'm so proud of you."

My dad and Julia also came, bringing a massively huge teddy bear into the room. "That big bear is from all your Buckley cousins up north," my dad said as he rocked the baby, while Julia peeked over his shoulder. "They can't wait to meet you."

"Everyone sends their love," said Julia. "I'm supposed to give you at least twenty hugs."

"I feel it," I said, worn out but happy.

Joe spent the night in a pull-out chair in my hospital room, even though I told him he didn't have to. He only left the hospital once, to feed Cleo and pick up the little bag I'd packed with a change of clothes for me and pajamas for the baby. He had three days' paternity leave, and he said he didn't want to waste a single minute of it apart from us.

The doctor cleared me to go home the following afternoon, and by six o'clock that evening, I was nursing our son in the rocking chair in his bedroom while Joe cooked spaghetti for us. Afterward, I snuck in a shower, and when I came out, I discovered him sitting on the couch with Nicky sleeping on his bare chest.

"My book said this is important so he bonds with me too," he said softly.

I touched my chest. "Just reach in and rip my heart out next time. It will be quicker."

He smiled. "Come sit with us."

Wearing just a T-shirt, I went over to the couch and cuddled up beside him, laying my damp head on his shoulder. "How's dad life so far?" I asked.

"Fucking perfect. My brother Gianni was right—which is not a sentence I enjoy saying at all."

"What was he right about?"

"He said something about how I wouldn't even remember not wanting to be a father. And I don't. I can't believe there was even one second where I didn't want this."

Placing a hand across his stomach, I thought back to the day I'd told him. "We were sitting right here on this couch when I told you. Remember?"

"Yes. Pretty sure I was about to put the moves on you."

I laughed. "Your moves are what got us into this in the first place."

"True." He was silent a moment before dropping a kiss on my head and stroking Nicky's little round back. "I know this isn't what either of us planned. But now that we're here, I couldn't imagine it any other way."

"Me neither."

Nicky made a sweet little noise, and we looked at each other in amazement, like he'd just solved a very complex mathematical equation. Then we laughed.

"You know, I've never been able to picture my life after hockey before," he said, shaking his head. "Now everything I really want is right here in this room."

"Same," I said softly, happiness cascading from my heart like a waterfall.

"Does that mean you're ready to marry me?"

"Maybe I am." I smiled and snuggled closer. "You're the one, after all."

"Damn right, I'm the one."

"Although you really need to stop proposing to me without a ring."

"Who says I don't have a ring?"

I froze. Then I picked up my head. The grin on his face had me gasping. "Joe. You don't."

"Hmm. Maybe you should take the baby so I can check my

pocket." He placed Nicky in my arms and stood up. Reaching into his pocket, he pulled out a small black velvet box. "Look at that."

"Oh my God." It was a good thing I was seated, because my legs would have given out had I been standing.

He went down on one knee and opened the box. I wasn't sure what had me squealing louder—the sight of Joe, shirtless and messy-haired and sexy as hell, holding out that open box, or the ring inside it, which was almost an exact replica of the one I'd admired on his mom's hand. I stared at the ring until it grew blurry, and then looked up at the love of my life. "I can't believe this."

"Mabel Jane Buckley, the day we met, you said you'd never gotten married, you'd never had kids, and you'd never had a hot one-night stand with a stranger. I can't say I knew right then and there I was going to check all those boxes for you—in reverse order, because I like forging my own path—but I can say right now that I love you, that I'll take care of you forever, and that it would mean everything to me if you'd be my wife. Will you marry me?"

By now I was ugly crying, but I nodded and held out my left hand. Joe slipped the ring on my finger, and we both looked at it.

"This is a design *almost* identical to my mom's," he said, "which was a replica of a ring my great-great-grandfather gave his wife. My parents said they were madly in love and married for nearly seventy years."

I smiled and sniffed. "I saw your mom's ring at Christmas and asked about it."

"She told me," he said sheepishly. "Yours has a few new touches, because you deserve your own ring. But I know how much you love history and how important family is to both of us."

"It's exquisite," I whispered, staring at the way the diamond caught the light. "It's absolutely perfect. But how did all this happen?"

"After you said you'd marry me the first time, I got the idea. So I called my mom and asked her to send me photos of her ring, then I took them to a jeweler to have a custom version made."

"Joey! How long have you had this?"

"Only for a week. But believe me, the moment it was in my possession, I wanted to put it on your finger. I was trying to force myself to wait until the season was over, like we said."

"But you couldn't."

He shook his head. "I couldn't. When Nicky was born, I just—" His eyes filled. "I just couldn't wait any longer."

I placed my palm on his cheek. "You don't have to."

He leaned forward and kissed me, then sat on the couch again, his arm circling my shoulders. "So what do you think about eloping?"

I laughed softly. "That's right. Elope or no deal, right?"

"Well, I can't live without you. So I take that back."

"Good, because we are not going to elope."

"Dammit."

"We don't have to have a big crazy wedding. Something small and simple is fine. But I would like our families there."

He sighed heavily. "Fine. For you, I will participate in a wedding."

"Thank you." I kissed his chin. "How about somewhere up north this July? Maybe your mom would like to plan it."

"She would love to. But she'll cry when you ask her."

I smiled. "I'll call her tomorrow."

His arm tightened around me. "Good. The sooner, the better, cupcake."

Nestling into the warm, protective curve of his body, I looked at the sleeping baby in my arms, overwhelmed by my love for both father and son. Awed by love's power to turn two strangers into a family. Excited about the future that lay before us, rose gold with possibility.

Happy beyond my wildest dreams.

Epilogue

JOE

THREE MONTHS LATER

*M*abel and I definitely had different opinions on "small and simple." Or maybe it was my mother's fault.

Either way, when I went out to my parents' backyard the third Saturday in July—one year to the day after nearly missing that flight—and saw the gigantic floral arch, fifty white chairs on either side of a white aisle, a tent strung with party lights, a dance floor, a multi-tiered wedding cake, rows of champagne bottles and a tower of glasses…I knew there would be nothing small and simple about this wedding.

But that was fine. Mabel deserved the wedding of her dreams.

My mom had planned everything, with Mabel giving input from Chicago. When they'd struggled to find a venue with an available Saturday on short notice, my parents had suggested having the wedding in their backyard, and both Mabel and I loved the idea. Even the weather was made-to-order, warm but not sweltering, blue skies with just a few puffy white clouds here and there.

"You call this small and simple?" I teased, surveying the scene with my mom a couple hours before the ceremony would begin.

She looked slightly horrified. "I never said I'd do small and simple. I said it would be intimate and elegant."

In all honesty, I hadn't paid much attention to the planning process, but Mabel assured me I was forgiven for that. I was very busy being a new dad and winning the Stanley Cup.

Yes, it happened.

And even though it was every bit as thrilling as I'd imagined it would be, it still didn't compare to the joy of becoming a father. To the pride I felt when I carried my infant son around in that little kangaroo pouch shirt. To the love that engulfed me when I watched Mabel nursing him. To the gratitude I held in my heart for her.

She made me a better man in every way.

I'd extended my contract for one more year, and after that I'd retire. Mabel and I were looking at land up here, not far from the arena Tyler Shaw would turn into Bayside Hockey Training, where I'd be the director of the program. Mabel thought she might contact the Traverse City Historical Society at some point and see if they needed any help, but she loved being a mom to Nicky and wanted more children.

I did too.

I couldn't imagine what my life would have been like if I'd missed that flight out of Chicago. Every day, I thanked my lucky stars it had been me by her side, holding her hand. Now I'd be there for the rest of my life.

I couldn't wait to get started.

• • •

I'll just admit it—I cried when I saw her walk down the aisle.

I couldn't help it. She looked like an angel, floating toward me in a long white dress, her dark hair loose and wavy around her shoulders. She carried Nicky in one arm, and the other hand was looped through her father's elbow. It was the most beautiful sight I'd ever seen in my entire life. She passed row after row of people we knew and loved—every single Lupo and Buckley family member and several good friends, even some of my teammates and their wives—but she only had eyes for me.

Standing there in my tux, I tried blinking the tears away. Pinching the bridge of my nose. Clearing my throat. Shifting my weight side to side. But I couldn't fight it, and by the time she kissed her father on the cheek and handed Nicky to Ari, I was weeping like a baby.

We faced each other, and I was so blown away by her beauty and the idea that she was about to become my wife, I swear to God I didn't hear a word the officiant said. But when it was Mabel's turn to say her vows, I listened closely. When it was my turn, I spoke with feeling. When I placed the ring on her finger, I squeezed her hand. When she slipped the band on mine, it was like the final piece of me slipped into place. I knew I was the man I was supposed to be.

When we were pronounced Mr. and Mrs. Joe Lupo, I took her in my arms and kissed her like no one was watching. As our family and friends stood and cheered, I put my lips to her ear. "Mrs. Lupo," I said.

She laughed and threw her arms around me, and I lifted her right off the ground, kissing her again. Our guests whistled and shouted, the string quartet began to play, and the sun came out from behind a cloud.

Life was fucking great.

I wouldn't change a thing.

. . .

MABEL

Joe and I spent our wedding night in a luxurious suite at Abelard Vineyards, a wedding gift from the Fourniers. Austin and Veronica had taken Nicky for the night.

"Well? Was it agony?" I slipped into bed beside my husband. *My husband.*

"Waiting for you to finish getting ready for bed so I could ravish you?" He reached for me, pulling me close. "Yes."

I laughed as he ran his hand along my leg and hip, beneath the white satin nightgown I wore. Lowering his head to my chest, he pressed a row of kisses along the lace-edged bodice that clung to my breasts. Moving my hands into his hair, I closed my eyes and savored every sensation.

Joe had loved my body this way all throughout my pregnancy, and he adored the changes it caused—the curvier hips, the bigger breasts, the softer stomach, even the stretch marks. He made me feel beautiful and desired every day, even when I was exhausted, bedraggled, milk-stained, and bleary-eyed, wearing the same sweatpants I'd been in for days.

"No, silly," I said. "The wedding. Was it torture?"

"It wasn't torture." He pushed the nightgown up to my waist and grabbed the back of my leg, tossing it over his hips. "Except when I cried and everyone saw."

I sighed as I recalled him standing there in his tux, so

handsome I couldn't believe he was mine, tears dripping from those gorgeous midnight blue eyes. "I love that you cried. It made me feel so good."

"But other than that, it was not torture. I actually had a great time." He pulled the edge of my nightgown aside and teased my nipple with his tongue.

"What was your favorite part?"

"Mmmm. Can this be the last question?"

I laughed. "Yes."

"Hearing us pronounced Mr. and Mrs. Joe Lupo. That sounded pretty fucking cool."

"It did." I smiled as his impatient hands tugged at my nightgown, trying to get it off me. "Hey, I got this special for our wedding night. I figured you were tired of me coming to bed in your T-shirts. Don't you think it's pretty?"

"Yes. But I will never think anything is as pretty as your naked body." He tossed my new lingerie aside and turned me beneath him, his hips settling between my thighs, his erection caught between us, his lips hovering over mine. "Wife."

My whole body tingled. "Husband."

He kissed me, his mouth opening wide over mine. I wrapped my arms and legs around him, eager for him to fill me, the fire burning hot. But Joe was endlessly patient and attentive, never rushing, always a gentleman.

"Ladies first," he said, easing down my body until his face was cradled between my thighs. I moaned at the first stroke of his tongue and didn't stop until the climax shattered me.

Growling with hunger, he moved up until his chest covered mine. Reaching between us, I wrapped my hand around his cock. It was hot and thick and hard, and he groaned as I worked my fist up and down its solid length. "I want you," I whispered. "Now. Please."

"Forever," he said as he filled me the way only he could.

"Forever."

"God, Mabel." Buried deep within me, he tipped his forehead against mine. "I know a good marriage takes work, and relationships are sometimes hard, but loving you is so damn easy."

I smiled, feeling it with my whole heart. "I love you too."

He began to move, and words were lost to us. The room around us disappeared. Our bodies and souls intertwined, and we celebrated the promises we'd made, the love we shared, the family we'd grow.

Which, of course, would expand nine months after our wedding night.

Joe Lupo was a man who knew how to score.

Acknowledgments

As always, my appreciation and gratitude go to the following people for their talent, support, wisdom, friendship, and encouragement...

Melissa Gaston, Kristie Carnevale, Brandi Zelenka, Jenn Watson, Hang Le, Corinne Michaels, Catherine Cowles, Elsie Silver, Anthony Colletti, Rebecca Friedman, Flavia Viotti & Meire Dias at Bookcase Literary, Julia Griffis at The Romance Bibliophile, Michele Ficht, One Night Stand Studios, the Shop Talkers, the Sisterhood, the Harlots and the Harlot ARC Team, Club Harlow, and my amazing readers! To Jessica Turner and the team at Entangled, what a pleasure it has been to partner with you! I look forward to all the excitement ahead.

And once again, to my family, for putting up with me while I disappeared every day into a fictional small town... I love you.

*Don't miss the exciting new books
Entangled has to offer.*

Follow us!

f @EntangledPublishing

○ @Entangled_Publishing

♪ @EntangledPub

an imprint of Entangled Publishing LLC